THE CURIOUS
MR. TARRANT

BY
C. Daly King

DOVER PUBLICATIONS, INC.
NEW YORK

This Dover edition, first published in 1977, is an unabridged and unaltered republication of the work first published by The Crime Club, London, in 1935.

International Standard Book Number: 0-486-23540-8
Library of Congress Catalog Card Number: 77-78591

Manufactured in the United States of America
Dover Publications, Inc.
180 Varick Street
New York, N.Y. 10014

FOR
JANETT
BECAUSE SHE PREFERS EPISODES

*All the persons and events
are fictitious, as usual*

Contents

CONTENTS

THE EPISODE OF THE CODEX' CURSE

Characters of the Episode

JERRY PHELAN, the narrator
JAMES BLAKE, Curator of Central American Antiquities
MARIUS HARTMANN, a collector
ROGER THORPE, a Director of the Metropolitan Museum
MURCHISON, a Museum guard
TREVIS TARRANT, interested in the bizarre
KATOH, Tarrant's butler-valet

THE EPISODE OF THE CODEX' CURSE

I HAD not wanted to spend the night in the Museum in the first place. It had been a foolish business, as I realised thoroughly now that the lights had gone out. A blown fuse, of course ; but what could blow a fuse at this time of night ? Still, it must be some-thing of that nature, perhaps a short in the circuit somewhere. Murchison, the guard in the corridor outside, had gone off to investigate. Before leaving he had stepped in and made his intention clear ; then he had closed the door, whose handle he had shaken vigorously to assure both of us that it was locked. The lock had had to be turned from the outside, for the door was without means of being secured from within. I was alone.

The room was in the basement. It was compara-tively narrow and about fifty feet long ; but, since it was situated at one of the corners of the great building, its shape was that of an L, with the result that, from where I sat near its only door, no more

9

than half of the room could be seen. Of the three barred windows near its ceiling, the one in my half of the room was already becoming dimly visible as a slightly lighter oblong in the darkness.

The darkness had given me quite a jolt. Earlier, at half-past ten, when I had propped my chair back against the wall and settled down to read my way through the hours ahead with the latest book on tennis strategy, it had been very quiet ; I had seen to it that the three windows were all closed and fastened, so that even the distant purr of the cars across Central Park had been inaudible. Murchison, from outside, had reported every hour, but of course he had other duties than patrolling this one corridor, although he was giving it most of his attention to-night. We had considered it better, when he was called away, to leave the door locked and this he had done on each occasion. At first he had unlocked it and either come in or lounged in the doorway when reporting, but lately he had been contenting himself with calling to me through the closed entrance.

The silence, which to begin with had been complete, seemed somehow to have gotten steadily more and more profound. Imperceptibly but steadily. Oppressive was the word probably, for by two a.m. I had the distinct feeling that it would have been possible to cut off a chunk of it and weigh it on a scales.

I am a person who is essentially fond of games and outdoor life generally ; being cooped up like this was uncongenial as well as unusual. As the silence grew deeper and deeper and Murchison's visits farther and farther apart, the whole thing commenced to get on my nerves. Inside, I undoubtedly began to fidget. There was no possibility of backing out now, however. The diagrams showing just how one followed the ball to the net for volley (the proper time to do so being explicitly set forth in the text) made less claim upon my attention as the hours drew past. I had finally ended by closing the book and dropping it impatiently to the floor beside me.

Could there possibly be anything in this Curse business? Absurd! I stared across at the Codex lying on the little table near the closed door. What power for either good or evil could be possessed by some unknown Aztec, dead hundreds of years ago? It was an indication of my unaccustomed nerviness that I found it of comfort to reflect that I was in a world-famous Museum in the centre of modern New York, to be specific on upper Fifth Avenue; there must be a score of guards in the Museum itself, a precinct station was but a few blocks away, the forces of civilisation that never sleep surrounded me on all sides. I glanced at the Codex again and gave something of a start. Had it moved ever so slightly since I had looked at it before? Hell, this was ridiculous. Then the lights went out.

The effect in any case is startling and in the present instance it was doubly so. Nothing could have been more unexpected. Unconsciously, I suppose, one becomes accustomed to hearing the click of a button or a switch when lights are extinguished; even in a roomful of people, unexpected darkness descending suddenly causes uneasiness. And I was not in a roomful of people by any means. The unbroken silence preceding and following made a sort of continuity that ought to have prevented any abrupt change. Darkness, silently instantaneous, for a moment was unbelievable.

Murchison's voice through the door a minute later was, I admit, a bit of a relief. He opened the door, flashed his light about for a moment, then locked it again and hurried away.

The guard's light had shown the Codex quietly in its place on the table. Well, naturally; how could it have moved, since I had not been near it and no one else was in the room? A Curse from the dark past of Aztlan. The third night. Nonsense. Here was merely a matter of a short circuit. It suddenly occurred to me that that, too, might not be un-important. Where there are short circuits, there are sometimes fires. The door was locked on the outside. I could break any of the windows, of course, if they couldn't be unfastened, but what then ? All of them were guarded by sturdy iron bars set in the stone-work of the building. It was plain enough that in any emergency I couldn't get out by myself.

I simply couldn't help thinking how often these coincidences seemed to happen. An ancient warning and a modern calamity. It was a silly notion ; it persisted in running through my head. In that inanimate manuscript written by dead Aztec hands there couldn't possibly be anything——

   .   .   .   .

When I had come into town that morning, nothing had been further from my mind than spending the night in the Metropolitan Museum. At most I had anticipated no more than calling there for a few minutes around noon to take Jim Blake out to lunch. Blake is considerably older than I am, being in fact a friend of one of my aunts ; our common interest, however, is not the aunt but the game of golf, as to which we are both enthusiasts. Thus, having some business in town, I thought I might run up and compare notes with him about a recently opened course in New Jersey which we had both played, though not together. Blake had been with the Museum for years and, I understand, is now the Keeper, or whatever they call it, of their Central American antiquities.

When I found him in his basement office, however, I discovered Marius Hartmann already with him, a fellow about my own age whom I knew slightly at college and never liked very much. A quiet, studious chap, though I suppose that's nothing against him. What I really disliked was his contempt for all sports, a matter he took little trouble to conceal. I had not

seen him since graduation but had heard that he had
come into a large inheritance and taken up collecting.
This interest, I suppose, had brought him and Blake
together but, not knowing of their acquaintance, I
was considerably surprised to find him in the office.

He shook hands with me pleasantly enough but it
was evident that his interest had been excited and
was wholly taken up by the subject he had been
discussing with Blake.

" Why, a Codex like that is priceless, literally
priceless ! " he exclaimed, as soon as the greetings
were over. " Such a find isn't reported once in a
century. And when it is, it's usually spurious."

Blake, leaning back in his chair with his feet
resting on a corner of his desk, grunted acquiescence.
" Fortunately there's no question of authenticity
this time," he asserted. " Our own man found it,
sealed away in a small stone wall-vault in the
teocalli. More by chance than anything else, he
says himself. The place where it was must have been
rather like a safe ; they never did find out how it
was properly opened. It was partly broken open
during the excavation work and when they saw that
some sort of storage chamber had been struck, they
finished it up with a pick. As I say, it was only a
small receptacle, a few feet each way, I understand."

" I suppose that accounts for its preservation,"
Hartmann reflected. " Over seven hundred years,
you say ? It's a long time, that, but if this temple
safe was sealed up—— Of course, we do know of
manuscripts as old as seven hundred years. The
oldest Codex I have is about four hundred," he added.

I thought it was high time to find out what a
Codex is, so I asked.

" A Codex, Jerry," replied Blake with half a
smile," is a manuscript book. Strictly speaking, the
thing we're talking about is not a Codex ; it's
written on stuff resembling papyrus and it is rolled
rather than being separated into leaves and bound.

But so many of these Central American records *are*
Codices written by Spaniards or Spanish-speaking
Aztecs after the conquest, that we have been calling
this record a Codex, too."

" But seven hundred years ? " I was puzzled.

" Oh, yes, it far antedates the conquest. In fact,
it purports to have been inscribed by the Chief
Priest of the nation at Chapultepec on the occasion
of the end of one Great Cycle and the beginning of
the next. ' Tying up the bundles of bundles of years,'
they called it ; a bundle, or cycle, being fifty-two
years and a bundle of bundles being fifty-two cycles,
or twenty-seven hundred and four years. The end
of the particular Great Cycle in question has been
pretty well identified with our own date, 1195 A.D."

Hartmann's eyes were glistening as he leaned
forward. " What a treasure ! "

" You knew of it some time ago, I believe ? "
Blake asked him.

" Yes. Yes, I did. Roger Thorpe, one of your
directors, told me. I offered the Museum forty
thousand dollars for it, through him, before it ever
got here. Turned down, of course . . . But I had
only the vaguest idea about the contents. It appears
to be even more valuable than I realised ; undoubtedly it contains an historical record of the
whole preceding Great Cycle."

" More than that," Blake chuckled, " more than
that. When this is published, it is going to make a
sensation, you can be sure . . . I don't mind telling
you in confidence that the Codex contains the
historical high spots of the preceding five Great
Cycles, including place names and important dates
of the entire Aztec migration. In some way we have
not been able to ascertain as yet, the occasion of its
writing was even more impressive than the end of a
Great Cycle ; apparently it was the ending of an
especially significant number of Great Cycles in their
dating system. Possibly thirteen ; we're not sure."

Frankly the subject wasn't of much interest to me. I couldn't work up the excitement that Hartmann obviously felt, and Blake, too, to a lesser degree. But I didn't want to mope in a corner about the thing. More to stay in the conversation than for any other reason, I asked what sort of writing was employed in the manuscript.

" Eh, what sort of writing ? Why, picture writing, naturally. Much more developed than the American Indian, though ; more like the Egyptian hieroglyphs. Some ideographs ; Chapultepec, for example, which means ' grasshopper-hill,' is represented by a grass-hopper on a hill. But there is a lot of phonetic transcription also, in which the symbols stand for their sounds rather than the objects pictured. The curious thing is that this Codex, by far the earliest Aztec manuscript we know of, uses a much more highly developed script than the later writings just preceding the conquest. It certainly makes the Popol-Vuh look just like what some of us have always suspected—the ignorant translation by a Spanish priest of traditions that had already been badly mangled and half forgotten by the natives them-selves."

Marius Hartmann had been doing some rapid calculation. He said : " But if this covers five Great Cycles, it goes back thirteen thousand five hundred years or more from 1195. Thirteen thousand five hundred years ! Why, that's—why——"

" Oh, yes," acknowledged Blake with an under-standing grin. " It is indeed. You know the con-troversies concerning the origin of the Aztecs, the location of the original Aztlan from which they traditionally migrated. I've only had a chance for one look at the Codex myself but it appears to me to be a highly circumstantial history without any embroidery at all. The writer states definitely that Aztlan is nothing else than the Atlantis mentioned by Plato. He even gives the clear location of the ancestors of the Aztecs in one of the western, coastal provinces of the continent. After the catastrophe the survivors found themselves on the North American coast, apparently in the vicinity of what have now become the Virginia capes. From there, after the passage of thousands of years and through the operation of a good many different causes, their migrations finally carried them into central Mexico."

Hartmann's mouth was partly open and his eyes, I thought, would soon be popping out. " You—you believe this is an authentic record ? " he stammered.

" I can only tell you this, but I really mean it. I've been here a good many years now, Hartmann, and so far as my own experience goes, it's the most authentic document that I have ever come across. I'd be perfectly willing to stake my reputation on it."

There could be no doubt about it ; the man's eyes would pop out in another minute. That would never do.

I said, " How about getting some lunch ? I'm empty as a football, for one."

.   .   .   .   .

The lunch was highly unsatisfactory from my point of view at any rate. Highly so. I had no opportunity to discuss the new course with Blake, or anything else about golf, for that matter. Marius Hartmann came with us ; he stuck to Blake like a leech and there was no getting rid of him. Worse, they both continued to discuss the matter of the Codex with undiminished zeal. Most of the time I ate in silence and by the approach of the end of the meal I was pretty thoroughly fed up on everything connected with Aztecs.

It was during lunch that the question of the Curse came up. It appeared that the Codex really comprised two separate parts, although both were written on the same manuscript. The second part was the historical section already mentioned, while the first dealt with a religious ritual or training of some kind. "Curious," Blake observed, "very curious. The title of the first part is almost identical with the actual title of the Egyptian Book of the Dead, *Pert em Hru*, 'Coming into Light.' The Aztec title is *Light Emergence*, but the contents are certainly not concerned with a burial ritual or anything like it."

Preceding this part of the Codex and introducing the entire manuscript, a species of warning had been placed. Blake quoted some of it. "Beware," it ran, "lest vengeance follow sacrilege. Who would read the Sacred Words, let him be instructed, for ignorance conducteth disaster. Quetzalcoatl, the Reminder, (goeth) in dread splendour. The desecration of Light-Words is an heavy thing; in an unholy resting-place the third night bringeth the Empty." And considerably more to the same general effect.

"It doesn't sound much like the Codex Chimalpopoca, does it?" ventured Hartmann.

"Not a bit. No, we have to do with something along different lines here. The Chimalpopoca is not much more than folklore at best, written some time after the conquest, even if it is in the native language. Our Codex is a genuine article; the man who wrote it was quite certainly the religious head and he had no doubts as to what he was writing about. Not only is the form of expression quite different but the content is, too; even the language is far more evolved. The author isn't guessing, in other words; he gives the strongest impression both of accuracy and of knowledge."

"How do you mean, Blake? Are you hinting that you take the opening Curse seriously?"

"Well, no. I didn't mean that exactly. I was referring more to the historical section and even to the ritual part itself. That seems to be a good bit more explicit, in parts at least, than most such compilations; from what I had a chance to read, one section appears to lead up to and introduce the following one, quite otherwise than in the usual haphazard collections. It gave me rather a strange feeling, just glancing through it. . . . As a matter of fact I've heard that you take such passages as the prefatory Curse more seriously than most of us."

Hartmann looked up from his salad. " As a matter of fact, I do. When I meet the real thing. Of course there was a lot of pseudo-magic in Greek times that couldn't affect a child. I mean the real thing," he repeated. " I can assure you that I'm much more sceptical about the dictum of a modern scientist than I am about that of a High Priest of, say, the Fourth Dynasty."

Blake smiled at our companion's earnestness. " Can't say I feel your way entirely. However, if that's your opinion, to-night is your night."

" Why ? How is that ? "

" ' In an unholy resting-place the third night bringeth the Empty.' We've finally gotten the Codex to its permanent resting-place and I've no doubt at all that the writer would consider it unholy. To complete the point, to-night is the third one." He paused and smiled again. " If I took it literally, I'd expect the Codex to vanish or undergo spontaneous combustion or something of the kind before morning. I shouldn't feel any too pleasant myself, either, for I happen to be its custodian now."

" Oh, you're all right. It doesn't say anything about the custodian," Hartmann answered. I was surprised, I must admit, at the entire seriousness of his words, which were accompanied by no hint of a smile. " About reading it, that's another matter ; I don't know whether I'd be prepared to try it or not, ' uninstructed.' But its custody, especially in an official capacity, will surely be harmless. It's not as if you had stolen it or even been the one to dig it up."

Blake looked a touch astonished himself, though

not as much as I was. He explained to me later that
enthusiasts often get these notions. He had known
a man once who had been determined to obtain an
Egyptian mummy and had finally procured one
which he kept in his library as his most prized
possession ; but he had assured Blake that were he
ever prevented from doing a proper obeisance—
" purification ceremony," he called it—night and
morning upon entering the room, he would get rid
of the mummy the same day, I, however, had not
met this man and Hartmann's sentiments, I confess,
were strengthening my disposition to consider him
something of an ass. Too much learning—some
old fellow said once, I think—is worse than not
enough.

But he was continuing. " About to-night, though,
that's a different thing. *If* it will really be the third
night and *if* it was set forth literally in the warning
just as you said, I should be frankly anxious, in your
place. What precautions have you taken ? "

" It's really the third night," Blake acknowledged.
" And the threat, or whatever you want to call it,
is not ambiguous ; it is simply and literally that the
third night will bring ' the Empty.' But, thank
heaven, I haven't your idea about it and I'm not
anxious at all. My word, if I worried about those
things, I'd have been out of my mind long ago ;
I'm surrounded every working day by more curses
and threats from the past than I can count. I just
don't bother about 'em. To tell you the truth, I
haven't taken any precautions," he finished, " and
I don't intend to."

" Surely you've got it locked up somewhere ? "

" Oh, surely. Your friend, Thorpe, by the way,
is of your mind ; he seems quite worried over the
matter. You ought to talk to him about it . . .
Yes, it's down in one of the extra rooms in the basement, locked up naturally. No one could get at it
down there. In the first place, a thief wouldn't know

where to look for it, in the second, although the room isn't a bank vault by any means, it *is* locked ; and in the third place, the usual patrols will be on duty near it anyhow. That's safe enough from my point of view."

" Oh, thieves." Hartmann snorted contemptuously. " I wouldn't be concerned about modern sneak-thieves ; no market for such a thing, anyhow. I'm thinking of something quite different than that, I assure you."

" So is Thorpe apparently. I can't make him out this time. He has insisted upon putting the Codex into the same room every night with his precious statue from Palestine, until we are ready to put it on exhibition in the main halls. *I* believe he has some superstition about that statue ; thinks it will be a guardian angel or something. He surprised me, really. You do too, if you're serious. What do you imagine could happen, thieves ruled out ? "

The other man shrugged. " Nothing—possibly. These warnings don't materialise sometimes but in my opinion that is because we don't know enough to interpret them correctly. Neither you nor I have any definite knowledge as to what ' the Empty ' means. Maybe your Codex will disappear to-night, although a thief would be the last thing I should look for in such a case. I don't know ; but I am certain of this, that something, and something more or less unpleasant, will happen on the third night that that bit of ancient wisdom rests in a museum. . . . After all, a museum is simply an exhibition house for the ignorantly curious, or vice versa."

Blake grinned his appreciation. " No reflections, I take it ? A lot of us have to earn our bread and butter, you know. . . . Well, why don't you sit up with it to-night and see what happens ? I'll get you permission."

" Not a chance ! I'm going to a ball at the Waldorf to-night ; but if I had nothing to do, you can take it I wouldn't do that. I don't want to be anywhere near your Codex on the third night."

" I believe you're more than half in earnest," said Blake, regarding our companion with an estimating glance. " It's tosh, you know."

Hartmann suggested, " Ask Jerry. He has heard both sides." Turning to me. " What's your idea, old man ; will anything happen, or won't it ? "

It was an opportunity I couldn't resist. I said briefly, probably all too briefly, " *Nuts !* "

He leaned back, smiling as he lit a cigarette. " Nuts, eh ? . . . Well, Jerry, I'll give you a thousand you won't stay up with the Codex and, further, if you do, that something will happen and you won't be able to prevent it . . . On ? "

Doubtless I looked as bewildered as I felt at the offer. Before I could pull my wits together and reply, Blake volunteered : " Wish I could take you myself. As a matter of fact, though, I'm taking Jerry's aunt to the opera to-night and I don't intend to miss out on that. You might tell her sometime, Jerry, that I paid one grand, extra, for the pleasure of seeing her this evening."

" Sure, glad to." My impatience with the whole business had reached a crucial point and I was feeling fairly irked. Not a word about golf the entire time and in another minute or so I should have to leave. " Look here," I said, " I can't afford to take you for a thousand but you're on for a hundred. I'll spend the night with your damned Codex and nothing will happen to it at all or about it at all. So what ? "

" So there's a hundred for me," came the exasperating answer.

" Nuts again. Draw your cheque."

Suddenly he was serious. " You mean this ? You really intend to go through with it ? "

" Naturally."

" All right. Now listen to me. A hundred isn't enough to make me want to have you take a risk,

And you'll be taking one, no matter what you think about it. I'm sorry now that I made the proposition. I'd much rather call it off. Shall we ? "

Let him crawl out like that ? " Nothing doing, my lad. It was your suggestion. It's on now ; I'm chaperoning the Codex to-night and collecting in the morning." If there's one thing I can't stand, it's these fellows who know more than every one else about everything. Except golf, of course.

" As you will." He shrugged, as who remarks that sagacity is wasted on any but sages. " Do you mind, Jerry, if I call you up once or twice during the night ? I'd feel a little easier."

" Call away. All you want."

" It can be arranged, Blake, can't it ? "

" Easily. I'll have the phone in the room plugged through before I leave." He smiled broadly, with more pleasure than I could muster over the tedious performance. " I don't think, though, that I'll stay up fretting over Jerry," he added.

" No ? " The tone had just that accent of the sceptical tinged with the supercilious that is appropriate, I suppose, to these occasions.

The waiter was bringing our check.

.   .   .   .   .

Late that afternoon Blake showed me the room. As I have said it was L-shaped. There was a roll-top desk in it and a flat one, both obviously unused. Several piles of bundles, pamphlets no doubt or some of the monographs the museum is frequently publishing, were stacked against the long back wall. There were also a few small boxes, various odds and ends that accumulate in a disused apartment. The statue, still in its skeleton crate whose sides were covered with sacking, stood at the farther end of the room beyond the flat desk on which rested the telephone instrument. Life-size, apparently, to judge from the crate. " Thorpe's sweetheart," said Blake in a dry voice. " He won't even let us see it.

It's a particularly nifty one of Astarte, I understand. Came in ten days ago from the Palestine expedition and he insists on unpacking it himself. Hasn't gotten around to it yet."

He laid the Codex on the small table in the other half of the room, near the entrance door. It was contained in a cylinder of wood, black with age, on one side of which two symbols, or letters, had been skilfully inlaid in white shell. " Sacred very-very," Blake translated them, explaining that the Codex was in its original package, as found. He had taken it carelessly from one of the drawers of his own desk.

As we turned to the door, he said : " Here's a note I've written for you to Murchison, the guard who will be on duty down here to-night. He's not here yet. And I'll introduce you to the supervisor as we go out, so there will be no trouble when you come in after dinner."

On the way up to the main entrance I surprised an unwonted expression on Blake's face. He said abruptly, " Of course, Jerry, I don't really know much about that Codex or its origin. Something might happen—I suppose. Watch your step. And if anything does begin to break, get out."

I stared at him in plain amazement. Through the big doors the sunlight was slanting cheerfully across Fifth Avenue. " Forget it. I'm making the easiest hundred bucks I've ever found. . . . Remember me to Aunt Doris."

    .   .   .   .   .

There wasn't any sunlight now. I sat back on my chair, staring into black murk. I couldn't fool myself into believing that I was relaxed ; I realised in fact, that my muscles were tensed as if for a spring. Not that I had any idea where to spring or for what purpose.

Funny, how thick the darkness seemed to be. One's eyes usually become accustomed to lack of light within a relatively short time, but the window

continued as dim as at first, minute after minute.
I couldn't see the table, only a few feet away. This
darkness was like the silence—it had weight—it
pressed. The cigarettes I had been smoking all
evening, perhaps ? That was a comforting thought
and I clung to it as long as I could. Still, cigarette
smoke doesn't show a preference, in a closed room,
for one part rather than for another. I became more
and more certain that the gloom was deeper in the
corner where the Codex rested than anywhere else.
Where the mischief was Murchison ? How long *did*
it take him to plug in a new fuse, anyhow ?

A little rustle ! Little enough, it would not even
have been perceptible ordinarily ; in the silence
of the room it was not only perceptible but it just
couldn't be put down to imagination. Thank God
it didn't come from the direction of the table. It
was only momentary and the silence resumed, as
leaden as ever. *Had* I imagined it ? As I strained
my ears for a repetition, Blake's words occurred to
me—" If anything breaks, get out." It also occurred
to me that the Codex was between me and the door.
The fact that the door was locked, if I remember
correctly, didn't occur to me till later.

Why hadn't I brought a flashlight ? I hadn't
brought a thing, actually. A gun would have helped
a lot, too. I'm a good shot with an automatic ; but
a good shot without an automatic is about as useful
as a fine yachtsman in the subway. I couldn't blame
myself for that, however. When I had left home in
the morning I hadn't foreseen a night of conflict
with the nebulous menace of a piece of manuscript.

I suppose your eardrums, if you are listening
intently, become supersensitised. Something about
" sets," I think. At any rate the noise that broke
out was terrific ; it seemed as if fifty devils had
started screaming simultaneously. I don't know
whether I yelled or not (probably did) but I gave
such a jump that I upset the chair and found myself

sprawling on the floor, supported by one foot, one knee and one hand. As I scrambled to my feet, still instinctively crouching, I was too scared to do any thinking. It was only when the noise stopped and then began again, that I realised the telephone was ringing.

I was relieved. For the moment I just straightened up and felt like singing the first song that came into my head. Then I became annoyed, suddenly, at the infernal din the thing was making. I started toward the bend in the room and the instrument beyond it ; and of course knocked a couple of bundles off the pile at the corner. With a hearty " Damnation ! " I took up the receiver.

" Hallo."

" Hartmann speaking from the Waldorf. Jerry, is everything O.K. so far ? "

That fellow certainly wouldn't find out how uncomfortable I was, if I could help it. I felt grateful to him, though, for the steadying effect of his silly voice. But I wasn't prepared yet for much talking. " Certainly. Why not ? "

" You're sure ? Nothing a bit out of the way has happened ? "

" Well, the lights seem to be out for the moment."

" What ? . . . My God ! . . ."

I waited but there wasn't any more.

" What do you mean, my God ? "

The quiet over the wire continued for so long that I began considering the possibility that he had left the phone. Then his voice came through excitedly.

" Jerry, get out of that room ! Listen, Jerry, please, *please* will you get out ? I'll pay you the hundred, I'll——. Get out now ! Before it happens. Now ! "

I'll admit I had a hard time answering that one, but I did. I said, " I won't get out at all. Anyhow, I can't ; the door's locked——"

" Oh my God ! You say the door's *locked* ? "

Hartmann's voice rose into a kind of wail that, under the circumstances, wasn't the pleasantest sound I could have thought of. " Jerry, Jerry ! Listen to me ; listen carefully. If you can't get out, you must do this. You must ; understand, you must ! Don't go near the Codex. Get as far away from it as you can, even if only across the room. And lie down on the floor. Do you hear me, Jerry ? You must lie down on the floor ; get as——"

Click.

And there I was, inanely banging the hook of the telephone up and down. It was dark as pitch in the room. There was silence over the wire. There isn't much that is deader than a dead telephone line, but somehow the silence over the wire didn't seem half as dead as the silence in the room.

.   .   .   .   .

I couldn't go one way, nor could I go the other. I stood there, with the telephone receiver still in my hand. The telephone had gone now, too. The lights had gone, the guard had gone, the telephone had gone ; what price those " forces of civilisation ? " What is unavailable, it was being borne in upon me, might just as well not exist. . . . What could he possibly mean, about lying down ? Why lie down ? It didn't——

The lights came on.

Instantaneously. Just as they had gone off.

Light is truly a blessed thing. I only realised that I had been trembling when I stopped, after the first dazzle was over. There were the blank walls, the two black windows, the piles of bundles, the crated statue. All motionless, with the stolidity of the prosaic. It was all right ; it was all right, I repeated, it was all right. I drew a deep breath of the heavy air and expelled it in a long " whew." Automatically I put the receiver on the phone. I started back to my chair in the other part of the room.

Right then I got the biggest shock of my life.

The table was absolutely bare. The Codex had vanished !

I jumped to the door and shook it ; it was locked as tightly as ever. I turned and stood stock still, staring down at the table, disbelieving my eyes.

From somewhere I heard an unmistakable chuckle.

．　　　．　　　．　　　．　　　．

I whirled around. And saw him.

There he stood, leaning negligently against the corner of the wall where the room turned, and regarding me with amusement in his grey eyes. A tall, lean man in an ordinary tweed suit. A sensitive face, ending in a long, strong jaw.

A number of thoughts chased themselves through my head in the space of that first second. Amazement was one of them. How had he gotten in ? And if he had (which was impossible, unless he could walk through locked doors), how had he managed to get behind me ? He hadn't been in the other half of the room when I had put down the telephone receiver ; and during my trip from the flat desk to the door, he could not have passed me, for the lights had been on then. Hostility was another of the thoughts. Had I not been overwrought by what had gone before, I might have reflected that, once in, he certainly couldn't get out again until the guard returned, and I might have acted differently. But as it was, I would probably have flung myself upon anything in the room that moved or betrayed an appearance of animation.

I flung myself upon the man at the corner, glad that he no more resembled an Aztec bird-god in armour than did any one else to be met with on Broadway in the daytime. Here was some one I could deal with adequately, at any rate.

It soon turned out that I was wrong in that, however. Unexpectedly as my sudden attack must have been, he slipped back in a quick turn and landed a powerful blow against my shoulder. I got

in with a few then on my own account, while he
contented himself with little more than parrying.
Within a short time, however, he appeared to have
come to the conclusion that I meant business. He
stepped closer ; just as I was launching a smash
toward his chin, he ducked with an agility that
caught me unprepared, grasped my arm in a grip
like a vice, and twisted.

The arm was bent back behind me. My face was
forced suddenly forward and collided smartly with
a bony knee that moved into its path at the proper
instant. Then the knee moved on and I was forced
to the floor with my opponent kneeling over me.
Pain shot along my arm from the wrist and began
spreading over the shoulder. I grunted with it and
tried in vain to twist away ; all I accomplished was
to rub my face along the floor until it was turned
once more in the direction of the doorway.

I had just achieved this position, surely no improvement upon its predecessor, when the door
opened. Murchison stood in the entrance, his mouth
partly open in amazement. But not for long. Like
the other museum guards, he was a special officer
and the gun that came up in his hand was business-
like and steady. Although it was pointing too near
my own head for comfort, I have seldom been more
pleased with the sight of any weapon.

"Get up outa that," commanded Murchison.
"Stand away."

They were the first words, except my short replies
to Hartmann, that had been spoken in the room
since he had left.

.   .   .   .   .

"Who is the man ? " Murchison demanded.

I said : "I don't know. I never saw him before."
I had gotten to my feet now and crossed over to the
guard beside the doorway. Opposite us the fellow
stood nonchalantly in the centre of the room, his
hands in his coat pockets, and regarded us quizzically

but with evident good humour. Murchison still had him covered.

"Don't worry, he's got the Codex," I went on grimly. "It was here when you left to see to the lights. When they came on, it was gone and he had gotten into the room somehow."

"Search him. . . . Up with your hands, my man."

I made the search, to which he acceded willingly enough, with that amused half-smile still on his lips. Most of it I conducted with the left hand, for my right arm was growing no less painful and was now beginning to swell. There was no sign of the Codex; and since it was a good two and a half feet long and a number of inches in diameter, it could scarcely have been concealed on his person. I found a bunch of keys and took from his coat pocket (where his own hand had so recently been) a wicked little automatic. I realised abruptly that he could easily have shot down Murchison, and myself too, a few seconds before. I looked at him perplexedly; this was certainly a funny sort of chap.

I tried his keys on the door immediately. None of them fitted and I tossed the bunch back to him. There was no other key on him. He said, "Thanks, old man," and pocketed them.

"Now," he went on, "you'll want to search the room. You have my word that I won't interfere, nor will I attempt to get away. Let's get it over with."

The easy sincerity in his voice impressed me, but Murchison, I noticed, continued to keep a wary eye on him. We began at the door and went completely through the room. Every bundle was moved, every box was opened, the desks were thoroughly searched and also moved about. No sign whatsoever of the Codex could we find.

When we came at last to the crated statue at the end of the room, there was a long slit down one side of the sacking. Before I could say anything, our prisoner remarked conversationally, " Yes, that's where I was. Of course. The lady with me looks hot but feels cold. If you have to lean against her for a few hours."

I hadn't an idea what he meant until I enlarged the slit somewhat and peered inside the crate. I recalled vaguely that Astarte was never considered as a symbol of the virginal and this conception, chiselled some thousands of years ago in Palestine, even from the small glimpse I could get, was sizzling. It struck me as a side thought that the basement was probably destined to be her permanent home at the Metropolitan.

The crate yielded nothing either. And that was the end. Definitely, the Codex had vanished from this locked room.

Our companion suggested calmly : " It's getting late and I should like to leave presently. Will you please call up Mr. Roger Thorpe on that telephone ? The number is Butterfield 7–8344."

For want of anything better to do, the truth being that my mind was filled with bewilderment, I followed the suggestion. But I decided not to be too naïve about it. First I called Information and verified that the number was that of Roger Thorpe.

After a minute's ringing Thorpe himself answered the phone ; and since he was already acquainted with the situation, it took little time to tell him what had happened. He received the news with rumbles of excitement. " Let me speak to Tarrant at once," he snorted through the receiver.

I placed the receiver against my side and turned about. " What is your name ? " I asked the man across the room.

He was bending forward, lighting a cigarette. When he had finished, he said : " My name is Trevis Tarrant. Thorpe wants to speak with me ? "

I handed the instrument over to him and heard

him confirming the information I had just given.
. . . " And kindly speak to this guard here, so I
can go home. . . . Oh, forget it, Roger ; and stop
that snorting. You'll have it back by noon
to-morrow, one o'clock at the latest. . . . Yes, I
give you my guarantee."

More bewildered than ever, I hardly caught the
end of Murchison's words through the instrument.
The upshot, however, was a complete change in the
guard's attitude. He now treated Tarrant with the
utmost respect and seemed prepared to follow any
directions the latter might give.

" Well," said Tarrant, " first of all I'll take back
my little gun. And then I shall bid you good-night,
if you will be so good as to show me the way out.
How is your arm, young man ? "

I winced with pain as he touched it and his
concern was apparent at once. " That's a bad
wrench," he ejaculated. " Worse than I meant. See
here, you must come along with me and spend the
night. No, I insist. I can fix that arm up for you ;
I owe you that much at the very least. Yes, yes, it's
decided ; let us be getting along."

I was too tired and in too much pain to argue.
I merely went with him.

. . . . . .

We picked up a cab opposite the Museum and in a
few minutes were set down before a modern apartment house in the East Thirties. As Tarrant opened
the door of his apartment a little Jap butler-valet,
spick-and-span in a white coat, came hurrying into
the entrance hallway, despite the lateness of the hour.

" Katoh," Tarrant advised him, " this is Mr.
Jerry Phelan. He will spend the rest of the night
with us. Let us have two stiff whiskies for a night-
cap, please."

In the lounge-like room, pleasant and semi-
modernistic, which we entered, the butler was
already coming forward with a tray of bottles,

glasses and siphon. The drinks were quickly mixed.

" Bless," said Tarrant raising his glass. He took a long pull. " Mr. Phelan is suffering from a severe ju-jitsu wrench in his right arm. See what you can do for him, Katoh."

Once again the man hastened away, to return in a moment with a small bottle of ointment. He indicated a couch upon which he invited me to rest and helped me out of my coat and shirt. The arm was now throbbing with pain and was almost unbearable when he first touched it. His fingers were deft, strong—and gentle ; and within a short time the peculiar massage he administered began to have a soothing effect.

To distract my attention, Tarrant was talking. " Katoh is as well educated a man as either you or I," he was saying. " He is a doctor in his own country in fact. Over here he is a Japanese spy. I found that out some time ago."

Katoh, busy with the muscles of my shoulder, looked up and grinned impishly. " Yiss." He poured out more ointment. " Not to mention, pless. Not everybody so broad-minded."

" Oh, I don't mind a bit," my host assured me. " If he wants to draw maps of New York when he could buy much better ones from Rand McNally for fifty cents, it's entirely all right. . . . I heartily approve of spy systems that permit me to hire one of my equals as a butler. . . . A hobby of mine, as you saw to-night, is investigating strange or bizarre occurrences and he's sometimes invaluable to me there also. No ; I'm not only amused by the spy custom but I am actually a beneficiary of it."

My arm was now so greatly improved that I was becoming aware of a tremendous fatigue. I sat up, mumbling my thanks, and finished off my drink. Tarrant said : " I think you'll sleep very well. Show him where to do it, Katoh."

I hardly saw the room to which the little Jap

conducted me and where he assisted me out of my clothes and into a pair of silk pyjamas. The events of the evening had worn me out completely ; I remember seeing the bed before me, but I don't remember getting into it.

. . . . .

At quarter of ten the next morning Katoh came into the room just as I was preparing to open one eye. As he advanced toward me, he grinned cheerfully and observed, " Stiff, yiss ? "

In a moment I was sufficiently awake to perceive the justice of the remark. My whole arm and shoulder were incapable of movement and as I inadvertantly rolled over on my side, I gave a grunt of pain.

" Pless."

The butler very gently removed my pyjama top and got to work with the same bottle of ointment. His ability was amazing ; it could have been no more than a minute before the arm was limbering up. Within five minutes the pain had gone completely.

" All right now. You rub to-night, then all finish. Your shower ready, sair."

Tarrant was waiting for me in the lounge, beside a table upon which two breakfast places had been laid out. As soon as we had greeted each other I lost no time in attacking the ice-cold grapefruit before my place. I was hungrier, in fact, than I can ever remember being.

During an excellent repast, of which I evidenced my appreciation in the most practical way, little was said. But when we had finished the last cup of coffee and were leaning back enjoying that first, and best, cigarette of the day, Tarrant remarked : " I see you know Marius Hartmann."

This was surprising. I was sure I had not mentioned Hartmann to him during our brief acquaintance.

He smiled at my puzzled expression. " No," he remonstrated, " I am not trying to emulate Holmes and bewilder a Dr. Watson. His card dropped out of your pocket last night when Katoh helped you out of your coat. There it is, over on the smoking stand."

" Oh, I see. Yes, I know him, worse luck. And by golly I shall have to step round and see him this morning." I explained how I had come to be in the Museum the night before and related the matter of the wager. " So there it stands," I finished. " I'm out a hundred dollars I certainly never expected to lose."

" Bad luck," my host observed. " Still, it was a foolish bet to have made. As I believe I mentioned last night, I interest myself in the sort of peculiar affairs with which we had to do ; and whatever else may be said about them, they always come out un-expectedly. Very poor subjects for wagers. I should never risk anything on them myself."

" I am altogether in the dark," I confessed. " I can't imagine what happened to the Codex. You— you don't think it's possible that that Atzlan Curse thing really worked, do you ? " With the sunlight streaming in brightly I was viewing the matter quite differently than a few hours before. And yet, what could have happened ?

" If you are asking whether I take a seven-hundred-year-old Mexican threat literally, I can tell you I don't. I have seen older warnings than that take a miss ; very much older. You heard me talking to Thorpe over the phone ; he was afraid something would happen and, at my suggestion, he smuggled me into the room in the basement to discover what it might be."

I grinned. " So I'm not the only one out of luck this morning."

" I'm afraid you are," Tarrant stated calmly. " In spite of your own unexpected presence which kept me much closer to the charmingly immoral Astarte than I had intended, I know exactly what occurred, and why."

" Well——"

" Yes, I think you are entitled to an explanation, but I should rather let you have it a little later. Before the morning is out, I'll be glad to tell you. Meantime, if you intend calling on Marius Hartmann, I should like to go with you, provided you have no objection. It happens that I should like to meet him and this will be a good opportunity, if you are sure you don't mind."

I expressed my entire willingness; indeed I was finding my new friend a pleasant companion. And presently we alighted in front of Hartmann's sumptuous apartment on upper Fifth Avenue, somewhat above the Museum.

His rooms were ornate, with the stuffiness of classic furnishing, and filled with *objets*, as I am sure he called them. We had little time to notice them, however, for he made an immediate appearance. His smile was just what I had expected, as he greeted me. " I take it you have come to make a little settlement ? You're very prompt, Jerry."

With the best grace I could summon I admitted his victory; and seeing a spindly kind of desk against one wall, I sat down and wrote out a cheque for him without more ado.

As I got up and waved the paper in the air to dry it (the desk had a sand trough instead of a blotter), I remembered Tarrant with sudden embarrassment. Hartmann had so exasperated me that I had forgotten my manners. I stammered some apologies and made the introduction.

They shook hands and Tarrant appropriated the only decent chair in the room. " By the way, Mr. Hartmann," he asked, " how did you know so soon what happened at the Museum last night ? "

" Eh ? Oh, I telephoned Roger Thorpe first thing

this morning and he told me all about it. I felt pretty sure something unusual would occur ; the ancients possessed strange powers on this continent as well as in the East. But this is more remarkable than I imagined. Really inexplicable."

" Why, I wouldn't say that exactly." Tarrant crossed one long leg over the other, as he lounged back comfortably. " I was there myself last night during the—phenomenon and a rather simple explanation occurs to me."

" Is that so ? You have discovered what type of power is in the Codex ? " Hartmann leaned forward with every appearance of interest.

" There is undoubtedly a certain force in the Codex," my companion agreed, " though not quite the sort you are thinking of. The recent phenomenon, however, was modern, very modern. And in a way estimable ; scheduled simplicity is always a characteristic of the best phenomena. I almost regret that it didn't come off."

" How do you mean ? I thought——"

" Oh, surely, the Codex vanished. But I have the strongest reasons to believe that it will return before one o'clock this afternoon. If you know what I mean ? "

" But I don't know at all. I can't imagine. You suppose that in some way it became invisible last night and will materialise again to-day ? "

" No, Mr. Hartmann," said Tarrant softly, " I do not look for anything so astonishing. The Codex will reappear in a much more prosaic manner, I expect. It would not surprise me, for instance, if it should be handed in at the entrance of the Museum by a messenger, addressed to the Curator of Central American Antiquities. Of course, it might be delivered otherwise, but that, I should think, would be perhaps the best way."

" You surprise me," Hartmann declared. " Why should such a thing happen ? "

"Chiefly because a certain Deputy Inspector Brown is a great friend of mine. He is a very busy man, handling cases turned over to him by the District Attorney, signing search warrants, but I am sure he would be glad to take a few minutes any time to see me. Ours is a very close friendship ; he has actually sent two of his men with me this morning, simply on the chance that I might have some unexpected use for them. . . . Yes, that, I think, is the real reason why the Codex may be expected to reappear before my time limit runs out. It would embarrass me somewhat if the prediction I made to Roger Thorpe should fail in any particular."

Hartmann had plainly been giving the words his serious attention. He said, " I see."

Tarrant got unconcernedly out of his chair and, on his feet, extended his right hand. " It has been a pleasure to make your acquaintance, Mr. Hartmann, I should be glad of your opinion about my little prediction. Of course, I can come back later—I should be delighted to see you again—but in that case I fear it will be too late to justify *all* my claims as prophet."

The other apparently failed to observe Tarrant's hand. He said, " I should really prefer not to interfere further with your day. Pleasant as your visit has been, I feel that we might not get on if we saw too much of each other. On the other hand, I may say I feel certain that so *brilliant* a man as you cannot be mistaken, especially when he has gone so far as to confide his expectations to one of the Museum Directors."

It was evidently our cue to leave and I followed Tarrant across the room puzzled by the enigmatic fencing with words to which I had been a witness. At the doorway he turned.

" Oh, I'm afraid I nearly forgot something, Mr. Hartmann. Experiments of the kind we engaged in last night naturally carry no other penalty than failure. There is, however, a small fine of one hundred dollars, to cover the necessary experimental expenses and I have arranged that my friend, Phelan, should be empowered to deal with it rather than my other friend, Inspector Brown. To save every one's time and trouble. Brown, as I said, is so busy he has doubtless forgotten all about it by now and it would be a shame to impose on his time unnecessarily."

Marius Hartmann did a most surprising thing. He said, " I fear I shall be forced to agree with you again. Fortunately the matter is simple, as you have arranged it."

He took from his pocket the cheque I had given him and, tearing it into small bits, dropped them into a tall vase.

.   .   .   .   .

In the taxi, on the way downtown, I turned to Tarrant. " But what—how—what *is* this all about ? "

Tarrant's expression was one of amusement. " Surely you realise that Hartmann has the Codex ? "

" Well, yes ; I suppose so. I couldn't make head or tail of most of the conversation, but when he tore up my cheque, I realised he must be on a spot somehow. But I don't see how he *can* have gotten hold of it. He was at the Waldorf telephoning me just before it disappeared. . . . Or was that a fake ? Wasn't he at the Waldorf at all ? "

" Oh, no," said Tarrant, " I'm sure he was at the Waldorf ; and almost certainly had a friend with him at the telephone booth, to make sure of his alibi. His accomplice took the Codex, of course, and delivered it to him later."

" His accomplice ? "

" Murchison, the guard. That is the only way it could have happened. The affair was run off on a time schedule. Murchison turned the lights off at an arranged time. A few minutes later Hartmann phoned, calling you into the other part of the room, and while you were talking to him, the guard quietly opened the door, secured the Codex in the dark and locked the door again. His cue to do so was the ringing of the telephone bell. I've no doubt Hartmann did everything he could to upset you while the lights were out so that you would be too nervous to connect anything you might hear with an ordinary opening of the door."

"Yes, he certainly did. He pretended to be frightened half out of his wits about me. Told me I must get as far away from the Codex as I could. But look here, Hartmann was the one to suggest that I be there, in the first place. Surely he wouldn't have done that, if——"

"A brilliant idea ; he is really a smart chap. He didn't know I was going to be there ; didn't know anything about me. But if no one was present, it is obvious the guard would be suspected, as the only person to have a key, and be grilled unmercifully. He might break down. But this way, here was some one else, present at Hartmann's own suggestion, who would give evidence that the door had not been opened at the crucial time. Provided everything worked out as planned. No, that was a clever notion of his."

"How could you figure all this out, when you were inside that crate, if I'm right, during the theft ? "

"Why, it's the only way it *could* have happened. Although I didn't see it, I was there in the room and knew just what the conditions were. If you attack the problem simply with reason—dismiss the smoke screen, an Aztec Curse this time—there cannot be any other solution."

I thought that over. After a few moments I said : "That might do for Murchison. But how did you know who had bribed him ? "

"Oh, that. Well, it was a longer shot. But Thorpe had some suspicions of him, to begin with.

Hartmann had suggested the possibility of some-thing supernatural about the Codex when his offer was turned down. And when he heard about the opening warning, he mentioned it again. He slipped there. Thorpe felt sure, though, that Hartmann wouldn't plan an ordinary theft ; that was why he fell in with the idea that I should be smuggled in. I wasn't entirely certain, until he made that other slip, giving away his knowledge of what had happened. when he first saw you just now. I talked with Thorpe this morning myself and asked especially whether Hartmann had called him. He hadn't."

" The man's no better than a common thief. It will be a good thing to have him arrested." By golly, I never had liked that man ; and for the first time I was beginning to feel my animosity justified.

" Wouldn't think of having him arrested," was Tarrant's calm comment.

" Why not ? He's a thief," I repeated.

" Nonsense. The episode was more in the nature of good entertainment than theft. The Codex will be back unharmed within an hour, which in itself is a very mitigating circumstance. All that talk of mine about Inspector Brown was pure bluff. Arrest one of the future benefactors of the Museum ? He'll be on the Board some day. Don't be silly.

" As for me," Tarrant concluded, " I should dislike greatly seeing him arrested. There are far too few such clever fellows at large as it is. With Hartmann confined there would be just one less chance for my own amusement."

THE EPISODE OF THE TANGIBLE ILLUSION

Characters of the Episode

JERRY PHELAN, the narrator
MARY PHELAN, his sister
VALERIE MOPISH, beautiful and frightened
JOHN MOPISH, her brother ; an architect
DR. USALL BACKENFORTH, a psychiatrist
TREVIS TARRANT, interested in mysteries
KATOH, Tarrant's butler-valet

THE EPISODE OF THE TANGIBLE ILLUSION

MARY threw her golf bag into the rumble of the roadster. " Sorry to keep you waiting, Jerry. Whatever is the matter with Valerie ? She looks like a perfect hag."

" Is *that* so ? " I slipped the clutch into second and jerked the car around the curve beside the clubhouse. " Listen to me, big girl ; she could be twice as worried and still make you and all the rest of them look like hags. If you were dumb enough to let any one see you in the same room with her." Mary has been told by so many golf club idiots that she is beautiful, that she has almost come to believe it. She isn't ; she's just a red-headed mug. Mary's my sister.

When the jerks stopped and we straightened out on the drive at about forty-five, she managed to sit up. " Hey ! Bee in your pants, or what ? Val's a sweet kid, even if you think so, too. But you're such a mooing calf about her you can't see how terrible she looks. What *is* wrong with her, anyhow ? "

" I don't know."

" And just after she's gotten into that darling house. How long has she been there ? A couple of months, isn't it ? No, more than that ; a little over three months. Just the same, something's the matter. . . . Probably," Mary considered, " it's simply your hanging around so much. Your face at the window twice a day, darling, would give any girl the jeeby-hoobeys."

After that we finished the rest of the drive home in silence.

For once in her life, though, Mary was right. Something was desperately wrong and I couldn't find out what it was. Valerie wouldn't tell me and if I pressed the question, she got so upset that I had to stop.

Valerie Mopish had come to Norrisville with her brother five years ago when she was eighteen. Although they were orphans and nobody knew them, they were so pleasant, especially Valerie, that they made friends everywhere ; within a year they were in all the clubs and on intimate terms with the crowd to which Mary and I belonged. Why she liked me, heaven only knows, but she did, from the start. Why I liked her, is easy ; she is the loveliest-looking girl that ever got into a one-piece bathing suit. She has blonde, yellow hair and violet eyes— violet, mind you—and she's sweet and sort of fragrant ; and she always wears high-heeled shoes and her ankles give you a feeling as if you were tied to an operating roller coaster. I could just sit and look at her ankles all day long. . . . Maybe it's not a very good description, but how could I even begin to describe Valerie ? It's just one of those things. They took all the very best parts of all the beautiful girls in the world and put 'em together and called it Valerie. Never heard a sweeter name, either, did you ?

After lunch I hung around for an interminable

hour until I thought it would be all right to walk over and see her. " Strong, active man," said Mary looking across at me fidgeting on the window seat. " I'm playing a round with the Busbeys, taking the roadster."

" Take it and ram it into the Courthouse. I hope you do."

I came out of the woods and across the field just as Valerie stepped on to the terrace that runs along one side of her new house. I vaulted over the low, stone railing and said, " 'lo, Val. Marry me ? "

She looked pale and there certainly were little circles under her eyes, but she smiled. " Sorry." When she smiles that way, it makes me feel like Mary's underdone custard inside.

" How many times is that, Jerry ? "

" I don't know ; stopped counting six months ago. I've been asking you for over a year, though. Mary says I'm strong and active, and that's a long time to resist a strong and active Irishman. Too long. . . . What's the idea, Val ? Don't you like me ? "

" Jerry, you know I like you." The smile faded as she looked straight at me. It came back a little as she went on. " As a matter of fact, I had the noose almost ready for you a month or so ago ; it would have served you right, you great big, wonderful dunce." She hesitated and the smile went out like a light, leaving just trouble. " Oh, Jerry, go away and forget about me. I—I—I can't."

We were pretty close together when she began ; when she ended, we were a good deal closer. As my arms went around her, she sort of collapsed and lay back in them. Then she raised her face and kissed me. . . . We did this a number of times, I think . . .

" Jerry, let me go. . . . Please."

I felt foolish, standing there all alone, so I sat down on the railing. Valerie had taken one of the big, wicker chairs and was patting at her hair. She looked like a well-groomed but disconsolate kitten.

"I called up Dr. Backenforth yesterday and he's coming out to see me this afternoon ; any minute now."

How she gets herself together so quickly, I don't know. I can't. I said, " Huh ? Who's he ? "

" He's the man who treated me when I—when I had the nervous breakdown, before we moved to Norrisville. He's a psychiatrist."

" A who ? "

" A whoozie-doctor, I suppose you'd call him. He got me over a lot of complexes and things once. I thought maybe——"

Along the road leading in from the highway a mile to the south a very snooty town car was covering itself with dust ; it was a long car, and low, and still very shiny in spots, although it wouldn't be shiny any longer after it finished the last half mile.

" There he comes now," said Valerie.

" Eh ? That looks more like Mr. Rockefeller or Mr. Morgan out for an airing than like a doctor."

" No, that's he. He's gone fashionable since I first knew him."

Her judgment was borne out when the car, as incongruous in the country as a lap dog on a duck hunt, rolled up to the terrace. The chauffeur opened the door and Dr. Backenforth got out, dressed in a cut-away and holding a silk hat in one hand. "Better tell him he's come too early for the wedding," I whispered; " we're not even engaged yet, worse luck."

Valerie said, " Shush," and walked over to the steps to meet him. The fellow had one of those faces that look calm because there is no expression on it. I didn't care for him. He was of medium height and his eyes were good enough, I guess, but his nose was a little crooked and his lips were too thin and he wore some kind of goatee or little beard. I had the feeling that there wasn't any chin under it. He said, " Ah, Miss Mopish," in a sleezy sort of voice.

She explained that they would go into the living-room for their conference and told me I could wait if I wanted to ; Dr. Backenforth never conferred for more than forty-five minutes at a time. " Do stay, Jerry. I'll have Annie bring you a drink."

Annie brought better than a drink ; she brought the bottle and a good Irish grin to go with it. But when I asked her about Val, she looked distressed. " She's worritted, poor child. Oh, Mr. Jerry, couldn't you be persuading her to come back to the big house with us ? It's quare things is happenin' here, I'm thinkin', though she'll tell me little enough."

I said I'd see what I could do when the wizard inside had left. Annie went away and I sat sipping my highball. All this hinting and suggesting made me angry. " Queer things " were happening ; what queer things ? And why go back to the big house when Val had just gotten settled in this one ? Even I could see that the new house was practically perfect for her. " . . . fear complex . . ." came drifting out one of the windows. " . . . claustro-phobia." " But you know I never had claustro-phobia, doctor . . . " Then the voices subsided to a murmur again. I considered sneaking up closer where I could hear what they said ; but with the chauffeur lounging just below the terrace I couldn't very well carry that out.

At the end of the second highball they came out on the terrace. " You must bring them up from the subconscious," Backenforth was saying. " You will be sure to send me those dreams the end of this week ? Well, well ; good-bye, Mr. Phelan. I hope for improvement, Miss Mopish ; good-bye, good-bye." With a most lugubrious expression he climbed into his town car.

" Cheerful chap to have around for a week-end," I remarked. " I see now that he gets himself up for funerals rather than weddings."

Val sat down silently. After a moment she said :
" You don't understand. He did me a lot of good."
And, for a fact, she looked tired but much less upset
than before she had talked with him.

Maybe I had been too hard on the man, for he had
relieved her to the point where, for the first time, she
was willing to talk. Presently she continued, " I
know you care for me, Jerry, and I'm going to tell
you about this. I think I ought to. . . . Before
John and I moved out to Norrisville, I had what they
call a nervous breakdown. You know that, but you
don't know how bad it was. I felt terrible and I got
morbid and it went on and on and got worse instead
of better. Finally I began to *hear* things——"

" Hear things ? "

" Things that weren't there. Oh, Jerry, it was
awful. I knew I was going crazy and there wasn't
anything I could do about it. . . . Then, finally,
I had Dr. Backenforth and he showed me how these
hallucinations came out of my unconscious mind
and, after about six months or so, he helped me to
get rid of them. One of the things I heard was some
one following me ; he showed me why I heard that
—because I wanted to—and that went away first.
By and by all the other horrors went, too, and I
was cured. I never thought another thing about it
or worried at all until just recently."

" Why worry now ? I don't know what could
have been the trouble, but if you're cured, you're
cured."

She looked at me almost beseechingly. She said
simply, " I've got 'em again."

" Oh, come on, Val. If——"

" No," she hurried on, " there's no use saying it
isn't so when it is. About a week after I moved
in here, the day after John sailed in fact, I began
to get frightened of nothing ; that's the way
it started before. And it's gotten worse and worse.
And I'm so tired of trying to hide it and not tell

any one, and they all see it anyhow. I know there's
nothing really to be afraid of, but I am. And now,
now I've begun to hear the footsteps again. Jerry,
I'm scared."

A reasonable explanation occurred to me. " Of
course you get nervous all alone here," I offered ;
" no one within a mile of you at night. Why don't
you have Annie stay with you instead of going
back to the big house every night ? Or better yet,
go back yourself for a while, until you get over
your nervousness."

" I can't do that. I can't run away from it, or
I'd be licked for the rest of my life. Don't you understand, Jerry ? I'm not afraid of tramps prowling
around or anything like that. It's just because I
know there's no one here that it's so awful. When
some one follows me up the stairs and there just isn't
any one there and I can hear him as plainly as I hear
you now, I get so that I nearly scream. And then
there are other things, too. It hasn't anything to do
with living here alone ; it would happen to me
anywhere I went."

" Then it's only imagination," I remarked in-
adequately. " Why don't you just forget about it ? "

" You don't understand. I can't do that. But I
can fight it the way I did before. Dr. Backenforth
has helped me start again and I guess I can do what
I did six years ago. It hasn't been so bad lately,
anyhow ; it seems to come and go, sort of."

It didn't make much sense to me but " Then
that's all right," I said, with more confidence than
I felt. " You'll be O.K. again in a jiffy. If you'd
only marry me, I'll bet you'd never think of this
stuff again. We'd go for a swell, long trip and——"

" I told you this, Jerry, so you'd know why I can't
marry you. I can't get married until I'm absolutely
sure there isn't something funny about me. And I
don't see how I can be sure ; maybe I'll never be
sure. I'm terribly fond of you and it isn't fair at all.

You can always be friends with me, but go get married to some one else, Jerry. Can't you ? "

I got up and crossed over to her chair. I said : " Listen, lady. Sooner or later you're going to marry me. Sooner is best, but later is a lot better than never. I don't care if you're goofy as a loon, which obviously you're not." I pushed her over in a corner of the big chair and perched on the edge. " Val, darling, I love you. Don't you know . . ."

When I left, I was sure that Valerie, in spite of her obstinacy, was feeling a lot better.

.   .   .   .   .

Everything went well for a couple of weeks. I saw lots of Val ; we danced, swam, played tennis, and she was just as she always had been. Even Mary remarked on it, in her flat-footed way. Then, late one afternoon I walked over to the new house for cocktails before dinner ; it was only a six or seven minutes' walk from where we lived and we frequently went over for that purpose ; or vice versa, Val dropped in on us. I liked the latter arrangement better, for then I could walk home with Valerie instead of with Mary. On this occasion I had come in rather late from a tennis match and, finding Mary already gone, had started after her.

Perhaps I should explain about Val's two houses. When she and John Mopish had come to Norrisville originally, they had picked up a place outside the town at a bargain price. It comprised roughly fifty acres of ground, mostly wooded, although there were some farm fields now disused, on which stood an old-fashioned residence, a cut above a farm-house but far from modern. It wasn't exactly what they wanted, but it was close enough and they moved in with two servants, a cook and a maid. No attempt was made to cultivate the farm.

Valerie, however, was very fond of modern things, appliances and what not, and the old house never suited her. So, when building costs took a depression tumble, she decided to put up just the sort of house she had always dreamed of, on a remote part of the land. In a straight line, of course, it was no more than a quarter of a mile away from the former house, but, due to the configuration of the ground and the woods that covered it, the actual journey came almost to a mile. She and her brother had mulled over the project for a year before the building was undertaken.

John, being an architect, had naturally drawn the plans and supervised the construction. Everything about it was ultra-modern, but since John was really talented in his profession, it escaped being ridiculous and was a perfect example of what can actually be put into a house under present conditions. It had flues for air conditioning, of course, in conjunction with its oil furnace ; it had the usual electric refrigeration and more unusual gadgets such as no-shadow lighting in the bathrooms and disappearing wall-beds on the small sleeping porch outside Val's own room. The doors of the little garage underneath opened automatically when you drove up to it and closed again after you were inside. One of the bathrooms had a nine-foot plunge in it. Both inside and outside the style was modernistic, as were the entire furnishings.

Not only to save construction costs but because she wanted it only for herself, the house was very small. Beyond the terrace that stretched across the front was the big, sunken living-room (radio and electric victrola built into the walls and a concealed modernistic bar, disclosed by a sliding section of panels) where Val could give a reasonable party when she wanted to. Besides this room there were on the first floor only an entrance hallway, with closets and a dressing-room and lavatory off it, and the small but complete kitchen. Between the living-room and the hallway a broad staircase led upward, spiralled for its upper half.

The second floor had two comfortable bedrooms, each with a bath, and one smaller room that could be used as a study or a tiny library or for sport equipment or whatever. Val's own bathroom was quite large, having a dressing-table and long closets for clothes and shoes. The other bath had the plunge. And that was all there was, with the exception of the garage and the cellar for furnace and storage space. Annie came over in the daytime to prepare the meals and attend to the cleaning, but otherwise Val lived alone. The place was really tremendously attractive in its compactness and conveniences, and it would have been a shame if she had been scared out of it just when it had turned out to be such a success. Well, that had been avoided now ; old Dr. Backenforth appeared to have done his stuff to some purpose.

It was a beautiful day with a clear, blue sky and the sunlight was still strong enough to dapple the green leaves with yellow along the short-cut path I took through the woods. I felt that combination of relaxation and revival that comes after a hard match followed by a stinging shower. I was about to see Val, I was about to enjoy some delicious cocktails, in another minute or so I would be able to look at Valerie and listen to Valerie's voice. Excellent, excellent ; I deemed the occasion worthy of a cheerful tune and began to whistle one light-heartedly.

I had already come around the corner and up on to the terrace from one end, I had already gone perhaps ten feet along the terrace, before I stopped whistling in the middle of a bar and stood still with my mouth part way open. On the wicker lounge Mary sat with her arms around Valerie and Valerie was sobbing violently ; not pretty sobbing but great wrenching sobs that seemed to come from way down inside her somewhere.

I stood there for quite a long while. And then I said, " Huh ? "

Mary looked up. " Oh, you're here, are you ? "

" What's the matter with Val ? If you've been picking on her, you——"

" I don't know what's the matter. She won't tell me. Shut up and go away."

I'm never very comfortable seeing Val with no one around but Mary ; she has a way of looking at me every once in a while that is just as bad as if she opened her mouth and said, " Mooing calf " right out. I can practically hear it. But with Val in tears it was much worse ; the sound of her crying both embarrassed and frightened me ; it seemed as if I *must* do something instantly. I felt like running pretty badly but I said, " I won't go until I know what's the matter."

Mary had forgotten all about me, apparently. She was patting Val's head and muttering at her. I caught, " There, poor darling, go ahead and cry ; you'll feel lots better. . . . Don't mind Jerry, anything you do goes with him." It was an unusually sensible remark for the girl.

Valerie had stopped sobbing and started gasping. " D–don't ma–make Jerry go. He knows ab–about it."

I opened my mouth and heard a perfectly blank, " Heh ? "

They were both busy now with powder and stuff out of Mary's vanity case, which is easily big enough for a whole theatrical troupe. Valerie sniffled a couple of times and patted her hair and said : " I'm awfully sorry ; I shouldn't have broken down like that. I look like a fright."

She looked very sweet and dewy. Forgetting Mary for a moment, I declared : " You look so sweet. What did I do ? "

" You didn't do anything. I just said you knew about it."

" About what ? Oh."

" It was terrible last night," Valerie said in a low

voice. " It was simply awful. And now to-night's almost here. When the afternoon began going and the sun started to set, I just——. I guess I'm no good."

" What was terrible last night ? " Mary demanded. " What is this all about ? "

" None of your business," I told her. " And if you open that trap of yours about this——"

Valerie said, " Jerry ! " and Mary looked as if she were going to get mad, then decided not to. She smiled, " God will probably forgive you ; and I certainly realise you don't know what you're doing. So far I haven't anything to open, in your elegant phrase, my trap *about*."

" You won't have, either . . . Val, you've got to come and spend the night with us. You will, won't you ? "

" No."

" But Val, please. You must."

" I can't run away from it, Jerry. I can't."

" See here," Mary announced in her Competent Voice, " I don't care what it's about if you don't want to tell me. I'll stay here with Val to-night, if she wants me."

But Valerie shook her head. " It's sweet of you, Mary ; you're swell to me. But I can't let you. You don't know. Honestly, I don't want any one."

The thing was impossible. I started to walk up and down. I growled for a while and then I spoke. " It's no go. You won't come with us and you won't let Mary stay here. All right ; then I'll stay. I'm here and I'm staying here. You can't make me go. I won't leave you. That's that."

Valerie said nothing for a whole minute. Then she looked up. " I can't throw you out ; you're too strong. And after all, you do know. I'd rather you wouldn't, but I see the mood you're in now. . . . Oh, Mary, please understand. You've been awfully good to me but I don't want to tell any one else—

yet. You'll know soon enough, one way or the other."
She finished with a quiver under the words.

"It's all right, Val. I can't imagine what this is,
but I don't want to know till you're ready to tell
me. For goodness' sake, don't worry about *me*. . . .
If you really want to get rid of Jerry, phone me and
I'll come over and bring him back. I can, all right.
But I think you're perfectly safe with him ; I don't
believe he'd touch your finger unless you said he
might. . . . The dolt."

I started to say something but Mary went right
on. "Those cocktails ! If you don't mind I'm going
to have a couple of quick ones ; then I'll have to
dash back for dinner."

"Do," said Valerie. "I mean, do and don't."

"No, *I've* got to go, even if my chump of a brother
does insist on forcing his unpleasant company on
you. . . . Lucky I'm broadminded. If necessary,
I'll swear he was in his own little beddie all night
to-night."

So there *is* some use in a sister, after all.

. . . . .

It was Annie's day off and Val and I got our own
supper in the little kitchen. She continued to
apologise for her outbreak and to urge me to go
home, but underneath it I sensed her nervousness
increasing as the daylight faded. I was sure she
would be less frightened with some one there and
nothing on earth could have dragged me away.

After supper we had coffee out on the terrace,
while the dusk deepened and a glorious moon, verging
toward the full, came up above the eastern trees.
We also had liqueurs. The evening was balmy with
late spring and I stretched back in my chair, enjoying
myself thoroughly. It had been fun getting supper
with Valerie, it was nice sitting here talking to her,
and whenever I realised that I was going to stay
right here all night, it gave me a nice, tingling
feeling. If she would only marry me, every evening

would be like this ; why the dickens wouldn't she ?

We talked casually for quite some time. Then I got us both a couple of highballs and we talked some more. The time went before I knew it ; it was nearly twelve o'clock when Val ground out a cigarette and stood up. She had been perfectly calm all evening, but now I could almost feel a wave of nervousness sweep across from where she stood. In the moonlight pouring down on the terrace I saw her shiver.

She gave a little shake. " I'm going up, Jerry." There was a forced tone in her voice that made it sound as if she had just avoided adding—to the execution chamber. " You — you don't have to stay, really."

" So ? . . . I'm staying, Val."

I followed her into the hallway and, at the foot of the stairs, took her hand and kissed it. It was a cold little hand. But she walked up the staircase steadily enough. " Don't you worry," I called after her, " I'll be right here in the living-room all night long. And the lights will be on and I'll be awake. Just you give a yell if there's any nonsense." As she went around the turn of the stairs and disappeared, she forced a smile and gave a little wave with one hand. I was listening pretty hard but I couldn't hear a sign of any one following her up the steps. Well, of course not.

If it was half as bad as she imagined, though, she was a brave kid, I thought, as I glanced into the kitchen and saw that the windows were closed and locked. I also turned the bolt on the front door and on the door of the steps leading down to the basement and garage. If there was any funny business around, I wasn't going to guess where it came from, anyhow. But of course there wasn't ; how could there be ? Valerie herself said she was sure nobody was prowling about her house. It was just imagination and overwrought nerves. Nothing at all would happen to-night and the reason it wouldn't happen would be because I was there. I made a note to advance this in the morning as an excellent reason why I should always be there.

Now I was in the living-room, where I turned on the indirect lighting and secured all the windows except two of the French ones giving on to the terrace. I intended to sit down between these myself when I had picked out a book from the shelves across the room. Valerie's taste in books was unusual and it took me some time to find one I could use. Finally, however, I picked out *A New Model of the Universe* by one Ouspensky and took it over to my chair. It seemed a peculiar piece of work as I skimmed through it ; I read all of the chapter on Sex and had to admit that the fellow wrote as if he knew what he was talking about.

By the time I had finished this it was after two in the morning. The slight noises of Valerie moving around upstairs and drawing water in the bathroom had long since ceased. I didn't feel like reading any more and the radio was in the wall right beside me. I turned the volume down low and fiddled with that for an hour ; it was a first-class set, of course, and even at such a time I got plenty of stations, even boats.

I tired of that, too. I got up, lit a cigarette and stood in one of the open windows looking out over the terrace. The moon had gotten into the west now but it was still shining brightly, a beautiful night, cool and fresh—and peaceful. Not a sound anywhere ; even the crickets and bugs and the little animals that still lived in the woods had gone to sleep. The calm, quiet peace of the countryside was everywhere. I drew a deep breath and lounged comfortably against the side of the tall window.

Then Valerie screamed.

It broke the quiet like a ton of rock crashing into a still pool. I jerked up and stood in motionless surprise for a moment ; to this day I don't know what happened to the cigarette. But I wasn't motionless for long ; if I have any idea of what terror is, there was sheer terror in that cry.

I ran for the hallway ; and as I ran, I shouted some stupid thing, like " What's the matter ? " I started to take the stairs two steps at a time and stumbled ; I wasn't familiar enough with that particular stairs. It is important to note that I swarmed up them a step at a time, as fast as I could. Because a third of the way up, before I had reached where they spiralled, some one began to follow me. There was no question about it at all ; even in my haste to get to Valerie (and there was no question of that, either) the pounding footsteps behind me were so clear and unmistakable that, when I reached the place where the stairs turned, I turned too, with my arm drawn back to slug the fellow, who could not possibly have any business there.

And the stairs behind me, in the unambiguous light of the hall, were absolutely empty !

I couldn't wait, I ran on and dashed into Valerie's room. After the lights in the hall it seemed pitch black but luckily I knew where the light switch was, and found it. She was sitting up in bed, clutching the blankets and sheets around her, and shaking with fear. I was a little jolted myself, after that business on the stairs.

" Where the devil is it ? " I demanded fiercely. Without the slightest idea of what I meant.

But Valerie didn't answer. She had collapsed on to the bed and was pushing frightened sobs into the pillows. I suppose if I'd had any sense I'd have gone over to her and taken her in my arms, but I'm not a very wild sort of fellow and I've never been much in bedrooms with beautiful-looking girls like Valerie. I couldn't get up my nerve to get practically into her bed. So I just stood where I was and kept asking what it was all about. Not that it did me much good ; all I could get out of her, even after the sobbing had subsided to whimpering, was that

" It " had gone. Curiously enough, she asked me to turn the lights *off* in order to make sure of this.

Naturally I made a careful search of the room and went out on the adjacent sleeping porch. I found nothing and came back to look through the other two rooms and the bathrooms on the second floor. Nothing there, either. Valerie had quietened down now and insisted that she would be all right and go to sleep again. I wasn't especially satisfied to leave her but she insisted and, also, I was anxious to go through the rest of the house. I hadn't said anything about being followed as I ran up, but I couldn't see for the life of me how any one could have come half-way up the stairs behind me and then vanished ; there wasn't any place for him to jump to so suddenly. The more I thought of it, the less I understood.

So I went down, still a little reluctantly, and searched through the lower floor. Here again there were no results, no sign of any one except myself having been in the house and the windows and doors were all locked just as I had left them. I locked the two open windows in the living-room and descended to the garage and the little cellar. The same answer over again ; nothing disturbed, everything fastened.

I came back, opened one of the windows again and stood in it. Neither head nor tail could I make out of what had happened. Of course I didn't know what had frightened Valerie but what I myself had met on the staircase was beginning to make me doubt that overwrought nerves could be a complete explanation any longer. I simply could not believe that the sounds behind me had been imagined ; they had been as clear and distinct, as loud and plain as any ordinary sounds I had ever heard ; they had been unmistakable footsteps, heavy and solid. If I had invented them out of my own imagination, then I was now doing the same thing as concerned the occasional chirping of the birds in the woods across from the terrace as they stirred and awoke just before the dawn. And I knew I wasn't inventing them; I knew I was hearing birds that were really there.

At the same moment I heard something else. No scream this time; what came to my ears was the sound of running feet above. For the second time I made for the hall.

I was just in time to see Valerie begin a rush down the stairs, her face once more a mask of terror. She came around the curving steps all right and half-way down the straight steps below them. The lights were on and I could see perfectly plainly. Just about where the footsteps that had followed me had ceased, she suddenly pitched forward, as if some one had given her a shove from behind. There was no person, nor anything else, near her.

She landed at the foot of the steps with a crash, unconscious. As I reached her and raised her body to a sitting position, I saw that her right leg was doubled up under her in a posture that could only mean it was broken. I looked around desperately for some one or something that had attacked her. I saw nothing whatsoever; the lights burned steadily and brightly, there was not a sound in the house.

I carried her into the living-room and laid her on a lounge. I slid back the panel of the bar and drew a glass of water, grabbed a brandy bottle in the other hand. When I got back to the lounge, she was already stirring; and I gave her a sip of water first, then the straight brandy. She groaned, tried to sit up and clung to me. " Jerry, Jerry, something pushed me." She groaned again.

I was so upset that for some minutes I couldn't think what to do. Valerie had to have a doctor; I couldn't leave her alone and I mustn't be found with her at an hour like this. What a nasty thing conventions are, anyhow. I laid her back on the lounge as gently as I could and walked over to the telephone. I wouldn't have been much surprised if it had failed to work, but it didn't. The dial-tone was clear and

the little clicks came back in succession as I moved
the disc.

" Hallo," said a sleepy voice.

My tone was probably fairly strained and excited.
" Get a doctor for Valerie ! Get him out here as
quick as you can ! And get here yourself ; you've
got to get here before him. Do you——"

Mary is pretty quick on the trigger, I'll say that
for her. And she isn't one of those silly females who
ask a hundred questions when there is something to
be done. She said sharply, " I'll get him. Coming,
Jerry." And snapped the phone down. Not that
I'll ever tell her so, but her brisk words did a lot to
pull me together.

Twenty minutes later Mary walked through the
French window and I made another search of the
house, once more a futile one. As I jumped over the
rail of the terrace, a headlight beam shot up in the
dim light above the woods to the south ; so the
doctor was coming too.

I walked aimlessly through the trees in the general
direction of home. I was bewildered and I was angry,
but I hadn't anything on which to focus the anger.
What the devil was going on ? Something was
attacking Valerie, but when you looked, nothing was
there to hit back at. Imagination and tricky nerves
were out now, definitely. I had heard the footsteps on
the stairs and in full light I had seen Valerie thrown
down the steps—by nothing. For a time I cursed with
vigour and, unusually, it didn't relieve a single
feeling. " What the hell, what the *hell* ?" I groaned
in a fury of futility. She had been hurt and she
would be hurt again, unless something were done.
But what *could* be done ? Just the same, it *had* to be,
it——

For no reason I can think of, a picture formed
itself all at once in my mind. Only a month before
I had stood in a basement room in the Metropolitan
Museum, in complete darkness, facing an ancient

Aztec curse contained in an old, a very old manuscript. A strange thing had happened there—or so it had seemed at the time. The picture I had now was that of the man who had so abruptly appeared at the height of the phenomena, a clear-cut picture of his steady eyes, his unruffled, even amused calm, his complete unbluffableness.

I quickened my steps and my walking took on an intended direction.

.   .   .   .   .

I drove into New York in the sedan. I almost got a ticket on the Skyway over the Jersey meadows but talked my way out of that. It had been dawn when I left Norrisville but an hour later the sun was bright as I turned out of the Holland Tunnel and took the Elevated Highway uptown.

At the door of the apartment Katoh, the little Japanese butler who was a doctor in his own country and a spy in this one, answered my ring. Despite my dishevelled appearance and the peculiar hour of my visit—it was just six forty-five—his welcoming grin held no element of surprise.

" How do, Misster Phelan. Come in, pless. Mr. Tarrant out now for ride in Park, but back soon. You have breakfast ? Yiss."

While Katoh set another place beside the one already prepared, I had time to reflect on the strangeness of my mission and even to become somewhat embarrassed. After all, I had only met Tarrant once ; he had been friendly, certainly, but there was no reason to suppose he would wish to interest himself in this affair of mine. Well, I'd put it up to him, anyhow ; it was too late to reconsider now. Besides, Valerie's danger was more important than anything else. Then he came in.

He walked through the hallway and stopped in the living-room entrance, in well-worn riding togs. He, at least, looked at me in surprise, then more keenly. " Well, Jerry Phelan. What brings you in

so early ? Something on your mind—you look
worried and dragged out. You haven't been sitting
up with any more Aztec demons, have you ? "

" I've spent the night fighting a ghost. And the
ghost won."

Tarrant smiled. " It sounds promising," he
commented. " But no more now. I'll jump into
the shower and then we'll both have some breakfast.
After that, I'd like to hear about it."

In an astonishingly short period he reappeared,
this time in a lounging robe. We ate another of
Katoh's delicious meals with only a few casual
remarks interspersed. After we had finished,
Tarrant got up and crossed the room for cigarettes,
then stretched out in a big chair opposite me. " Go
ahead," he invited, drawing the smoke up through
his nostrils ; " tell me about it."

I told him about Valerie. Once started, there
seemed to be quite a lot to tell and he interrupted
me occasionally with questions. " This Miss Mopish
must be rich ? " he ventured at one point.

" She is very well off," I replied, " though she
isn't tremendously rich. She and her brother are
orphans, you see, and they were in very poor circumstances, practically poverty-stricken, she told me,
until some distant relative died and left her his
whole estate which was considerable."

" Just to her ? The brother got nothing ? "

" No, John didn't get anything. He is still as
poor as he ever was, but his profession will bring him
in plenty some day, with the progress he's making
now. Meantime Valerie is very generous with him ;
I'm sure she makes him a pleasant allowance. They
always seem to be very fond of each other."

" He's an architect, you say ? Yes, I believe I've
heard of him. Didn't he do those modern houses
they were showing at Radio City last month ? "

" Yes, he did those. He's getting quite a reputation
now. Three months ago he went over to Rome as a

result of some prize he got. His design won a competition and they wanted him to come across and supervise the finishing touches on the building. . . . He's on his way back now ; he'll be landing in another day or so, I believe."

I got back then to our real business and told him of Valerie's increasing nervousness after John's departure and how I had come to insist on staying with her the night before. To the best of my ability I described what had occurred, but in Tarrant's living-room with the prosaic rumble of the city coming through the windows with the sunlight, it didn't sound very convincing, even to me.

He said : " From what you tell me, I should be inclined to agree with the psychiatrist. She must be desperately worried over something and she is taking it out this way."

" You believe in those fellows ? "

" Not in the details of their theories ; not by any means. But in the general descriptions of the situation that they give, yes."

" But I tell you I heard those footsteps myself and I'm not worrying over anything. I saw her taken and pushed off the stairs and I swear that nothing touched her."

My obvious sincerity impressed him. " Of course," he admitted, " if you are really right about it, it's an amazing performance. There's no need in asking whether you could be mistaken ; I can see you are convinced. . . . Well, I haven't any explanation I can offer you from this distance. I don't believe in haunted houses and I've never yet heard of a modernistic house equipped with ghosts."

The crucial moment had arrived. " Will you come out for a few days and see these things for yourself ? You said once you were interested in peculiar happenings, and this one is the most peculiar I've ever seen. I can't get anywhere with it and I'm worried to death about Valerie."

" I wouldn't worry too much about the girl,"
Tarrant said. " Her brother will be back in a day
or so to take care of her."

" No. He won't be any more use when he gets
here than I am. He lives at the big house, not with
Valerie in the new one. I don't believe she will let
him stay with her, anyhow ; she has a persuasion
that she has to fight the thing out alone. But it
isn't just imagination she's fighting, it's something
a good deal more dangerous than that." I knew I
was imposing on him but he was the only one I could
think of to turn to. " I wish you'd come, if you can."

For some moments he considered in silence. Then,
" Whom do you live with, Jerry ? Your parents ? "

" No. Since mother died, six or seven years ago,
dad has spent most of his time travelling. Right
now he's in Asia. There's no one but Mary and
myself . . . I came in in a car. I can run you out,
if you'll come."

Suddenly Tarrant seemed to have made up his
mind. He gave an unusual whistle and his valet
appeared in the doorway. " Katoh, pack a bag for
each of us. We are going to spend a few days in the
country."

For the first time since I had left Valerie at dawn,
I experienced an unfounded but sure sense of relief.

. . . . .

We stood in the small hallway of Valerie's house.
Valerie was upstairs in bed and Annie was with her.
We had had luncheon at home with Mary, who
assured us that everything had been done that could
be done. After luncheon we had come over to the
new house and I had taken Tarrant up and introduced him. Valerie, of course, looked perfectly
lovely sitting up in bed and I could see that my
friend was startled by her unexpected beauty.
Whatever misgivings I may have had about bringing
him into the affair vanished at once, for it was clear
with the first few words that Valerie liked him and

was prepared to trust him. And indeed his calm matter-of-factness and his low steady voice were reassurance itself.

Now we stood in the hall below, Tarrant and Katoh and myself. Tarrant said : " That sister of yours is a fine girl, Jerry. Most attractive."

I stared. How he could even think of Mary when he had just seen Valerie, was beyond me. " Oh, she's a good enough egg at times. Just a red-headed flop, though."

Tarrant stared. He smiled slowly and murmured : " I noticed a certain tendency in you toward missing the obvious once before ; you should have your eyes examined, my boy." Then more briskly : " Well, let us make a little experiment and see whether your ghost is still around. See if you can find a ladder, will you, Katoh ? "

A tall step-ladder was discovered and, placing it beside the stairs, Tarrant mounted it and perched on top. " Apparently the wraith is not afraid of light, so we might as well try to conjure him up now. Jerry, you had better tell them up above that we are making some experiments, so they won't be frightened. And Katoh, you walk up the stairs while I sit here and observe."

The little Japanese gravely mounted the steps. And nothing at all happened. At the top he turned and came down again. " No ghost," he remarked blandly.

" Now you, Jerry."

I ran up the stairs and there the footseps were, about two treads behind me, clear and audible. Tarrant's arm shot out and extended part way across the step I had just passed ; the footsteps went under his arm and continued. As I had done the night before, I stopped half-way up and turned on my pursuer. Although I had known what to fore-see, the recurrence of the phenomenon was so im-pressive that I really expected to find some one at

my back. As I stood there, Tarrant's expression
for the first time held more than polite incredulity.

" H'm," said Tarrant. " He's awake now,
evidently. You heard that, of course, Katoh ? "

" I hear." The valet's face was expressionless.

" All right. Come on down, Jerry. Now I want
you to do that again, only go all the way up this time.
Don't stop till you get to the hall upstairs. Katoh,
you run up about three or four steps behind him."

We did this and I was followed again. Not only
by Katoh. Between him and myself, other footsteps
pounded up the stairs. It was a weird feeling, this
business of an unknown behind you, and I had all
I could do to keep from stopping once more and
turning around. The thought of the valet, also
behind me, was distinctly pleasant. It may sound
incredible, but near the top of the flight he increased
his speed and reached vainly at the empty air at my
back. That's how overwhelmingly natural the
thing was. The footsteps followed me all the way
to the top.

As I watched Katoh returning to the ground floor
it seemed to me that at one point he made a peculiar
movement. I looked at him queerly. " Did you
feel a slight push on the way down ? "

He shook his head. " No. No push."

Tarrant slid down the ladder and stood with his
hands in his pockets. " There is no use doing any
more of this. There's something here I don't understand. Under some circumstances I'd think of mass
suggestion but I happen to know how to avoid that
for myself. It's an impressive demonstration of
magic." He looked over at the valet. " What do
you think, Katoh ? "

" Is mahg-ic. But not here. This more like
ju-jitsu, I think. Also might be dangerous."

" It *is* dangerous." Tarrant's tone was decisive.
" There is something here far more objective than
imagination. It is objective and it is in this house.

Miss Mopish must be moved to the other place. I shall insist on it. We three will spend the night here and we'll spend it alone, except for whatever this intruder is."

Valerie finally consented. I never thought she would, but Tarrant is a persuasive talker. After twenty minutes or so, most of which was spent in pointing out that something *was* in the house and that it simply could not be a matter of her own subjective nervousness, she agreed and even made the necessary arrangements over the phone.

I stayed a moment after Tarrant had left the room. " Jerry," said Valerie, " please take care of yourself to-night. I couldn't bear it if anything happened to you."

That made me feel grand. " I'll take care of whatever is around here," I said grimly, " if I can once get my hands on it."

.   .   .   .   .

That night we divided our forces. Katoh was stationed in the entrance between the hallway and the living-room, where he could observe all of the latter and at the same time be close to the foot of the stairs. I sat in Valerie's own room upstairs ; and Tarrant roved through the house, now here, now there. It was another beautiful night outdoors, with bright moonlight from an unclouded sky.

I was tired, I had had no sleep the previous night. We began our vigil about eleven in the evening and the hours dragged by interminably. Nothing happened ; I just sat in the dark and waited. At first the fact that I didn't know what I was waiting for, kept me keyed up but finally I decided to lie down on the bed and rest my body anyhow. Tarrant had come in a moment before to report the absence of anything unusual and had just gone out again. Of course I fell asleep.

I don't know how much later it was when I began dreaming of a forest fire. As the flames mounted

higher and higher in dazzling brilliance I woke and
sat up. For a moment I had no idea where I was,
nor was I concerned with that. Opposite the foot
of Valerie's bed a full-length mirror was set in the
wall and this mirror was mysteriously bright,
although no light in the room was on. That was
puzzling, though not especially terrifying ; but
something else was. In the centre of the mirror,
illuminated by the unexplained glow, was a clear
and gruesome image of a scaffold with a human
figure dangling from it !

I gasped and rubbed my eyes. Yes, there it was,
no doubt about it. Even as I stared at it, it began
to fade. It went, just like a fadeout in the movies,
and the light itself gradually departed. I called to
Tarrant, but when he came in I hardly believed that
I had seen anything real myself.

We sat discussing it in the darkness. I made no
concealment of the fact that I had been asleep and
that when I had first seen it I had not been fully
awake. It hadn't lasted long but it seemed to me
that, before it had faded out completely, I had been
plenty awake. As we went on talking I still sat on
the bed, supporting myself with one hand which was
buried in the pillow on which my head had rested.
Happening to glance down presently, I noticed that
the pillow was becoming bright, as if a light were
focused on it ; and almost at the same instant
Tarrant grunted with surprise.

We both saw it this time. The mirror glowed
again and we were treated to a close-up of the
previous picture. An agonised face stared out at us,
the noose knotted behind one ear, the rope leading
upward. And slowly, almost imperceptibly, the
mouth in the face sagged open.

As the image began to fade once more, Tarrant
was out of his chair and pressing the electric light
button across the room. Instantly the picture
vanished. A moment later he was knocking with

his fist over the now empty mirror, sounding it and the walls immediately beside it. There appeared no hint of any hollowness, however ; both glass and wood gave back a solid response to his pounding.

"I shall examine that mirror more carefully in the morning," he promised. "We can't do much now. Let us turn the lights out and see if there is any more."

But though we sat through the next two hours to daylight, no further display occurred. Nothing further of any kind occurred, in fact. The image of that face of agony kept haunting me, none the less, and I began to understand the added horror, were I convinced, as Valerie had been, that the thing was being projected from my own morbid mind. Even the position of the bed would add to that illusion, for the mirror was directly opposite it and in the natural course of events reflected the bed and its occupant.

I also realised why she had wanted the lights turned off the night before, in order to see if " It " were still there.

.   .   .   .   .

The following day I spent at home in my own bed. Sound asleep. Mary drove Tarrant into Norrisville and he returned with various instruments, such as a yard-stick, a saw, chisels and a hammer. He also procured from Valerie the original plans of the house.

"What did you want all that stuff for ? " I inquired the same evening, when I was told about it. " Were you looking for hidden passages or recesses in the house? "

" No," he assured me. " Even without the plans, you can see that there is no space anywhere for a secret passage large enough to be used by a monkey. And by the way, I took that mirror out and there was nothing behind it but solid wall. No signs of its being connected with any kind of mechanism at all."

" So what we saw was not the result of mechanical arrangement, then ? "

" No, it wasn't. I am certain that there is no mechanical contrivance in the entire house in any way connected with the phenomena."

" So what ? Damn it all, Tarrant, we're completely stymied. What in heaven's name can be causing those sights and sounds ? "

" I believe I could tell you the answer to that now," he asserted calmly enough. " Half an hour's more work to-morrow and I'm sure I shall have the whole answer . . . I'll need a good, high ladder, though."

" I'll see that you get the ladder. But what *is* the answer ? "

He would say no more, however. " I shall tell all of you, say day after to-morrow, when Miss Mopish's brother arrives home. He will certainly be interested in the things that have been going on in his house. I think, personally, that it would be best if he, too, were present."

I was bitten with a terrific curiosity, for I felt certain that Tarrant would not have claimed a solution he had not achieved. Nevertheless, try as I would, I failed to get any satisfaction. On the other hand, Tarrant, too, was disappointed. That very evening Valerie received a radio from John, saying that he had been taken ill during the crossing and would have to be transferred directly from the ship to a hospital in New York. Two days later, when it was learned that he was really desperately sick and would be confined for a considerable period at least, Tarrant gave up his notion and summoned us to the new house to exorcise, as he said, the ghost. Valerie was brought back, in a chair, and Mary and Katoh and I were there, of course. Also, at the last moment, Tarrant insisted that Annie, Valerie's maid, should come in, also.

When we were all present, and before he had said a word concerning the purpose of the gathering, a surprise occurred. Dr. Backenforth unexpectedly drove up to the house, explaining that he had been passing through Norrisville and taken the opportunity to stop and see his patient. At Tarrant's insistence, he was prevailed upon to remain.

The demonstration that followed was exceedingly simple. Tarrant, lounging against the long table in the living-room, began it by addressing the psychiatrist pointedly. For a moment a dark suspicion entered my mind ; could this fellow have been drumming up trade by arranging assorted scares for Valerie in some devious way ? But no ; the absence of any mechanical fear-gadgets seemed to rule that out.

Tarrant, however, was speaking. " I understand, Dr. Backenforth, that Miss Mopish has called you in to assist her as to the recurrence of certain illusions which she suffered during a previous ' nervous breakdown.' Prominent among such illusions there is said to have been the sound of footsteps following her, when in fact no person was present to whom the footsteps could be attributed.

" When this case was first brought to my attention, I must confess that your own explanation, involving the projection of subjective phantasies, appeared to me to cover the situation. It is necessary, however, that any such explanation now be abandoned, finally and absolutely."

" How so, sir ? " demanded the doctor. " These phenomena are far from unusual. In Miss Mopish's own case which I treated——"

" I shall show you very shortly," Tarrant interrupted grimly, " why that type of explanation will not serve here. For the present I will only say that we are dealing in this house with entirely objective sounds of footsteps. They follow not only Miss Mopish ; they likewise follow Mr. Phelan, who is far from a neurotic subject. Mr. Phelan has heard them, my assistant—" he nodded in Katoh's direction—" has heard them ; I myself have heard them. Presently you will hear them. Since at any rate both my assistant and myself are quite immune to mass suggestion, there is not the slightest doubt that we have to do with phenomena of an objective character. I could establish this very easily with a microphone to record the objective sounds, but l consider it scarcely worth while. . . . Well, come along ; I shall demonstrate it for you."

We all trooped out into the hall after him and stood grouped about ; I noticed at once that a step had been removed from the staircase and through the aperture could be seen a slanting strip of wood, backing it. Valerie's house was certainly well constructed.

" I want you, Mr. Phelan, to walk up those stairs, then turn around and walk down them."

I did so, climbing over the missing step. Somewhat to my own surprise no sound accompanied me other than my own footsteps on the hard wood. As I returned, Dr. Backenforth released an audible sniff.

Entirely unruffled, Tarrant continued, " Now, Mr. Phelan, kindly run up the stairs as fast as you can. But when you come down, walk ; please be sure of that, *walk*."

This time there could be no question of it ; three treads behind me the ghostly footsteps followed my own to the floor above. Tarrant watched my descent, then spoke quietly.

" One would hardly suppose that so simple a thing could be so terrifying. The sounds that followed Mr. Phelan are, of course, no more than an echo. Here "—through the missing step he tapped the slanting wood behind it—" is an ingenious sounding board, so made that it reflects the echo *downward* ; thus the echoed steps appear always to be just behind the person mounting the stairs. When they are taken at a walk, nothing happens ; the echo functions only for running footsteps. I am sure that Miss Mopish could be guaranteed to run—at times, anyhow.

" But the staircase is more dangerous than yet appears. In a house where all the furnishings and all the fixtures, even the construction itself, is modernistic, the eye is led away and confused by curious angles, by surfaces and planes at unaccustomed slants. It is not remarkable, therefore, that, seen from this hallway, the various steps appear uniform. But they are not uniform ; I have measured them carefully and at a point just below the turn in the stairs three steps in succession have such dimensions that a foot, accustomed to the equal heights of the other steps, sooner or later will slip there. That is what happened to Miss Mopish a few nights ago ; she was not pushed off the stairs, she slipped forward so suddenly that the impression was the same. It happened in a much less degree to my assistant when he came down the stairs, and we are indebted to his excellent leg reflexes and his quick recognition for the first hint of what sort of thing was happening here."

He turned suddenly to Valerie, seated in her chair by the living-room entrance. " Both Mr. Phelan and I have seen the apparitions in your mirror, Miss Mopish ; you may dismiss entirely any notion that you manufactured them yourself. For these the arrangement is more difficult than in the matter of the stairs, but equally simple, once one gets on to it.

" At the end of your room upstairs are two French windows opening upon a sleeping porch and above each is a permanent transom of leaded glass. In these transoms are set four prisms. The most interesting are the two which contain tiny replicas of the images seen in the mirror ; the other two simply concentrate the moonlight upon the pillow of the bed just before the former function, so that it will frequently happen that any one sleeping there will be awakened. Then the second one functions, concentrating its light, and its image, in the mirror.

The angles, of course, are very carefully worked out, to correspond with certain positions of the moon in the sky. To the naked eye the moon's motion is imperceptible but, actually, it is always moving. The prisms, protected by the overhang of the roof, only function fully for a period of seconds, the image then fading out and making it more probable than ever that the vision was due to a disordered imagination. By the time a witness arrives, the picture is gone. I am certain these pictures have appeared at particular times, when the moon has been full, or nearly full, for example."

Valerie nodded, with sudden acquiescence.

" As a matter of fact the images are not nearly as clear as they seem to be in the middle of the night with one's eyes accustomed to darkness after some hours' sleep. The lighting in the room overwhelms them completely ; that is also why the sun, even should it occupy the same relative position as the moon, does not cause them in the daytime when the room is bright.

" There was a somewhat similar arrangement in a temple in Egypt in the old days, called *Het Abtit* or the House of the Net. I do not know whether your brother is interested in Egyptology, but, if not, then he has struck upon a very similar arrangement. The temple arrangement ensured that at high noon upon one special day of each year the Net, for which the building was named, should be illuminated through the temple roof in such a fashion that its ordinary outlines vanished and a resplendent picture of the miracle of the Virgin Birth appeared in its place. In the present instance we find the same principles used for a far less worthy purpose. . . . I have taken the liberty of removing the prisms from your transoms. I do not know of any further phenomena in the house. Have there been any, Miss Mopish ? "

" No," Valerie answered in a low voice, so low as

to be scarcely audible. " That is all, the mirror and the stairs. It was enough."

" In the case of a girl only a few years recovered from so serious a breakdown as I understand occurred," Tarrant went on, looking about at the rest of us, " it will readily be appreciated how such apparently inexplicable events would work upon her. Especially as one of them, the footsteps, if not the other phenomena also were devised to correspond with previous obsessions. She would naturally suppose a return of her former troubles, which this time, however, could be guaranteed not to yield to any subjective technique at all, since they depended upon quite objective arrangements, having nothing to do with her personal imagination. It was a cruel and miserable performance ; fortunately we have discovered its nature in time."

From my interest in Tarrant's explanation I abruptly awoke to its implications. I cried out : " Why, the God-damned skunk ! But what could he—but what—but why ? "

" That is something I do not feel myself commissioned to find out, Jerry. But money has caused plenty of trouble and is still doing it. I do not know who is the beneficiary under Miss Mopish's will, nor do I wish to. I might also point out that, after a few years in a sanitarium, an administrator is usually appointed for the patient's estate."

I was so mad I could have knocked the stairs down with my bare hands ; I have never been so mad in my life. I felt like yelling curses that could have been heard for miles. But Valerie was sobbing. So I went to her instead.

· · · · ·

John Mopish died the following week in his New York hospital. And it was damn lucky for him that he did. I don't know whether Valerie was glad or sorry, for we never mention him. I do know, though, that she only kept me waiting a month, the darling.

THE EPISODE OF THE NAIL AND
THE REQUIEM

Characters of the Episode.

JERRY PHELAN, the narrator
GLEEB, manager of Tarrant's apartment house
WICKS, apartment house electrician
BARBARA BREBANT, wealthy débutante of bohemian
    tastes
MICHAEL SALTI, an artist in oils
MULLINS, a lieutenant of police ; large and loud
PEAKE, deputy inspector ; tall, thin, soft voiced
WEBER, patrolman ; a regular cop
TREVIS TARRANT, interested in sealed rooms
KATOH, his butler-valet

THE EPISODE OF THE NAIL AND THE REQUIEM

THE episode of the nail and the requiem was one of
the most characteristic of all those in which, over a
relatively brief period, I was privileged to watch
Trevis Tarrant at work. Characteristic, in that it
brought out so well the unusual aptitude of the man
to see clearly, to welcome *all* the facts, no matter
how apparently contradictory, and to think his way
through to the only possible solution by sheer logic,
while every one else boggled at impossibilities and
sought to forget them. From the gruesome beginning
that November morning, when he was confronted
by the puzzle of the sealed studio, to the equally
gruesome denouement that occurred despite his own
grave warning twenty-four hours later, his brain
clicked successively and infallibly along the rails of
reason to the inevitable, true goal.

75

Tarrant had been good enough to meet us at the boat when Valerie and I had returned from our wedding trip ; and a week later I had been delighted with the opportunity of spending the night at his apartment, telling him of the trip and our plans and hearing of his own activities during the interval. After all, he was largely responsible for my having won Valerie when I did; our friendship had grown to intimacy during those few days when the three of us, and Katoh too, had struggled with the thickening horror in Valerie's modernistic house.

It was that most splendid time of year when the suburban air is tinged with the smoke of leaves, when the country beyond flaunts beauty along the roads, when the high windows of the city look out every evening through violet dusk past myriad twinkling lights at the gorgeous painting of sunset. We had been to a private address at the Metropolitan Museum by a returning Egyptologist ; we had come back to the apartment and talked late into the night. Now, at eight-thirty the next morning, we sat at breakfast in Tarrant's lounge while the steam hissed comfortably in the wall radiators and the brisk, bright sky poured light through the big window beside us.

I remember that we had nearly finished eating and that Tarrant was saying : " Cause and effect rule this world ; they may be a mirage but they are a consistent mirage ; everywhere, except possibly in subatomic physics, there is a cause for each effect, and that cause can be found," when the manager came in. He wore a fashionable morning coat and looked quite handsome ; he was introduced to me as Mr. Gleeb. Apparently he had merely dropped in, as was his custom, to assure himself that all was satisfactory with a valued tenant, but the greetings were scarcely over when the phone rang and Katoh indicated that he was being called. His monosyllabic answers gave no indication of the conversa-

tion from the other end; he finished with "All
right; I'll be up in a minute."

He turned back to us. "I'm sorry," he said, "but
there is some trouble at the penthouse. Or else my
electrician has lost his mind. He says there is a
horrible kind of music being played there and
that he can get no response to his ringing at the
door. I shall have to go up and see what it is all
about."

The statement was a peculiar one and Tarrant's
eyes, I thought, held an immediate gleam of curiosity.
He got out of his seat in a leisurely fashion, however,
and declared: "You know, Gleeb, I'd like a breath
of fresh air after breakfast. Mind if we come up
with you? There's a terrace, I believe, where we
can take a step or so while you're untangling the
matter."

"Not at all, Mr. Tarrant. Come right along. I
hardly imagine it's of any importance, but I can
guarantee plenty of air."

There was, in fact a considerable wind blowing
across the open terrace that, guarded by a three
foot parapet, surrounded the penthouse on all sides
except the north, where its wall was flush with that
of the building. The penthouse itself was rather
small, containing as I later found, besides the
studio which comprised its whole northern end,
only a sleeping room with a kitchenette and a
lavatory off its east and west sides respectively.
The entrance was on the west side of the studio and
here stood the electrician who had come to the roof
to repair the radio antennæ of the apartment house
and had been arrested by the strange sounds from
within. As we strolled about the terrace, we observed
the penthouse itself as well as the wide view below.
Its southern portion possessed the usual windows
but the studio part had only blank brick walls;
a skylight was just visible above it and there was,
indeed, a very large window, covering most of the

northern wall, but this, of course, was invisible and inaccessible from the terrace.

Presently the manager beckoned us over to the entrance door and, motioning us to be silent, asked : " What do you make of that, Mr. Tarrant ? "

In the silence the sound of doleful music was more than audible. It appeared to emanate from within the studio; slow, sad and mournful, it was obviously a dirge and its full-throated quality suggested that it was being rendered by a large orchestra. After a few moments' listening Tarrant said : " That is the rendition of a requiem mass and very competently done, too. Unless I'm mistaken, it is the requiem of Palestrina. . . . There ; there's the end of it. . . . Now it's beginning again."

" Sure, it goes on like that all the time," contributed Wicks, the electrician. " There must be some one in there, but I can't get no answer." He banged on the door with his fist, but obviously without hope of response.

" Have you looked in at the windows ? "

" Sure."

We, too, stepped to the available windows and peered in, but beyond a bedroom that had not been used, nothing was visible. The door from the bedroom to the studio was closed. The windows were all locked.

" I suggest," said Tarrant, " that we break in."

The manager hesitated. " I don't know. After all, he has a right to play any music he likes, and if he doesn't want to answer the door——"

" Who has the penthouse, anyhow ? "

" A man named Michael Salti. An eccentric fellow, like many of these artists. I don't know much about him, to tell the truth ; we can't insist on as many references as we used to, nowadays. He paid a year's rent in advance and he hasn't bothered any one in the building, that's about all I can tell you."

" Well," Tarrant considered, " this performance

is a little peculiar. How does he know we may not be trying to deliver an important message ? How about his phone ? "

" Tried it," Wicks answered. " The operator says there isn't any answer."

" I'm in favour of taking a peek. Look here, Gleeb, if you don't want to take the responsibility of breaking in, let us procure a ladder and have a look through the skylight. Ten to one that will pass unobserved ; and if everything seems all right we can simply sneak away."

To this proposal the manager consented, although it seemed to me that he did so most reluctantly. Possibly the eerie sounds that continued to issue through the closed door finally swayed him, for their quality, though difficult to convey, was certainly upsetting. In any event the ladder was brought and Tarrant himself mounted it, once it had been set in place. I saw him looking through the skylight, then leaning closer, peering intently through hands cupped about his eyes. Presently he straightened and came down the ladder in some haste.

His face, when he stood beside us, was strained. " I think you should call the police," he grated. " At once. And wait till they get here before you go in."

" The police ? But—what is it ? "

" It's not pleasant," Tarrant said slowly. " I think it's murder."

Nor would he say anything further until the police, in the person of a traffic patrolman from Park Avenue, arrived. Then we all went in together, Gleeb's pass-key having failed and the door being broken open.

The studio was a large, square room, and high, and the light, sweeping in through the north wall and the skylight, illuminated it almost garishly. It was sparsely furnished ; a couch, a chair, a stool, an easel and a cabinet for paints and supplies stood on a hardwood floor which two rugs scarcely covered. The question of the music was soon settled ; in one corner was an electric victrola with an automatic arrangement for turning the record and starting it off again when it had reached its end. The record was of Palestrina's Requiem Mass, played by a well-known orchestra. Some one, I think it was Tarrant, crossed the room and turned it off, while we stood huddled near the door, gazing stupidly at the twisted, bloody figure on the couch.

It was that of a girl, altogether naked ; although she was young—not older than twenty-two certainly —her body was precociously voluptuous. One of her legs was contorted into a bent position, her mouth was awry, her right hand held a portion of the couch covering in an agonised clutch. Just beneath her left breast the hilt of a knife protruded shockingly. The bleeding had been copious.

It was Tarrant again who extinguished the four tall candles, set on the floor and burning at the corners of the couch. As he did so he murmured : "You will remember that the candles were burning at eight-forty-seven, officer. I dislike mockery."

Then I was out on the terrace again, leaning heavily against the western parapet. In the far distance the Orange mountains stood against the bright horizon ; somewhat nearer, across the river, huddled the building masses that marked Newark ; overhead a plane droned south-westward. I gagged and forced my thoughts determinedly toward that plane. It was a transport plane, it was going to Newark Airport; probably it was an early plane from Boston. On it were people, prosaic people, thank God. One of them was perhaps a button salesman ; presently he would enter the offices of Messrs. Simon and Morgetz and display his buttons on a card for the benefit of Mr. Simon. . . . Now my insides were behaving less drastically. I could gasp ; and I did gasp, deep intakes of clear, cold air.

When I came back into the studio, a merciful blanket covered the girl's body. And for the first time I noticed the easel. It stood in the south-east corner of the room, diagonally opposite the couch and across the studio from the entrance doorway. It should have faced north-west, to receive the light from the big north window, and in fact the stool to its right indicated that position. But the easel had been partly turned, so that it faced south-west, toward the bedroom door; and one must walk almost to that door to observe its canvas.

This, stretched tightly on its frame, bore a painting in oil of the murdered girl. She was portrayed in a nude, half-crouching pose, her arms extended, and her features held a revoltingly lascivious leer. The portrait was entitled " La Séduction." In the identical place where the knife had pierced her actual body, a large nail had been driven through the web of the canvas. It was half-way through, the head protruding two inches on the obverse side of the picture; and a red gush of blood had been painted down the torso from the point where the nail entered.

Tarrant stood with his hands in his pockets, surveying this work of art. His gaze seemed focused upon the nail, incongruous in its strange position and destined to play so large a part in the tragedy. He was murmuring to himself and his voice was so low that I scarcely caught his words.

" Madman's work. . . . But why is the easel turned away from the room. . . . Why is that ? . . ."

. . . . . .

It was late afternoon in Tarrant's apartment and much activity had gone forward. The Homicide Squad in charge of Lieutenant Mullins had arrived and unceremoniously ejected every one else from the penthouse, Tarrant included. Thereupon he had called a friend at Headquarters and been assured of a visit from Deputy Inspector Peake, who would be in command of the case, a visit which had not yet eventuated.

I had gone about my business in the city somewhat dazedly. But I had met Valerie for luncheon downtown and her presence was like a fragrant, reviving draft of pure ozone. She had left again for Norrisville, after insisting that I stay with Tarrant another night when she saw how excited I had become over the occurrences of the morning. Back in the apartment Katoh, who, for all that he was a man of our own class in Japan, was certainly an excellent butler in New York, had immediately provided me with a fine bottle of Irish whisky (Bushmills, bottled in 1919). I was sipping my second highball and Tarrant was quietly reading across the room, when Inspector Peake rang the bell.

He advanced into the room with hand outstretched. "Mr. Tarrant, I believe? . . . Ah. Glad to know you, Mr. Phelan." He was a tall, thin man in mufti, with a voice unexpectedly soft. I don't know why, but I was also surprised that a policeman should wear so well-cut a suit of tweeds. As he sank into a chair, he continued, " I understand you were among the first to enter the penthouse, Mr. Tarrant. But I'm afraid there isn't much to add now. The case is cut and dried."

" You have the murderer ? "

" Not yet. But the drag-net is out. We shall have him, if not to-day, then to-morrow or the next day."

" The artist, I suppose ? "

" Michael Salti, yes. An eccentric man, quite mad. . . . By the way, I must thank you for that point about the candles. In conjunction with the medical examiner's evidence it checked the murder definitely at between one and two a.m."

" There is no doubt, then, I take it, about the identity of the criminal."

" No," Peake asserted, " none at all. He was

seen alone with his model at 10.50 p.m. by one of the apartment house staff and the elevator operators are certain no one was taken to the penthouse during the evening or night. His fingerprints were all over the knife, the candlesticks, the victrola record. There was a lot more corroboration, too."

"And was he seen to leave the building after the crime ? "

"No, he wasn't. That's the one missing link. But since he isn't here, he must have left. Perhaps by the fire-stairs ; we've checked it and it's possible. . . . The girl is Barbara Brebant—a wealthy family." The inspector shook his head. "A wild one, though ; typical Prohibition product. She has played around with dubious artistics from the Village and elsewhere for some years ; gave most of 'em more than they could take, by all accounts. Young, too ; made her debut only about a year ago. Apparently she has made something of a name for herself in the matter of viciousness ; three of our men brought in the very same description—a vicious beauty."

"The old Roman type," Tarrant surmised. "Not so anachronistic in this town, at that. . . . Living with Salti ? "

"No. She lived at home. When she bothered to go home. No one doubts, though, that she was Salti's mistress. And from what I've learned, when she was any man's mistress he was pretty certain to be dragged through the mire. Salti, being mad, finally killed her."

"Yes, that clicks," Tarrant agreed. "The lascivious picture and the nail driven through it. Madmen, of course, act perfectly logically. He was probably a loose liver himself, but she showed him depths he had not suspected. Then remorse. His insanity taking the form of an absence of the usual values, he made her into a symbol of his own vice, through the painting, and then killed her, just as he mutilated the painting with the nail. . . . Yes, Salti is your man all right."

Peake ground out a cigarette. " A nasty affair. But not especially mysterious. I wish all our cases were as simple." He was preparing to take his leave.

Tarrant also got up. He said : " Just a moment. There were one or two things——"

" Yes ? "

" I wonder if I could impose upon you a little more, Inspector. Just to check some things I noticed this morning. Can I be admitted to the penthouse now ? "

Peake shrugged, as if the request were a useless one, but took it with a certain good grace. " Yes, I'll take you up. All our men have left now, except a patrolman who will guard the premises until we make the arrest. I still have an hour to spare."

It was two hours, however, before they returned. The inspector didn't come in, but I caught Tarrant's parting words at the entrance. " You will surely assign another man to the duty to-night, won't you? " The policeman's reply sounded like a grunt of acquiescence.

I looked at my friend in amazement when he came into the lounge. His clothes, even his face, were covered with dirt ; his nose was a long, black smudge. By the time he had bathed and changed and we sat down to one of Katoh's dinners, it was nearly half-past nine.

. . . . .

During dinner Tarrant was unaccustomedly silent. Even after we had finished and Katoh had brought our coffee and liqueurs, he sat at a modernistic tabouret stirring the black liquid reflectively, and in the light of the standing lamp behind him I thought his face wore a slight frown.

Presently he gave that peculiar whistle that sum-moned his man and the butler-valet appeared almost immediately from the passage to the kitchen.

"Sit down, doctor," he spoke without looking up.

Doubtless a small shift in my posture expressed my surprise, for he continued, for my benefit, "I've told you that Katoh is a doctor in his own country, a well-educated man who is over here really on account of this absurd spy custom. Because of that nonsense I am privileged to hire him as a servant, but when I wish his advice as a friend, I call him doctor—a title to which he is fully entitled—and institute a social truce. Usually I do it when I'm worried . . . I'm worried now."

Katoh, meantime, had hoisted himself on to the divan, where he sat smiling and helping himself to one of Tarrant's Dimitrinoes. "Sozhial custom matter of convenience," he acknowledged. "Conference about what?"

"About this penthouse murder," said Tarrant without further ado. "You know the facts related by Inspector Peake. You heard them?"

"I listen. Part my job."

"Yes, well that portion is all right. Salti's the man. There's no mystery about that, not even interesting, in fact. But there's something else, something that isn't right. It stares you in the face, but the police don't care. Their business is to arrest the murderer; they know who he is and they're out looking for him. That's enough for them. But there *is* a mystery up above, a real one. I'm not concerned with chasing crooks, but their own case won't hold unless this curious fact fits in. It is as strange as anything I've ever met."

Katoh's grin had faded; his face was entirely serious. "What this mystery?"

"It's the most perfect sealed room, or rather sealed house, problem ever reported. There was no way out and yet the man isn't there. No possibility of suicide; the fingerprints on the knife are only one element that rules that out. No, he was present

all right. But where did he go, and how ? . . .
Listen carefully. I've checked this from my own
observation, from the police investigations, and from
my later search with Peake.

" When we entered the penthouse this morning,
Gleeb's pass-key didn't suffice ; we had to break the
entrance door in because it was bolted on the inside
by a strong bar. The walls of the studio are of brick
and they have no windows except on the northern
side where there is a sheer drop to the ground. The
window there was fastened on the inside and the
skylight was similarly fastened. The only other
exit from the studio is the door to the bedroom.
This was closed and the key turned in the lock ; the
key was on the studio side of the door.

" Yes, I know," Tarrant went on, apparently
forestalling an interruption ; " it is sometimes
possible to turn a key in a lock from the wrong side,
by means of pincers or some similar contrivance.
That makes the bedroom, the lavatory and the
kitchenette adjoining it, possibilities. There is no
exit from any of them except by the windows. They
were all secured from the inside and I am satisfied
that they cannot be so secured by any one already
out of the penthouse."

He paused and looked over at Katoh, whose head
nodded up and down as he made the successive
points. " Two persons in penthouse when murder
committed. One is victim, other is Salti man. After
murder only victim is visible. One door, windows
and skylight are only exits and they are all secured
on inside. Cannot be secured from outside. Therefore, Salti man still in penthouse when you enter."

" But he wasn't there when we entered. The
place was thoroughly searched. I was there then
myself."

" Maybe trap-door. Maybe space under floor or
entrance to floor below."

" Yes," said Tarrant, " well, now get this. There

are no trap-doors in the flooring of the penthouse, there are none in the walls and there are not even any in the roof. I have satisfied myself of that with Peake. Gleeb, the manager, who was on the spot when the penthouse was built, further assures me of it."

"Only place is floor," Katoh insisted. "Salti man could make this himself."

"He couldn't make a trap-door without leaving at least a minute crack," was Tarrant's counter. "At least I don't see how he could. The flooring of the studio is hardwood, the planks closely fitted together, and I have been over every inch of it. Naturally there are cracks between the planks, lengthwise; but there are no transverse cracks anywhere. Gleeb has shown me the specifications of that floor. The planks are grooved together and it is impossible to raise any plank without splintering the grooving. From my own examination I am sure none of the planks has been, or can be, lifted.

"All this was necessary because there *is* a space of something like two and a half feet between the floor of the penthouse and the roof of the apartment building proper. One has to mount a couple of steps at the entrance of the penthouse. Furthermore, I have been in part of this space. Let me make it perfectly clear how I got there.

"The bedroom adjoins the studio on the south, and the lavatory occupies the north-west corner of the bedroom. It is walled off, of course. Along the northern wall of the lavatory (which is part of the southern wall of the studio) is the bath-tub ; and the part of the flooring under the bath-tub has been cut away, leaving an aperture to the space beneath."

I made my first contribution. "But how can that be ? Wouldn't the bath-tub fall through ? "

"No. The bath-tub is an old-fashioned one, installed by Salti himself only a few weeks ago. It is not flush with the floor, as they make them now, but stands on four legs. The flooring has only been cut away in the middle of the tub, say two or three planks, and the opening extended only to the outer edge of the tub. Not quite that far, in fact."

" There is Salti man's trap-door," grinned Katoh. " Not even door ; just trap."

" So I thought," Tarrant agreed grimly. " But it isn't. Or if it is he didn't use it. As no one could get through the opening without moving the tub—which hadn't been done, by the way—Peake and I pulled up some more of the cut plank by main force and I squeezed myself into the space beneath the lavatory and bedroom. There was nothing there but dirt ; I got plenty of that."

" How about space below studio ? "

" Nothing doing. The penthouse is built on a foundation, as I said, about two and a half feet high, of concrete building blocks. A line of these blocks runs underneath the penthouse, directly below the wall between the studio and bedroom. As the aperture in the floor is on the southern side of that wall, it is likewise to the south of the transverse line of building blocks in the foundation. The space beneath the studio is to the north of these blocks, and they form a solid wall that is impassable. I spent a good twenty minutes scrummaging along the entire length of it."

" Most likely place," Katoh confided, " just where hole in lavatory floor."

" Yes, I should think so too. I examined it carefully. I could see the ends of the planks that form the studio floor partway over the beam above the building blocks. But there isn't a trace of a loose block at that point, any more than there is anywhere else. . . . To make everything certain, we also examined the other three sides of the foundation of the bedroom portion of the penthouse. They are solid and haven't been touched since it was constructed. So the whole thing is just a cul-de-sac ;

there is no possibility of exit from the penthouse even through the aperture beneath the bath-tub."

"You examine also foundations under studio part?"

"Yes, we did that, too. No result. It didn't mean much, though, for there is no entrance to the space beneath the studio from the studio itself, nor is there such an entrance from the other space beneath the bedroom portion. That opening under the bath-tub must mean something, especially in view of the recent installation of the tub. But what does it mean?"

He looked at Katoh long and searchingly and the other, after a pause, replied slowly: "Can only see this. Salti man construct this trap, probably for present use. Then he do not use. Must go some other way."

"But there *is* no other way."

"Then Salti man still there."

"He isn't there."

"Harumph," said Katoh reflectively. It was evident that he felt the same respect for a syllogism that animated Tarrant, and was stopped, for the time being at any rate. He went off on a new tack. "What else specially strange about setting?"

"There are two other things that strike me as peculiar," Tarrant answered, and his eyes narrowed. "On the floor, about one foot from the northern window, there is a fairly deep indentation in the floor of the studio. It is a small impression and is almost certainly made by a nail partly driven through the planking and then pulled up again."

I thought of the nail through the picture. "Could he have put the picture down on that part of the floor in order to drive the nail through it? But what if he did?"

"I can see no necessity for it, in any case. The nail would go through the canvas easily enough just as it stood on the easel."

Katoh said: " With nail in plank, perhaps plank could be pulled up. You say no ? "

" I tried it. Even driving the nail in sideways, instead of vertically, as the original indentation was made, the plank can't be lifted at all."

" O.K. You say some other thing strange, also."

" Yes. The position of the easel that holds the painting of the dead girl. When we broke in this morning, it was turned away from the room, toward the bedroom door, so that the picture was scarcely visible even from the studio entrance, let alone the rest of the room. I don't believe that was the murderer's intention. He had set the rest of the stage too carefully. The requiem ; the candles. It doesn't fit ; I'm sure he meant the first person who entered to be confronted by the whole scene, and especially by that symbolic portrait. It doesn't accord even with the position of the stool, which agrees with the intended position of the easel. It doesn't fit at all with the mentality of the murderer. It seems a small thing but I'm sure it's important. I'm certain the position of the easel is an important clue."

" To mystery of disappearance ? "

" Yes. To the mystery of the murderer's escape from that sealed room."

" Not see how," Katoh declared after some thought. As for me, I couldn't even appreciate the suggestion of any connection.

" Neither do I," grated Tarrant. He had risen and began to pace the floor. " Well, there you have it all. A little hole in the floor near the north window, an easel turned out of position and a sealed room without an occupant who certainly ought to be there. . . . There's an answer to this ; damn it, there must be an answer."

Suddenly he glanced at an electric clock on the table he was passing and stopped abruptly. " My word," he exclaimed, " it's nearly three o'clock. Didn't mean to keep you up like this, Jerry. You either, doctor. Well, the conference is over. We've got nowhere."

Katoh was on his feet, in an instant once more the butler. " Sorry could not help. You wish night-cap, Misster Tarrant ? "

" No. Bring the Scotch, Katoh. And a siphon. And ice. I'm not turning in."

I had been puzzling my wits without intermission ever since dinner over the problem above, and the break found me more tired than I realised. I yawned prodigiously. I made a half-hearted attempt to persuade Tarrant to come to bed, but it was plain that he would have none of it.

I said, " Good-night, Katoh. I'm no good for anything until I get a little sleep. . . . Night, Tarrant."

I left him once more pacing the floor ; his face, in the last glimpse I had of it, was set in the stern lines of thought.

. . . . .

It seemed no more than ten seconds after I got into bed that I felt my shoulder being shaken and, through the fog of sleep, heard Katoh's hissing accents. "——Misster Tarrant just come from penthouse. He excited. Maybe you wish wake up." As I rolled out and shook myself free from slumber, I noticed that my wrist watch pointed to six-thirty.

When I had thrown on some clothes and come into the living-room, I found Tarrant standing with the telephone instrument to his head, his whole posture one of grimness. Although I did not realise it at once, he had been endeavouring for some time to reach Deputy Inspector Peake. He accomplished this finally a moment or so after I reached the room.

" Hallo, Peake ? Inspector Peake ? . . . This is Tarrant. How many men did you leave to guard that penthouse last night ? " . . . " What, only one ? But I said two, man. Damn it all, I don't make suggestions like that for amusement ! " . . .

"All right, there's nothing to be accomplished arguing about it. You'd better get here, and get here pronto." . . . "That's *all* I'll say." He slammed down the receiver viciously.

I had never before seen Tarrant upset ; my surprise was a measure of his own disturbance, which resembled consternation. He paced the floor, muttering below his breath, his long legs carrying him swiftly up and down the apartment. . . . "Damned fools . . . everything must fit. . . . Or else . . ." For once I had sense enough to keep my questions to myself for the time being.

Fortunately I had not long to wait. Hardly had Katoh had opportunity to brew some coffee, with which he appeared somewhat in the manner of a dog wagging its tail deprecatingly, than Peake's ring sounded at the entrance. He came in hurriedly, but his smile, as well as his words, indicated his opinion that he had been roused by a false alarm.

"Well, well, Mr. Tarrant, what *is* this trouble over ? "

Tarrant snapped, "Your man's gone. Disappeared. How do you like that ? "

"The patrolman on guard ? " The policeman's expression was incredulous.

"The *single* patrolman you left on guard."

Peake stepped over to the telephone, called Headquarters. After a few brief words he turned back to us, his incredulity at Tarrant's statement apparently confirmed.

"You must be mistaken, sir," he asserted. "There have been no reports from Officer Weber. He would never leave the premises without reporting such an occasion."

Tarrant's answer was purely practical. "Come and see."

And when we reached the terrace on the building's roof, there was, in fact, no sign of the patrolman who should have been at his station. We entered the penthouse and, the lights having been turned on, Peake himself made a complete search of the premises. While Tarrant watched the proceedings in a grim silence, I walked over to the north window of the studio, grey in the early morning light, and sought for the nail hole he had mentioned as being in the floor. There it was, a small, clean indentation, about an inch or an inch and a half deep, in one of the hardwood planks. This, and everything else about the place, appeared just as Tarrant had desscribed it to us some hours before, previous to my turning in. I was just in time to see Peake emerge from the enlarged opening in the lavatory floor, dusty and sorely puzzled.

" Our man is certainly not here," the inspector acknowledged. " I cannot understand it. This is a serious breach of discipline."

" Hell," said Tarrant sharply, speaking for the first time since we had come to the roof. " This is a serious breach of intelligence, not discipline."

" I shall broadcast an immediate order for the detention of Patrolman Weber." Peake stepped into the bedroom and approached the phone to carry out his intention.

" You needn't broadcast it. I have already spoken to the night operator in the lobby on the ground floor. He told me a policeman left the building in great haste about 3.30 this morning. If you will have the local precinct check up on the all-night lunch-rooms along Lexington Avenue in this vicinity, you will soon pick up the first step of the trail that man left. . . . You will probably take my advice, now that it is too late."

Peake did so, putting the call through at once ; but his bewilderment was no whit lessened. Nor was mine. As he put down the instrument, he said : " All right. But it doesn't make sense. Why should he leave his post without notifying us ? And why should he go to a lunch-room ? "

" Because he was hungry."

" But there has been a crazy murderer here
already. And now Weber, an ordinary cop, if I ever
saw one. Does this place make everybody mad ? "

" Not as mad as you're going to be in a minute.
But perhaps you weren't using the word in that
sense ? "

Peake let it pass. " Everything," he commented
slowly, " is just as we left it yesterday evening.
Except for Weber's disappearance."

" Is that so ? " Tarrant led us to the entrance from
the roof to the studio and pointed downwards.
The light was now bright enough to disclose an
unmistakable spattering of blood on one of the steps
before the door. " That blood wasn't there when
we left last night. I came up here about five-thirty,
the moment I got on to this thing," he continued
bitterly. " Of course I was too late. . . . Damnation, let us make an end to this farce. I'll show you
some more things that have altered during the night."

We followed him into the studio again as he strode
over to the easel with its lewd picture, opposite the
entrance. He pointed to the nail still protruding
through the canvas. " I don't know how closely you
observed the hole made in this painting by the nail
yesterday. But it's a little larger now and the
edges are more frayed. In other words the nail has
been removed and once more inserted."

I turned about to find that Gleeb, somehow
apprised of the excitement, had entered the penthouse and now stood a little behind us. Tarrant
acknowledged his presence with a curt nod ; and
in the air of tension that his tenant was building up
the manager ventured no questions.

" Now," Tarrant continued, pointing out the
locations as he spoke, " possibly they have dried, but
when I first got here this morning there was a trail
of moist spots still leading from the entrance doorway to the vicinity of the north window. You will

find that they were places where a trail of blood had been wiped away with a wet cloth."

He turned to the picture beside him and withdrew the nail, pulling himself up as if for a repugnant job. He walked over to the north window and motioned us to take our places on either side of him.   Then he bent down and inserted the nail, point first, into the indentation in the plank, as firmly as he could. He braced himself and apparently strove to pull the nail toward the south, away from the window.   ,

I was struggling with an obvious doubt.   I said, " But you told us the planks could not be lifted."

" Can't," Tarrant grunted.   " But they can be *slid*."

Under his efforts the plank was, in fact, sliding. Its end appeared from under the footboard at the base of the north wall below the window and continued to move over a space of several feet. When this had been accomplished, he grasped the edges of the planks on both sides of the one already moved and slid them back also.   An opening quite large enough to squeeze through was revealed.

But that was not all.   The huddled body of a man lay just beneath ;   the man was clad only in under-wear and was obviously dead from the beating in of his head.

As we bent over, gasping at the unexpectedly gory sight, Gleeb suddenly cried, " But that is not Michael Salti !   What is this, a murder farm ?   I don't know this man."

Inspector Peake's voice was ominous with anger. " I do.   That is the body of Officer Weber.   But how could he——"

Tarrant had straightened up and was regarding us with a look that said plainly he was anxious to get an unpleasant piece of work finished.   " It was simple enough," he ground out.   " Salti cut out the planks beneath the bath-tub in the lavatory so that *these* planks in the studio could be slid back over the beam along the foundation under the south wall ; their farther ends in this position will now be covering the hole in the lavatory floor. The floor here is well fitted and the planks are grooved, thus making the sliding possible. They can be moved back into their original position by some one in the space below here ; doubtless we shall find a small block nailed to the under portion of all three planks for that purpose.

" He murdered his model, set the scene and started his phonograph, which will run interminably on the electric current. Then he crawled into his hiding-place. The discovery of the crime could not be put off any later than the chambermaid's visit in the morning, and I have no doubt he took a sadistic pleasure in anticipating her hysterics when she entered. By chance your radio man, Gleeb, caused us to enter first.

" When the place was searched and the murderer not discovered, his pursuit passed elsewhere, while he himself lay concealed here all day. It was even better than doubling back upon his tracks, for he had never left the starting post. Eventually, of course, he had to get out, but by that time the vicinity of this building would be the last place in which he was being searched for.

" Early this morning he pushed back the planks from underneath and came forth. I don't know whether he had expected any one to be left on guard, but that helped rather than hindered him. Creeping up upon the unsuspecting guard, he knocked him out—doubtless with that mallet I can just see beside the body—and beat him to death. Then he put his second victim in the hiding-place, returning the instrument that closes it from above, the nail, to its position in the painting. He had already stripped off his own clothes, which you will find down in that hole, and in the officer's uniform and coat he found no difficulty in leaving the building. His first action was to hurry to a lunch-room, naturally, since after a day and a night without food under the floor here, he must have been famished. I have no doubt that your men will get a report of him along Lexington Avenue, Peake; but, even so, he now has some hours' start on you."

"We'll get him," Peake assured us. "But if you knew all this, why in heaven's name didn't you have this place opened up last night, before he had any chance to commit a second murder? We should have taken him red-handed."

"Yes, but I didn't know it last night," Tarrant reminded him. "It was not until late yesterday afternoon that I had any proper opportunity to examine the penthouse. What I found was a sealed room and a sealed house. There was no exit that had not been blocked nor, after our search, could I understand how the man could still be in the penthouse. On the other hand, I could not understand how it was possible that he had left. As a precaution, in case he were still here in some manner I had not fathomed, I urged you to leave at least two men on guard, and it was my understanding that you agreed. I think it is obvious, although I was unable then to justify myself, that the precaution was called for."

Peake said, "It was."

"I have been up all night working this out. What puzzled me completely was the absence of any trap-doors. Certainly we looked for them thoroughly. But it was there right in front of us all the time; we even investigated a portion of it, the aperture in the lavatory floor, which we supposed to be a trap-door itself, although actually it was only a part of the real arrangement. As usual the trick was based upon taking advantage of habits of thought, of our habitised notion of a trap-door as something that is lifted or swung back. I have never heard before of a trap-door that slides back. Nevertheless, that was the simple answer, and it took me until five-thirty to reach it."

Katoh, whom for the moment I had forgotten completely, stirred uneasily and spoke up. " I not see, Misster Tarrant, how you reach answer then."

" Four things," was the reply. " First of all, the logical assumption that, since there was no way out, the man was still here. As to the mechanism by which he managed to remain undiscovered, three things. We mentioned them last night. First, the nail hole in the plank ; second, the position of the easel ; third, the hole in the lavatory floor. I tried many ways to make them fit together, for I felt sure they must *all* fit.

" It was the position of the easel that finally gave me the truth. You remember we agreed that it was wrong, that the murderer had never intended to leave it facing away from the room. But if the murderer had left it as he intended, if no one had entered until we did, and still its position was wrong, what could have moved it in the meantime ? Except for the phonograph, which could scarcely be responsible, the room held nothing but motionless objects. *But if the floor under one of its legs had moved, the easel would have been slid around.* That fitted with the other two items, the nail hole in the plank, the opening under the bath-tub.

" The moment it clicked, I got an automatic and ran up here. I was too late. As I said, I've been up all night. I'm tired ; and I'm going to bed."

He walked off without another word, scarcely with a parting nod. Tarrant, as I know now, did not often fail. He was a man who offered few excuses for himself, and he was humiliated.

It was a week or so later when I had an opportunity to ask him if Salti had been captured. I had seen nothing of it in the newspapers, and the case had now passed to the back pages with the usual celerity of sensations.

Tarrent said, " I don't know."

" But haven't you followed it up with that man, Peake ? "

" I'm not interested. It's nothing but a straight police chase now. This part of it might make a good film for a Hollywood audience, but there isn't the slightest intellectual interest left."

He stopped and added after an appreciable pause, " Damn it, Jerry, I don't like to think of it even now. I've blamed the stupidity of the police all I can ; their throwing me out when I might have made a real investigation in the morning, that delay ; then the negligence in overlooking my suggestion for a pair of guards, which I made as emphatic as I could. But it's no use. I should have solved it in time, even so. There could only be that one answer and I took too long to find it.

" The human brain works too slowly, Jerry, even when it works straight. . . . It works too slowly."

THE EPISODE OF "TORMENT IV"

Characters of the Episode

JERRY PHELAN, the narrator
VALERIE PHELAN, his wife
MORGAN WHITE, their host
LESTER BLACK, a neighbour
AMELIE BLACK, his wife
JULIE BLACK, their daughter
TOM CONSTABLE, Black's cousin
TOM CONSTABLE, JUN., his son
MARGARET CONSTABLE, his widow
JIM DUFF, hired man
TREVIS TARRANT, interested in puzzles

THE EPISODE OF "TORMENT IV"

WE were driving straight towards horror. Though we didn't know it yet.

Valerie said, "Dar*ling*, I do hope Trevis' friend has a decent place. I want a big room, with blinds to make it dim, and none of those awful New Hampshire spiders. And I want a nice, long bath."

"Oh, I guess his place is all right. Nothing much any one can do about New Hampshire spiders, though; they're big and nasty. But there won't be any in our room. The fellow probably has a good enough shack. Why shouldn't he?"

"Ugh! . . . Spiders." Valerie grimaced. "Yes, I suppose it'll be a good house. Trevis is rather tasteful about places himself."

We were motoring down from Canada and had arranged to pick up Tarrant at Winnespequam Lake where he had been staying with a friend named

Morgan White, whom neither Valerie nor I had met. Tarrant planned to come along with us to New York a couple of days later, for White had been good enough to write, asking us to break our trip at his place for a day or so. We had gotten well along now, had passed Lancaster and were scooting through the Crawford Notch as fast as we could. It was as hot as blazes.

I said, " Another hour and a half will get us there. Then a swim, before anything else. I feel like a strip of wilted cardboard."

" I want a nice, long bath," Valerie repeated.

Ahead of us a small truck and a touring car loaded with about eighteen sweating travellers in their shirt sleeves were creeping along the hot asphalt through the centre of the valley. I gave the horn some lusty digs and we swerved past them.

And that, though we didn't know it, either, was our introduction to the episode of " Torment IV."

. . . . .

" The most intriguing problem I have ever heard of," said Tarrant, " is the mystery of the *Mary Celeste*. It is practically perfect."

As he spoke, he leaned back in the hammock chair and the moonlight glinted through dusk against the sharp lines of his lean, strong face. Across the water came the twinkle of little, twin lights, red and green, where a motor-boat, a mere shadow on the darkening lake, put out from the opposite shore.

Valerie and I had arrived, hot and tired, about five in the afternoon. And I had had a most refreshing swim. Winnespequam, as a good many people know, is a New Hampshire lake. It is typical. Surrounded by hills, it has gathered around itself an almost unbroken line of the estates of prosperous merchants and professional men whose winter homes are in New York and Philadelphia. Some of the natives, too, boast modest bungalows nestling near the water, to which they repair during the summer months from their more permanent quarters in the little town that runs down to the northern tip of the lake. Even the motor highway that circles the shore, travels chiefly between forested slopes and does little to disfigure the scene. It is a pleasant and carefree resort.

White, a big man and a good host, grunted, "Don't know it. I'm sure you do. What's the *Mary Celeste*?"

"You don't know the *Mary Celeste*?" Tarrant was plainly surprised. "Why, it's the perfect problem of all time. Dozens of people have had a whack at it, including some fairly clever ones, but it remains to-day as unsolved and apparently insoluble as it was sixty years ago."

He paused ; then, as we were all quiet, obviously waiting for further information, he went on again. "The *Mary Celeste*, sometimes wrongly called the *Marie Celeste*, was a 200-ton brig owned by an American called Winchester. She was picked up by the barque, *Dei Gratia*, one pleasant afternoon early in December, 1872, about three hundred miles west of Gibraltar. This was what was wrong about her : there was not a soul on board and she was sailing derelict on the starboard tack against a north wind that was driving her off her course. Her chronometer, her manifest, bills of lading and register were missing. A further examination showed that a cutlass hanging in her cabin bore stains as if blood had been wiped from it ; but a medical officer in Gibraltar, who subsequently analysed these stains, declared that they were not of blood. There was a deep cut in her rail, as if made by an axe ; but no axe has been mentioned as having been found aboard. On both sides of the bows a small strip, a little more than an inch wide and six or seven feet long had recently been cut from her outer planking a few feet above the water line ; this strip was only about three-eighths of an inch deep and had no effect upon her seaworthiness. Her log had been written up to the evening of the twelfth day previous and the slate log carried to eight a.m. of the eleventh day before. In other words the log was not up-to-date.

"But what was right about her was more astonishing. In the galley were the remains of a burnt-out fire above which stood the victuals for the crew's breakfast. Some of their clothes were hanging upon a line to dry and their effects were in good order and undisturbed. In the master's cabin breakfast had been partly eaten; some porridge was left in a bowl and an egg had been cut open and left standing in its holder. A bottle of cough mixture had been left on the table, its cork beside it. An harmonium stood in one corner and in a sewing machine was a child's garment, partly sewed. None of these articles were in any way disturbed. In the first mate's quarters, moreover, was found a piece of paper with an unfinished sum upon it, just as he had put it aside when interrupted. For the eleven days during which the log had not been kept, the weather over the course from the point last noted in the log to the position where the *Mary Celeste* was found, had been mild. The cargo, some casks of alcohol for Genoa, was intact and securely stowed. The boat itself was staunch in all respects, hull, masts and rigging. There was no sign whatsoever of fire or other hazard. And last of all, the single small boat with which the brig was equipped, was upon its davits, untouched and properly secured.

"Those are the essential facts, as evidenced by many and reliable witnesses. They make a very pretty problem. . . . Of course, a good many hypotheses have been advanced. But actually not one of them is even as easy to credit as the curious state of affairs that was discovered when the *Mary Celeste* was boarded that December afternoon. . . . What could possibly have happened to make a competent crew, not to mention the captain's wife and small daughter, abandon a perfectly sound ship in fine weather, without so much as attempting to launch her boat ? . . ."

There was a little silence.

" Match your mystery," White grunted. " Right here."

Tarrant twisted round in his chair. " Yes ? I think you would be put to it to find another enigma with such simple and such contradictory factors."

" Judge for yourself," said our host. . . . " The Blacks. That big place just across the lake is theirs. Closed up now. They had the ' Torment IV ' and they were——"

Struck by his unusual expression, I interrupted. " What in heaven's name is a torment four ? " I asked. " How do you mean they had it ? "

" Oh, no mystery there," he assured us. " That is the name of their motor-boat. Blacks have been coming up here for years, and a good many years ago now they got their first boat. Just when steam launches were going out and gas engines coming in. Wasn't much of a boat ; jerky and spasmodic, and among other essentials it lacked a self-starter. A fairly thorough nuisance, and they named it, quite properly, *Torment*.

" Presently they got another ; though the second one had a self-starter it was just one more thing to be spasmodic and *Torment II* was a good name for that one also. The third was much better, really a proper boat, but by that time the name had become traditional. *Torment III* was turned in only a year ago and the new one, *Torment IV*, is a beauty ; long, fast, polished up like a new dime. I was out in her early this summer ; I remember at the time that *Torment* seemed a foolish title for such a beautiful piece of machinery, but now—well, I don't know."

He paused, and, " Yes, but what happened ? "
asked Valerie.

" All killed. Lester Black and his wife, Amelie,
and their small daughter. Just like your captain and
his family."

" I didn't say the captain had been killed."
Tarrant's reservation came softly across from the
railing.

" Touch," said White. " Wrong myself. They're
dead ; at least two of 'em are. Said they were
killed, but I don't even know that. No one knows
what actually happened to them."

The voice from the railing was plainly interested
now. " Come on, Morgan, what did happen ? "

" I tell you I don't know. It was really extraordinary. . . . Well, here's the story. Blacks came
up early this year and so did I. It occurred about
the end of June ; hot spell then, if you remember,
and we got it here, too. It was a beautiful, bright
day and very warm for that time of year. Middle of
the afternoon, *Torment IV* ran ashore a little way
up the lake from here ; that was the first we knew
anything was wrong.

" Let me take your method and tell you what was
right about her first. To begin with, her keel was
hardly scratched and that came from her grounding,
which happened by good luck on a strip of sand.
Later, when the affair turned into a tragedy, I went
over her carefully with the sheriff and there wasn't
another mark or dent of any kind on her. Engine,
transmission, and so on, in perfect condition—ran
her back to the Blacks' dock myself after we found
her. Have to tell you the cushions and pillows on
the after-deck are life preservers in themselves,
filled with some kind of stuff that will keep you
afloat if necessary. Not one of 'em had been disturbed in any way ; all present and accounted for.
Not a leak, not a single miss from the motor—
nothing.

" In fact, only two items were wrong. First, one of the chairs on the afterdeck was overturned ; might have happened when she ran ashore. Second, no one was in her. I know, for I saw the boat a hundred yards or so off land and watched her bump. . . . That's all."

Tarrant threw the remains of his cigar in a wide arc and, three second later, came a tiny *phizz* as it struck the water below. " You mean these three people simply vanished ? " he demanded. " How do you know they even went out in the boat, in the first place ? "

" Found that out when I took the boat back. They had gone out after lunch, apparently for a joy ride. And they were drowned somewhere in the middle of the lake—two of the bodies were recovered later, Black's and his wife's, not the child's—but how or why is a complete mystery."

" But in the middle of a bright afternoon——" Tarrant began. " There were no witnesses at all ? No one saw them ? "

" Well, they went up to the town dock at the end of the lake and got some gas ; that was established. Then they headed out again—Lester Black was running the boat—and that is the last any one saw of them. Of course, end of June, not many people around the lake, still a bit early for the summer people. Just the same it *is* strange. Inquiries were made all around the lake, of course, but no one was found to throw even a glimmer on the thing."

" H'm," remarked Tarrant. " There was no obvious cause, I suppose ? No trouble, financial or otherwise ? An estrangement between husband and wife, something serious ? "

" Not a chance," White grunted. " I wasn't an intimate friend but I've known them for years. Man had plenty of money, lived a leisurely life, great family man, as a matter of fact. Very fond of his

wife and daughter and they of him. Last thing in the
world he would do, kill them and drown himself,
if you've anything like that in your head."

Tarrant, meantime, had lit a cigarette and now
smoked silently for some minutes. Finally he spoke.
" Still, something like that is all you leave, if your
other facts are right, isn't it ? People don't jump
out of a perfectly good motor-boat in the middle of
a lake for nothing. Could they swim ? "

" They could all swim, though probably none of
them would have been good for a mile or more. And
I've told you about the life preservers, every one of
them in the boat. We made a careful check of that,
naturally."

" Well, there you are. The more you say, the
more it appears to have been a purposeful performance. . . . There are lots of things in people's lives
that are kept pretty well hidden. . . . What
happened to the boat ? "

" I don't believe there was a thing in Lester
Black's life that would account for that kind of
tragedy," our host insisted. " Prosaic man, prosaic
as hell. The boat was inherited by the Constables,
cousins of the Blacks. Live next them up here, down
the road a bit. They didn't use the boat for some
time ; didn't care to, I guess. Lately they've been
taking her out once in a while. Boat's really too
good to throw away."

Again there came a pause, but just as I was about
to enter an opinion, Tarrant summed the matter up.
" Let's see ; here it is, then. Black took his wife
and daughter out for a spin on a nice, clear day.
First they went to the village dock and bought gas.
Then they turned out into the lake once more. From
the time when they left the village—— By the
way, when was that ? "

" Between two and two thirty."

" And when did the boat come ashore ? "

" Just about four o'clock."

" Then some time during that hour and a half the man and his wife went overboard and doubtless the child, too. There is no way, apparently, of fixing it closer than that ? "

" No, none. Boat may have come ashore directly they were out of it or it may have cruised around for an hour or more. No one noticed it."

" The boat was entirely unharmed and, in any event, they would not have abandoned it ordinarily in the middle of the lake without the precaution of providing themselves with the life preservers so readily at hand. I'm sure there was no fire or you would have mentioned it."

" Absolutely not," White declared. " Not a trace of anything like fire. Anyhow, since it obviously didn't burn up, they would have had plenty of time to throw over *all* the preservers in that case."

I had a sudden thought. " How about some sort of fumes from the engine that might have affected all of them at once so that they were forced to jump without waiting for anything ? "

White merely grunted and Tarrant's tone was quizzical. " Hardly, Jerry. In an open boat proceeding at a fair speed no fumes would get much of a chance to affect the passengers. And some mysterious poison fumes that would make them jump instantly are simply incredible. If the engine burned ordinary gas, as it did, carbon monoxide is all that could possibly come off. So that if we grant the impossible and assume that it came through the floor instead of going out the exhaust—and then stayed near the deck—the result would surely have been to asphyxiate the people, certainly not to throw them overboard. . . . No, that's out.

" There remain, of course, several àlternatives," he continued. " The first is that White threw his wife and daughter out and followed them as a suicide. That's the one you don't care for, Morgan."

" Can't see it at all. Silly."

" There are a number of reasons to account for such an action. A bitter quarrel is only one of them. There is temporary aberration, followed by remorse, for example."

" Nonsense. Still silly. You didn't know Black."

" All right, we'll reverse it. The wife hits the man over the head while he is running the boat, throws him out and then follows *him* with the child. The aberration theory fits a woman better than a man, anyhow ; they are more highly strung. How about that ? "

" Trevis, come off it." White seemed almost provoked by the last notion. " Aside from Amelie's being incapable of such a thing psychologically, I'll tell you why it's absurd. She was a little woman, much smaller than Black. She couldn't possibly have tossed him out *unless* she hit him first. And he hadn't been hit. The autopsies showed that neither of them had a single mark of violence on them."

Undoubtedly Tarrant was smiling in the darkness as he said, " Very well, we'll leave that theory entirely. I was only thinking abstractly, you know ; no reflections intended. . . . Then we are left with one more hypothesis, the accident one."

" Ugh."

" Perhaps it's the most reasonable of all, anyhow. The child falls overboard, the mother jumps to save it, the father, who is running the boat, is the last to act. He jumps to save them both, and they are all drowned, while the boat, which in the excitement he has failed to close off, speeds away."

White answered at once. " Won't do, either. Naturally, we've been over that possibility up here. There is not merely one, but three or four points, against it. Altogether too many. As I said, they all knew how to swim and the daughter was about ten, not helpless in the water by any means, even with her clothes on. In the second place, the Blacks have been aquaplaning for years, and aquaplaning behind a fast boat is no joke. Matter of fact, not even aquaplaning ; they did it on water skis, much harder. The point is, if any one had fallen over, they would naturally have followed what they have done so often when there was a spill off the skis ; swung the boat about and come up to the swimmer. They were used to doing that ; they could do it quickly ; it was a habit. They were all used to the water, to being on it and in it ; couldn't possibly have lost their heads completely over a mere tumble.

" But last and most impressive of all, I tell you that Black was a prosaic and methodical man, known for it. Supposing some real emergency— though what it could have been, God knows— supposing the wife did jump and he prepared to go after her. He would never have left his boat empty without shutting off the motor, it doesn't take an instant. Granting even that impossibility, however, it is simply beyond belief that he would have jumped to their rescue himself before throwing them at least a couple of preservers, which would reach them more quickly than he and be of as much use. You must remember that they weren't at all helpless in the water, either of them. He would surely have done that first. Then, I grant you, he *might* have gone in, just to make sure. But the theory you built won't do. . . . No, it won't. . . . Really."

" The objections are strong," Tarrant acknowledged. " Of course, I didn't know the people at all. . . . Well, that's the end of the list, so far as I can see now. You discard them all ; the first as being impossible on grounds of character, the second on physical grounds, the third on grounds of habit and familiarity with the water and its hazards. I——"

For the first time during the discussion Valerie interrupted. She had been sitting quietly beyond Tarrant and smoking while the talk went on. Now she said, " May I suggest something ? Perhaps it's pretty wild. . . . What about this ? The parents had received some kind of threat, kidnapping or something. No, this is better. They were hailed from the shore while they were riding about and they landed. There the child actually *was* kidnapped. The parents were stricken with grief, they were quite out of their heads for a time. They went out on the lake again and presently made a suicide pact and both honoured it at once. That covers it all, doesn't it ? The child's body, I understood, hasn't been found."

Tarrant's chair creaked as he turned towards her and a match, flaring in his hand, showed his surprised and interested expression. " Valerie," he said, " you have constructed the best theory yet. Really, that's very good. It covers all the facts of the case except one. So I'm afraid it won't work, but I can see that you and I are going to get on famously. It's too bad you have forgotten that one little point. Black was a well-to-do man. Kidnapping is done for ransom ; and surely he would have paid a ransom as an alternative to his wife's and his own suicide. It is unreasonable to suppose that even a week's separation would cause him to choose so absurdly. The only possibility would be that the child was taken by some enemy for revenge and no return intended. That's too much like a bad shocker ; I'm afraid it won't do. . . . It was a good try, though."

He rose and stretched. " I'm going to take a stroll for a bit and then turn in early. I imagine Valerie and Jerry would like to, too, after their ride." He turned and wandered slowly down the verandah.

" So you give it up ? " White called after him. " No answer ? "

" No. All the first answers are washed out. I'll grant you this, though, Morgan. You have a very good replica of the *Mary Celeste* ; all the essential items are there. It's a problem all right ; I'm not through thinking about it yet."

.   .   .   .   .

The matter remained in this state of suspense while we were sitting about the following morning after breakfast. The day was bright and clear but gave promise of becoming even hotter than the previous one ; I was distinctly glad that Valerie and I were not to be touring the roads again.

A half-hour or so later Morgan White made the suggestion that we try his tennis court, since if we delayed much longer it might well become too uncomfortable for playing. Every one was agreeable and we trouped down to the court, which turned out to be of clay in excellent condition. " Jim Duff, the Constable's hired man, rolls it for me every other morning before he goes up to their place," White confided.

We proceeded to enjoy the fruits of Duff's labours. After several sets it was getting considerably hotter and Valerie voted for doubles. We won, though I am not at all sure it was due entirely to our play ; during the second and last set I, for one, was beginning to feel a touch weary.

Every one agreed, at the conclusion of that set, that swimming was the form of exercise now indicated. All of us except Val were dripping. In fifteen minutes or less we had reassembled at White's boathouse in bathing suits and stood smoking a final cigarette along the little platform by the side of the boathouse proper that covers his *Grey Falcon*. I remarked upon the diving-board protruding over the water at the platform's end and White assured us all that the lake here was seven or eight feet deep, so that diving was feasible. The afternoon before I had simply jumped off the end of his dock.

" I think I'll be trying it," I informed the rest, just as White turned to Tarrant and pointed out over the water.

" There, see that boat ? " he said. " About two-thirds across the lake, heading north. That's *Torment IV*, the one we were discussing last night. Wait till I get my glasses from the boathouse and you can have a good look at her, Trevis."

He unlocked the boathouse door and disappeared inside, returning at once with a pair of binoculars which he handed over. At the moment, however, I was more interested in getting wet than seeing a motor-boat. Valerie was already in the water, shouting that it was perfect and calling the rest of us Sissies. " You look," I told Tarrant. " I'm for a dive." White apparently felt the same way, for upon turning the glasses over to his friend, he immediately took a header into the lake.

Thus it happened that the first intimation of excitement reached me in mid-air. I had struck the end of the board hard and it threw me high. At the top of the spring I was just touching my feet for a jack-knife when Tarrant's shout came to me. " Morgan ! Morgan, come here ! Hurry ! We must get your——" Swish into the water went my head and his words were cut off ; but on the way I got an upside-down view of Tarrant holding the binoculars steadily to his eyes, his mouth suddenly grim as he called out.

Under the water I twisted back towards the dock and, reaching an arm over the platform above me, pulled myself partway up. " What ho ? " I demanded.

White was already clambering up and Tarrant disappearing through the door. " The boat," he called after him. " Hurry up ! How fast can we get her out ? "

Tarrant's calm is proverbial, but when he wants to, he can certainly work quickly. By the time I got inside he had the slide-door at the end almost up and White, dropping into the driving seat of the *Grey Falcon*, was pushing the starter-button. " All

clear," called Tarrant; the rat-tat-tat of the motor
fell to a grind as the clutch went into reverse. Just
as the boat began to back out, Valerie jumped down
into the rear deck.

We came around in a wide circle and headed out
into the lake, the motor coughing a little as it was
opened full without any preliminary warning.
Tarrant said, " They jumped. You'll have another
tragedy unless we can get there in time."

" *What is* this about ? " cried Valerie. " Who
jumped where ? Have you boys all gone crazy ? "
Valerie has noticed, I think, that men of Tarrant's
age rather like to have her call them boys.

His voice was unpleasantly serious as he answered.
" The people in that boat I was watching, this
Torment of yours, Morgan. There were two people
in her, a big man and a little one, or maybe a man and
a boy——"

" Tom Constable and junior, his son, undoubtedly," White put in, without turning his head.

" Suddenly the man who was driving scrambled
out of his seat and into the rear deck, where the boy
was riding. He grabbed the boy's arm and
immediately jumped overboard, pulling the boy with
him. . . . Here, Morgan, don't follow the boat !
There's no one in it. The place where they went out
is almost on a direct line between your boat and
that big rock on the other shore."

All of us except White were on our feet looking
helplessly across the water to where, a good two
miles away now, *Torment IV* was still speeding
up the lake with her bow waves curving high on both
sides. It gave me a queer feeling, that boat which I
could just see was empty (now that I had been told),
driving along as if operated by an invisible pilot.
The sun was burning down, making such a glare on
the lake that it was impossible to discern any small
object on the surface. Such as a man's head, for
example. Tarrant had the binoculars (being

Tarrant, of course, he had not failed to bring them) held to his eyes with one hand, attempting to shade their glasses with the other.

" Have you got her at top speed, Morgan ? " he demanded. " Best part of a mile yet to go, as I judge it."

"Everything she's got," grunted White. " Full out. Check my direction if you see anything."

" Thought I saw them a minute ago. Right together. Lost them now."

" Not good swimmers. Nowhere nearly as good as the Blacks. Doubt if they can stay up long enough."

" Oh," said Valerie, and sat down abruptly, her rubber bathing trunks making a squdging sound on a cushion. " Hurry, Mr. White. Oh, hurry ! "

White said, " Agh ! "

" Lost 'em," Tarrant announced definitely. " Not a sign."

Nor was there a sign when, some minutes later, we came up to the spot where, as closely as Tarrant was able to guess, the thing had happened. For five or ten minutes we floated, with the motor cut off, peering over the sides and in all directions around the *Grey Falcon*. Nothing but the calm, bright water of Winnespequam, ruffled by the lightest of breezes, met our gaze. Valerie, too, searched with the rest of us, although I could see from her expression that she wasn't very anxious to discover anything. " Of course," Tarrant pointed out, " I can't be positive as to the spot. The line is right, but the exact distance from your boathouse, Morgan, is another thing."

We began to circle slowly, in wider and wider courses.

" Any use diving ? " I asked, having some vague notion that these people could possibly be brought up and resuscitated.

" No good. Deep here ; take a deep-sea diver to fetch bottom. Besides we don't know where they went down. Even if the line is right, they may have swum some distance in any direction before they gave out. . . . Not to the shore, though. They never made that."

Our search went on. But though we circled over a large area for more than two hours, not a trace did we find either of the man or of the boy. Finally, "Nothing more we can do," said White gloomily. "They sink in this lake. Didn't recover the others for three days. . . . Might as well run up towards Winnespequam and see what happened to the boat." He turned the wheel and we headed north.

Scarcely had we gone a mile when on the shore off our starboard side we saw a knot of persons gathered at the edge of the lake ; and a little distance from them, what was obviously the boat we sought. I wondered, as we approached, at the unmistakable signs of excitement evidenced by the small group, for surely *Torment IV* must have grounded here nearly two hours previously.

We landed a hundred yards to the south at a disused and ramshackle dock, and made our way to the scene. An old man passed us as we drew near ; he was hobbling along, shaking his head, and his mumbling reached us clearly enough—" 'Tis bewitched, she be a devil's boat."

It took us some time to discover, from the excited replies of the people we came up with, that yet a further tragedy had occurred. They interrupted each other and told the story backwards rather than forwards, but at last we pieced together the following account.

Torment IV, after the affair that Tarrant had witnessed, had run ashore upon a small island so close to the town wharf that she had been seen by numerous loungers. Among these was Jim Duff, in the village on an errand, and he had at once procured another boat and been taken out to salvage that of the Constable's. The latter seemed, at any rate, to possess her own luck, for neither in running afoul of the island nor in her present landing had she suffered much harm. Duff had put himself aboard and, finding all in good order, had set off towards the Constable's dock alone, after expressing his fears to his companions that some ill must have befallen his employers.

The story then passed to four fishermen who, having been almost where we now stood, had witnessed the sequel. Duff, they asserted, had been passing not far from shore on his way south when, without any evident cause, he leapt from the seat he occupied and dived overboard. No doubt he twisted the wheel as he jumped away, for *Torment IV* turned and headed in. Two of the fishermen, however, seeing their friend struggling in the water, had immediately put out in their row-boat and gone to his rescue. Duff was a strong swimmer, accustomed to the lake since boyhood, but to their astonishment, no sooner did he note their approach than he turned and, in place of coming ashore, swam out into the lake with every appearance of panic. They were still some distance away from him when this happened and, though they made all possible efforts to overtake the man, he had sunk three times before they reached him, and he had drowned. Nevertheless, after much exertion they had been able to recover his body.

For the first time we noticed a still form, covered by one of the fisherman's blankets, lying farther up the bank among the trees.

" Have you tried resuscitation ? " asked Tarrant sharply.

" More'n an hour an' a half we tried," he was told. " He be dead, he be."

White and Tarrant walked over to the body and, after sending Valerie back to the *Grey Falcon*, I followed. When I arrived, they had drawn back the blanket and were looking at the corpse. It was not a pleasant sight. I have been led to believe that persons who have drowned wear a peaceful expression but this one assuredly did not. He was a man of about forty-eight or fifty, a native New Hampshire-man, bony and obviously strong. But on his face there was stamped a hideous grimace, an expression so obviously of extreme horror that it would have been essentially identical on any cast of features.

With a grunt Morgan quietly replaced the blanket. " That's him, all right ; that's Jim Duff."

When we returned to the shoreline, arrangements were being made to tow *Torment IV* back to the Constable's dock. No one seemed anxious to pilot her, and I noted a bit absently that our host did not volunteer his services this time, however willing he may have been on the first occasion he had told us about. Once more in the *Grey Falcon*, we backed out on the water and steered for home. A subdued party. It was Tarrant who broke the silence after it had continued for several minutes.

" No use trying to avoid the subject," he said. " We're all thinking about it. . . . If what I saw earlier, and what has just happened here, isn't due to some form of insanity arising with the utmost suddenness, God knows what it may be."

Silence again.

White spoke this time, gruffly. " How can a boat drive people insane ? Certainly not a hard-boiled old-timer like Duff."

" Could it, could it be sunstroke ? " Valerie asked in a small voice. " It's awfully hot."

Tarrant admitted, " There's no question it's hot. But I don't see a sunstroke theory. None of us feel any symptoms, do we ? And we have been on the lake longer than any of them were."

" But what *can* have made them do it ? "

" I don't know," said Tarrant in a low tone. " I confess I don't know. . . . At first I felt that some deep cause for suicide must be operating in the

Black-Constable family. What I saw surely looked like nothing so much as a determined suicide combined with murder, or perhaps a double suicide. . . . But that's out now, definitely. This man Duff could hardly be involved in such a thing and, furthermore, I don't believe for a moment that he had the least idea of doing away with himself when he started that boat down the lake."

No one had even a conjecture to add. The rest of our return was only the purring of the engine and the slap-slither of the little waves against our boat. As for me, I was completely bewildered. Here were a succession of calamities ; first three persons, then two, finally one, who for no reason at all had abruptly cast themselves into the lake to drown. The last two tragedies had been amply witnessed, one by Tarrant himself through the binoculars, the other by no less than four fishermen, friends of the unfortunate man, and this time at a reasonably short range.

One must suppose, at all events, that the first disaster had been similar to its successors, a finding that scarcely did much to account for any of them. The last victim's relations with the others had certainly not been of a nature so serious as to form a bond of death. What could possibly have caused such different types of people, in broad daylight, on this peaceful lake, and plainly menaced by no danger, to jump and die ? Duff's reported actions, surely, appeared to indicate that, once out of the boat, he was determined to drown. Suicide seemed absurd ; and yet his actions had comported with it. Both sight and sound—for his friends had shouted at him—had combined to assure him that help was close at hand. But he had renounced all aid. Involuntarily I shook my head. It just didn't make sense.

When we landed, Tarrant made an abrupt excuse and hurried off to the house in his bathing suit.

Apparently he changed with some speed, for he was nowhere to be found when the rest of us climbed the path.

. . . . .

He was late for dinner. We were half-way through the main course when he came in and sat down at the table. " Glad you didn't wait for me," he said, a little absently. On his forehead there still lingered the trace of the frown that always accompanies his most strenuous thinking.

" Didn't know whether you'd show up or not," White remarked in explanation. " Where have you been ? "

" Looking over that boat."

" Thought so. Find anything ? "

" Not a thing," answered Tarrant frankly. " That is, if you mean, as I take it you do, anything that throws light on these strange deaths."

For a time he applied himself to his meal, but when he had caught up with us at its end, he pushed back his chair and addressed us. " I examined this *Torment IV* from stem to stern. She is a beautiful boat, Morgan, no doubt about it ; and she has gotten out of these mishaps herself with no more than a few dents in the bows. And a long gash coming back from the bow on one side where she careened off a rock when grounding on the island. It's above the water-line and scarcely an eighth of an inch deep. No real harm ; but just another item resembling the *Mary Celeste*. You remember *she* had strips in her, running back from the bows, too. It's a strange coincidence how these circumstances match, even down to the condition of the boat—so far as a motor-boat *can* exhibit the same conditions as a two hundred-ton brig. . . ."

In the short pause I queried, " Still, that doesn't get us anywhere, does it ? "

He agreed. " As you say. Even if we had reason to believe that the same causes were operating—

since several of the same symptoms have appeared—
we have no further clue, since we don't know what
could have brought about the situation on the
Mary Celeste. And of course we have no right to
assume even similar causes ; a hundred to one this is
merely a superficial resemblance."

Came one of White's grunts. " Nothing at all,
eh ? Nothing ? What were you looking for ? "

" To tell you the truth," Tarrant confessed with a
smile, " I'm afraid I was looking for some sort of
mechanical arrangement. I don't know exactly what.
Something along the lines of Jerry's idea of a poison
gas, possibly. Since it obviously couldn't come from
the motor in the routine way, I considered the
possibility of a small, hidden tank concealed somewhere on board. With a blower or insufflator
arrangement, of course. Although I have some
knowledge of gases and have never heard of one
having the observed effects, it is still possible. That
would at least indicate malice, murder, in fact ;
and we should have a reasonable background for
these events. Pretty far-fetched, I admit. You see
to what conjectures I have been reduced by the
apparently inexplicable data. . . . I have never
cared much for supernatural explanations."

" Hmph. Why ' apparently ' inexplicable ? Looks
actually inexplicable to me."

" Nothing," said Tarrant shortly, " is actually
inexplicable. That is, if you credit Causation. I do.
What is loosely called the ' inexplicable ' is only the
unexplained, certainly not the unexplainable. The
term is quite literally a mere catchword for ignorance.
That's our present relation to the deaths ; we are
still ignorant of their cause."

" Guess we'll have to remain so this time."

" Oh, no. After our experience to-day, it's a
challenge I accept."

Something in his tone interested Valerie. She
said, " I'm glad you won't give it up. But what else

can you do now, if you have already examined the boat ? "

" I've examined the boat. Thoroughly. I even had the floorboards up ; I couldn't take the engine out but I did everything else. Had a boy go under her in the dock and he reported everything shipshape and just as it ought to be along the keel."

" Well, then," Val repeated, " what is left that you can do ? "

Tarrant smiled. " Now I'm disappointed in you, Valerie. Surely that is obvious. There is something pretty drastic that happens to people in that boat. There is only one alternative left now. With Jerry's help I propose to find out to-morrow what it is that happens. When we know that, it may be possible for us to deal with it."

" Oh. Oh, I see. Of course. You're going out in the boat yourself." Val paused ; and added suddenly, " Not with Jerry, you're not ! No, I won't listen to it. I won't let Jerry go anywhere near the horrible thing ! "

I expostulated. If Tarrant was willing to risk his neck, it seemed only fair that some one else should go with him. Morgan White offered to go immediately, but it appeared that Trevis preferred me for some reason.

" He won't have to go very near it, Valerie," Tarrant assured her. " I wouldn't myself permit him to come with me in the boat. I only want him to follow me at a respectful distance in the *Grey Falcon*, so that, if I jump over, he can pick me up. . . . There must be a reason why people jump."

In the end we persuaded her, though Tarrant did most of it. There are times when Valerie seems hardly to listen to *me*. He persuaded her not only to permit me to follow him but not to come along herself. As usual, he had his way.

. . . . .

We all went down to the boathouse after breakfast.

White explained to me how to run his boat, which was simple enough ; and Tarrant and I started off for the Constable's dock, leaving Valerie and our host behind. He agreed to run *Torment IV* up and down the lake opposite the boathouse, so that they could observe what happened, if anything.

On the way over, Tarrant produced the implements with which he had equipped the *Grey Falcon* earlier in the day—so as not to worry Valerie unnecessarily, he said. They made a curious collection. There was a shotgun and, somewhat redundantly, a rifle ; an axe and a long rope with a lasso at its end completed his equipment.

Naturally my attention was caught by the fire-arms. " But what can we use those for ? " I inquired curiously. " Is there some one to shoot at ? But no, there wasn't any one in the boat except the people who jumped out of it, each time. And this morning you are going alone, aren't you ? "

" I don't know. I'm going alone, yes. On the other hand, there is certainly villainy of some kind here, and where there is villainy, it has been my experience that there is usually a villain. . . . I'm glad it turned out a good, hot day again."

More puzzled than ever, I said, " We threw out the sunstroke theory, didn't we ? What in heaven's name has a hot day got to do with it ? "

" I don't know, Jerry, honestly I don't," Tarrant grinned. " I have the haziest notion about this thing, but it is much too vague for me to tell you. So far as I know, there are only two conditions leading up to these deaths, a ride in *Torment IV* and a bright, warm day. Since I want to see duplicated whatever happens, I am glad that both conditions are fulfilled."

There was no time for more, as we had now reached the Constable's dock. Tarrant, who had taken the precaution of donning his bathing trunks, landed and was admitted to the boathouse by a man who evidently had been waiting for him. After a short delay—no doubt he was making another examination of *Torment IV*—I heard him start the motor and, a moment later, the ill-omened motor-boat slid slowly out of its shelter.

The events that succeeded constituted a series of complete surprises for me, culminating in sheer amazement. He turned and headed the boat out into the lake, opening her up fairly wide, and I brought the *Grey Falcon* along in his wake as closely as I dared, constantly alert for any change of direction or other sudden action on his part. *Torment IV* had a driving seat stretching entirely across the centre of the boat, and my first surprise was to observe Tarrant clamber up on this and crouch there in a most uncomfortable position, as he manipulated the controls. Nothing further happened, however, and while continuing to watch carefully, I could not avoid wondering again for what purpose he had provided the weapons in my own craft.

I realised that it was foolish and yet I could think of no other type of explanation of the tragedies than a supernatural one. A ghost or ghoul? In broad daylight, on a motor-boat? Even so, a shotgun isn't of much use against a ghost. But of course that was nonsense, anyhow. Even the strange coincidence of sudden, self-destructive madness on the part of these diverse people in similar circumstances, was better. And again, you can't shoot madness. The rope and the axe I abandoned hopelessly.

By now we had reached the centre of the lake and Tarrant motioned to me, without turning around, that he proposed to slow down. As I did so, too, I saw that he had produced a length of stout cord and was lashing *Torment IV*'s wheel in such a way that the boat would continue forward in a large circle.

When he had done so, he scrambled out of the driver's seat altogether and, passing right by the rear well-deck with its comfortable chairs, gained the upper decking of the hull itself as far astern as he could get, immediately over the propeller, in fact. There he stood upright, balancing easily on both feet and intently observing the entire boat ahead of him, almost all of which was visible from his position.

And nothing happened. *Torment IV* continued to circle at a reduced speed and Tarrant continued to watch as tensely as ever. It went on for so long that I am afraid I was beginning to get a little careless. I must have been all of seventy-five yards away when suddenly I saw him stiffen, start to turn away, take one more glance forward—and dive !

I strained my eyes, but I could see no change whatsoever in his boat, which was keeping placidly on her circular course. It certainly looked as if he had seen something, but if so, it remained invisible to me. Abruptly I came to and swung the *Grey Falcon* towards where he was swimming with more speed than I had thought him capable of. Even yet I was not much concerned. Tarrant was neither a Philadelphian merchant nor a backwoodsman. Furthermore, he was a good swimmer and in his bathing suit. Accordingly my astonishment all but took my breath away entirely when, as I came up towards him, he gave a horrified glance over his shoulder and twisting abruptly away from the *Grey Falcon*, dug his arms into the water in a panic-stricken Australian crawl !

In that moment I realised we were up against something serious. I threw in the clutch and went after him. Fortunately I could always overtake him with the motor-boat I had ; and I prepared to jump in for him if he showed signs of sinking. I was sure that, no matter how good a swimmer he was, he would sink before he reached Winnespequam, some eight miles away, for he was heading up the lake directly towards the town, although the nearest shore was well within a mile.

I was drawing up to him again, but this time, instead of slowing down, I sent the boat past him as closely as I dared. And as I went past, I yelled at the top of my voice, " Tarrant ! For God's sake, what the hell has gotten into you ! "

Evidently one of his ears was out of the water, for he hesitated and raised his head. For a moment he regarded my boat and myself without recognition, then he trod water and looked anxiously all about. I was coming about now, having been carried beyond him, and I heard his hoarse shout, " All right. I'm coming aboard."

He was literally shaking when I helped pull him over the side and for a minute or so he merely stood in the *Grey Falcon* and gasped. Then he said suddenly, " Where is that devil's boat ? " I was struck by the same expression the old man had used the day before.

" There she is," he went on. " She's getting too close in to shore. She mustn't land again ! " In the chase after Tarrant I had almost forgotten *Torment IV*, but now I saw that she was, in fact, circling closer and closer to the edge of the lake.

" We shall have to get near enough, Jerry, so that I can rope that little mast on her bow," he grated. " Don't get *any* closer than you have to, though." And he added under his breath, " God, I hate to do this." Well, I gave up ; in view of these unbelievable happenings it didn't seem even worth while asking questions. No matter what occurred, I didn't think my friend had gone mad.

I settled down to the job and soon made a parallel course with *Torment IV*. " Not so close, for God's sake ! " yelled Tarrant. I eased off a little ; and he threw his coiled rope. The third time he succeeded ; the noose settled accurately over the small mast and he jerked it tight. " Make for the centre of the lake now, Jerry. Give it all you've got ; you'll have to pull the other boat out of her course. I didn't dare

stop her completely for fear it wouldn't happen."
As he spoke he was securing his end of the rope to a
cleat, and immediately caught up the axe and took
his stand above the taut line, looking anxiously
along it. So that was why he had brought the axe!
Apparently he foresaw the possibility of having to
sever the rope even before it could be released. It
was hard going, pulling against *Torment IV*'s
powerful engine, but finally we were well out in the
lake again. With an audible sigh of relief Tarrant
brought down the axe, the rope snapped.

"Now," he said, "the rifle," retrieving it from
the floor and slipping in a cartridge. It was a
regulation Winchester, a heavy weapon. "Go
parallel again but at least twice as far away from
her," he admonished me.

When this course had been taken up to his satisfaction and we were a good hundred yards and
more from *Torment IV*, he commenced firing at the
empty boat. The shots crashed out over the lake,
a round dozen of them, and I saw that he was quite
literally attacking the motor-boat itself. A little
series of spurts appeared just along its waterline as
the bullets punched a neat row of holes through the
hull.

"Enough, I guess," he observed, putting down
the rifle and catching up the shotgun, hastily loading
both chambers. We waited then, still accompanying
Torment IV at the same distance; and shortly she
began to list on the side towards us. This had the
effect of straightening her course somewhat but only
for a few hundred yards, for she was filling rapidly
now and beginning to plough down into the water.
Deliberately she settled on her starboard side until
the lake poured over her rail; then with a final
swirl her stern lifted a little and she went under.

But, just as she did so, something climbed up on
her port side and hopped away. At the distance I
couldn't see what it was, except that I should have

judged it to be about two feet or more in diameter. It made a dark spot against the bright water, and it did not sink. On the contrary it scrambled over the surface and it was making directly for our boat. " Easy, Jerry," Tarrant grated, as I instinctively put on speed ; " we've got to get it."

Reluctantly I swung to port in order not to catch the thing in our wake. It seemed to be coming towards us with the speed of lightning ; I doubt if we could have distanced it, anyhow. Tarrant's face was white and strained, and a tremor ran over his body as he raised his gun. For a few seconds he waited, then fired. Just behind the creature the water splattered where the shot struck the lake. He had one more shot ; the thing was closer now and still coming rapidly. It was so close I could begin to see it clearly—the most repulsive animal I have ever looked at. Spiders always make me creepy, but this monstrous creature with its flashing legs, its horribly hairy bulb of a body, was nauseating and worse than nauseating. There was something so horrifying about it that I very nearly jumped before it reached us. I could see, or imagined that I could, a beady, malignant eye fixed definitely upon me. If Tarrant had missed his last shot I don't know what would have happened. It's one of those things I don't let myself think about.

He didn't miss. Simultaneously with the roar of the gun, the water about it churned and the monster disappeared, blown to bits.

For the next ten minutes we drifted aimlessly. I was being sick over the side of the *Grey Falcon*.

.   .   .   .   .

" I think," said Tarrant that evening, " that it was some member of the *Lycosidæ* or wolf-spider species. Or else one of the larger species of *Aviculariidæ*, some of which grow to great size. Even so, I have never heard of anything as large as this having been reported. And judging from the experiences here I judge it unlikely that many observers will live to report it. Although the poisonous effects of most spider bites are exaggerated, I have a feeling that this one's bite was fatal.

" Of course I had some inkling as to what to expect. Oh, not such a spider, I couldn't guess that. Although I should have done. When I was examining the motor yesterday, I did see some heavy cobwebbing way up under the bow, but at that time I didn't think that any sort of spider could be so terrifying; I am not greatly upset by spiders myself. Just the same, reason told me that something appeared on that boat which drove people overboard in a panic. And since the motor was the only portion of it that I was unable to examine thoroughly, it was from that direction that I looked for it. That is why, as soon as I could, I lashed the wheel and got as far away from the driving seat as was possible. The heat, I believe, brought it out; not only the heat of the motor but also that of the sun pouring down on the forward deck. How it got into the driver's cockpit I don't know; the first I saw of it was when it sprang up on the back of the seat.

" I can't express the horror and loathing its appearance inspired. It was sufficient to make Jerry pretty ill—and it never got with twenty yards of him. Sheer panic, that's what one felt in its presence. When I struck the water, I had no thought of where I was going, only a hopeless conviction that I would surely be overtaken. I forgot everything, all my own preparations; and the mere swish of Jerry's boat when he first came toward me only increased my terror. That is why Duff turned away from his rescuers; in his panic-stricken condition he may even have imagined that the rowboat with its oars was the beast itself. . . . Well, thank God I recovered sufficiently to get into the *Grey Falcon* and finish the job."

"Suppose there'll be no trouble about the motor-boat?"

"Oh, no. I didn't see the widow, but she sent word that I could blow it up if I wished and good riddance. The loss of the boat was a small price, I think."

Valerie shuddered and reached for my hand. "Jerry," she said, "it's nice here, but take me home to-morrow, please?"

THE EPISODE OF THE HEADLESS HORRORS

Characters of the Episode

JERRY PHELAN, the narrator
VALERIE PHELAN, his wife
MARY PHELAN, his sister
JING DUCK, negro keeper of gas station
LINCOLN DUCK, his brother
CAPTAIN BABCOCK, of the New Jersey State
    Constabulary
TREVIS TARRANT, interested in the unusual
KATOH, his butler-valet

THE EPISODE OF THE HEADLESS HORRORS

OF course it was obvious enough when Tarrant had solved it. But for several weeks it kept the New Jersey State Troopers stationary before a stone wall of the inexplicable. And as for the readers of the metropolitan press, their bewilderment grew as the case developed and, towards its end, even the numerous suggestions that poured over the city editors' desks, ranging all the way from the use of numerology to a hint that here was a Nazi pogrom, dwindled from a flood to a mere trickle. Some of these theories, wild as they were, were adopted by the police in their baffled impotence ; but to no avail.

My own acquaintance with the case only came after it had progressed through a number of stages over a period of some weeks. I had seen a headline here and there but I hadn't bothered much about it.

Valerie and Mary were sitting out on the terrace and I had just come from the living-room with a

shaker of cocktails when up our road from the highway travelled one of the dilapidated taxis that hang
around the Norrisville station. Since our marriage
Valerie and I have been living in Val's little modernistic house, which is just about big enough for both of
us without an inch left over. It was really too
perfect a house for Valerie to leave and, since we
had chased the terror away from her room and from
the spiralled staircase, it was a happy and comfortable home.

We regarded the taxi with surprised interest, for
we were expecting no one ; and this interest changed
to undisguised pleasure when the car drew up and
an unmistakable rear view of Katoh was presented
as he struggled out of the cab first, lugging after him
a portmanteau almost as large as himself. Tarrant
followed, after paying off the taxi driver, and
advanced up the terrace with a smile playing over
his tanned face.

" Glad to see you," I declared. " What brings
you out to our midst so unexpectedly ? How are
you, Katoh ? "

The little Japanese grinned, jerking his head
violently in a series of nods. " Fine, pless, thank
you, How-do, Mrs. Phelan, Miss Phelan."

Tarrant said, " This ' Headless Horrors ' thing.
I'm interested in it. Thought I'd spend a few days
looking into it and I was a bit afraid you might be
offended if I came out here and didn't stop with you.
I've rung you up twice to-day ; once I couldn't get
through and once there was no answer. So we just
packed up and came along."

Valerie was looking as much like the worried
housewife as she can. " Golly, Trevis," she admitted,
" I'm delighted to have you but there isn't a place
in the house where I can put you up. We have only
two beds in the place. Though Jerry can fold himself
up on the lounge in the living-room. Yes, that'll do
it all right."

" I wouldn't think of it. Throwing an old man like Jerry out of his bed. Never. Seriously, though, Valerie, I had quite forgotten how small this house of yours is; it's so perfectly appointed that one carries away an impression of size too. I'm afraid I've made a nuisance of us." But his smile evidenced an entire lack of embarrassment. " We'll put up at an inn, of course. There must be one nearby somewhere."

" You'll put up at an inn, of course," Mary mimicked him sarcastically. " You'll put up at no inn, my good man, and you know it. You'll come to me; I've room enough to take in a dozen of you, now that Jerry has moved out. Val and he are coming to dinner, anyhow, and I won't even bother to phone about the extra place. As soon as we wrap ourselves around some of these cocktails, we'll shove along in the roadster—if Katoh can balance himself on top of that enormous suitcase of yours."

Now I thought Tarrant did seem a touch uncomfortable. He said : " Why, that's awfully good of you. But your father isn't home, is he ? I mean, I understood you were alone."

Mary looked at him in complete amazement, or in a very good imitation of it. Then she laughed whole-heartedly. " Good heavens, Trevis ! You can't be a day over forty and you talk like George Washington's great-grandfather. I don't need to be chaperoned in my own house ; the word's obsolete, anyhow. And I certainly don't need any protection from you. Vice versa, in my opinion. In fact," said Mary, " I wish to goodness you'd show a little more spirit."

" I am forty-six," Tarrant asserted with dignity. " And it is perfectly true that I am safe with little girls, even with very charming little girls. On the other hand, what would your friends say about it ? "

" You are simply wasting our time," Mary concluded. " I want my cocktails. . . . Any ' friends ' who talk about me, Trevis, are invited to scram and stay scrammed. The others like what I do and do the same themselves. So there isn't anything to talk about. My, what a doddering old fellow *you* turned out to be."

A little later, when I was helping Katoh hoist the big suitcase into the roadster, I asked him : " What about these ' Headless Horrors ' ? Is it a dangerous business ? "

" Not know much about," Katoh grunted. He grinned as Mary came down the steps. " I think maybe iss some dahnger for Misster Tarrant. But not headless, maybe."

. . . . .

In the library after dinner, I demanded, " Come on now, Tarrant, it's time you told us about this case you're on. Unless the whole story is a fake. Perhaps you just came out for a few free meals ? "

He looked surprised. " Surely, Jerry, you know about the ' Headless Horrors ' case. Why, it has been happening no more than ten miles away from you here. Don't you ever read the papers ? "

" Nothing but the sporting page, naturally ; that's the only part worth reading. No," I went on, indicating the girls, " they don't know about it, either. Val is a woman of responsibility, now that she has to take care of me. She hasn't any time to waste on newspapers ; and I don't think Mary knows how to read."

" You're a spoiled pup, Jerry, with two such lovely girls to bother about you." He smiled. " I don't know very much about the case myself ; I came to find out more about it. I got interested when Peake dropped in the other day and began discussing it— you remember, the man we met over the studio murder. Here's an outline of it, which is all I have.

" On the third of September, about three o'clock in the morning, the headless trunk of a man was found in the centre of Route 48, some eight miles beyond Norrisville, opposite a gas station that was then closed for the night. The finder was a motorist going home from a late party. He was drunk but not too drunk to turn around and drive back to the Norrisville police station. The police tried to pin it on him, but they couldn't ; he was obviously in no condition to have done a beheading. So they had his licence revoked for driving under the influence of alcohol ; that was his reward for the virtue of reporting his discovery.

" Five days later, on the eighth, a woman's body was found about half a mile beyond the first spot. She had also been beheaded. This time the discovery was made much earlier, ten-thirty in the evening, and the neighbourhood was kept disturbed during most of the night by the efforts of the police. There is a headquarters of the State Constabulary at Norrisville, I am told, and since the bodies had been found outside the town limits, the job was theirs. Briefly, I understand that they have been able to accomplish nothing. The second crime achieved a wide publicity—all the New York papers have been playing it up on account of the unusual method of killing. But the troopers have neither been able to find a trace of the heads belonging to the victims, nor the place or means whereby the crimes were committed. Moreover, the corpses have not been identified.

" That brings us to to-day, the thirteenth. Last night, at one a.m., still another victim was found, or rather his trunk, for this time it was a man again. The place was close to where the woman's body had been discovered on the eighth. The keepers of the gas station are reported to have placed some kind of guard near their premises on their own initiative but nothing was seen or heard by this guard that could indicate any detail of the crime. The whole thing remains a complete mystery and although it is more or less in the nature of routine police work, the unusual features of the case seem remarkably interesting to me. This is not a wild section of the country; it is well built-up and populated; how such murders can continue so openly despite the best efforts of the troopers, and without apparently leaving a single clue behind, I cannot imagine. I have a letter to Captain Babcock of the Constabulary from Inspector Peake and I propose to-morrow to take it in and see exactly how the case stands. . . . And, well, that is absolutely all I can tell you about it now."

So we made up a table of contract and played until well after midnight. How any one can play contract with Mary for a partner, I don't know. But Tarrant did. And they were 4000 up on us when we stopped. I guess it was just luck; it must have been.

.   .   .   .   .

The next morning Mary drove Tarrant in to the headquarters of the State Troopers. But Captain Babcock had already left, to be away until late in the afternoon, so they drove about the country (of all things) and ended up at the Club for luncheon. That afternoon Mary had a bridge engagement at Aunt Doris'; any one could see that she didn't want to keep it, but it was too late for her to sneak out, so she had to go. She took Valerie in the roadster, made a disagreeable face, and rolled off. Tarrant was left with me.

"If, as you say, Jerry, you've nothing to do, I'd like to take a look at the spots marked X," he proposed. "I wonder if you'd mind bringing Katoh, too."

The idea was a good one, so, after stopping for the Japanese, we rode over to Route 48. There was no difficulty in finding our destination. Just around a turn in the road we came upon a sizable wayside garage and gas station whose sign board proclaimed "Duck's Filling Station—Gas, Oil, Water, Air— Used Cars." Beside the road an old tyre was propped up and crude lettering glared from within its circle

—" Flats Fixed, 75c. " ; next to this invitation stood a large wheelbarrow with a depressed seat, such as is used for carrying cement, although this one had high sides and an equally high backing over its single wheel. The gas station itself was an ancient farmhouse in fair repair, with a shed on one side that constituted the garage. On the other side of the house an addition was in process of being built, perhaps an improved repaired shop ; a concrete floor had been half laid and the rest of the surface was prepared for further work. To the north of this unfinished structure a line of six or eight unfortunate-looking cars stood out in the open, the Used Cars department, no doubt.

All this I noticed as we passed by and Tarrant remarked : " That must be the station that figures in the case. Let us go on along the road now, though."

Hardly half a mile farther on we came up with a trooper in a smart blue and gold uniform leaning on his motor-cycle beside the asphalt. We drew up to one side and he walked over to us, informing us that this was where the last two bodies had been found and that he was stationed there for no other purpose than to prevent loitering. A brief glance, therefore, was all we could obtain before turning the car and retracing our way. However, there was little to see. Route 48 was here no more than an asphalt country road, three car-widths in breadth, bordered on both sides by fields and occasional trees. There were no houses in sight, we observed ; the trooper was posted near the middle of a straight stretch of the turnpike, about a quarter of a mile long, which then vanished around a pair of turns at either end.

At the filling station we stopped on the pretence of getting some gas and Tarrant got out. The proprietor himself advanced to serve us and was at once engaged in conversation. He was a tall, lean negro, quite light in complexion, almost yellow. He spoke in a peculiar voice, a kind of combination of negro intonation and British accent.

He replied to Tarrant's question : " Yassir, I comes from de West Indies. I was bo'n in Hayti and raised in Bar*ba*does. Bin in de States now fo' ten, twelve yea's." He applied himself to our gas tank while Tarrant sauntered about with the air of stretching his legs. The latter finally seated himself on the wheelbarrow beside the tyre announcement.

Katoh, too, had descended meanwhile and now addressed the negro. To my surprise I heard him saying : " Could look used cars, pless ? Might wish to buy old car cheap." At the other's nod he pattered across a ditch and was busy for some time peering into interiors, raising hoods and examining the small stock with all the appearance of a prospective customer. Presently he returned ; Duck had just finished putting water into our radiator.

" Might look more at Chevvy," announced Katoh, pointing to a disreputable old sedan on the far end of the line. " But moteh number scratched off. Might be stolen car, I think ? "

" Ain' no stolen ca's heah," the proprietor assured him with a chuckle. " Not that we knows of, anyways. My brothah have used ca' business oveh in Pennsylvania ; these jes' some o' his poorest ca's. He be bringin' oveh one or two mo' pretty soon ; maybe you come back an' look again."

Katoh agreed. " Maybe yiss. Some more days to be here maybe."

" Hm," murmured Tarrant, as we started off and the filling station disappeared around the bend, " I wonder if our friend Babcock knows about that obliterated motor number ? That was smart work of yours, Katoh."

The little Japanese was grinning with pleasure. " Might mean something, maybe no," he assented modestly.

·　　·　　·　　·　　·

Captain Reuben Babcock of the State Constabulary was a slender man of more than average height, with washed-out blue eyes and washed-out blond hair. When upright, his posture included a slight stoop. His appearance suggested a subtle hint of incompetence, strangely at variance with those of the hard-boiled young men of his command lounging about the headquarters building. In his very bright, natty uniform he somehow gave the impression that he himself was only too well aware how incompatible was his costume with his physique ; it was slightly embarrassing.

It was five o'clock in the afternoon. Tarrant and I had dropped Katoh and were making an official call. Captain Babcock sat in his office with its map-covered walls and had just finished reading through the letter Tarrant had presented. From his comments it appeared that he was prepared to go beyond a mere matter of professional courtesy ; there existed a personal friendship between himself and Peake.

Tarrant said, " I only know what I have read in the press, Captain. And a few details that Inspector Peake was able to give me ; not much. I wonder if you would bring me up to date ? "

When Babcock spoke, it was surprisingly to the point. " If you have read what is in the papers, you know as much as I do. We have gotten nowhere, so far. Not a single clue."

" It seems incredible," murmured Tarrant.

" It is good of you to say so," the officer replied, removing his glasses with a hand in which he continued to hold them aimlessly. " But the reports are unfortunately correct. We have not as yet succeeded even in identifying any of the victims. That, in fact, is the only progress we have made."

My companion's eyebrows were raised inquiringly at the apparent contradiction.

" Yes," went on Babcock, " of course this lack

of identification does suggest something. You
see, Route 48 is one of the main arteries in this
section ; it is not only one of the big channels
for north and south traffic through the State but
it is also a connecting link between two of the large
east-west routes. There is considerable movement
over it even at night and during the day it is frequently crowded. It is mainly tourist traffic ; most
of the trucks and all the big bus companies use the
routes farther east."

" I see . . . Yes, I see."

Perhaps for my benefit Babcock put it into words.
" Since we have had no local disappearances and
none that match from the neighbouring states
either and since the tourist traffic that passes here
originates in practically every state in the union,
the probability is that the victims are drawn from
the tourist stream. It is impossible to check over
the whole country in a short time ; it may be
impossible ever to do so. And these cars come from
California and Maine and Texas and Alabama and
from every state between them."

" Let us take it provisionally that your tourist
traffic is the source of the persons murdered,"
Tarrant suggested. " But surely they cannot be beheaded at the roadside. Where is the killing done ? "

" God only knows," sighed the Captain. " If
these bodies are those of interstate tourists, as seems
certain, it must be done not far from where they are
found. In the first place, they cannot wander far
from the arterial route hereabouts ; and, since the
second murder, this stretch has been under a heavy
guard—we have eliminated, I believe, any possibility
that the murders are committed along some other
highway and the bodies brought here and dumped.
Nevertheless, along the section of 48 which we are
guarding there is no place where the crimes can be
committed."

" But that is impossible. You are saying that the

murders are not committed nearby nor at a distance.
Yet they are committed somewhere, certainly."

" A week ago," said Babcock, " we received a
letter suggesting that an airplane was used to
convey the bodies here. But their condition, when
found, shows plainly that they have not been
dropped from any height at all."

Tarrant pointed out that there were fields all about
where a landing might be made.

" No. If so, it must be made near Route 48.
The corpses cannot be conveyed across country
for any distance from where they are found. The
country is either heavily wooded or stoutly fenced
in ; and there are no roads, not even a trail, leading
away from the section of the highway under guard.
An airplane could not land, let alone take off again,
within the necessary area without having been heard
or observed by my men."

We left it. " Is there anything peculiar, Captain,
about the bodies that have been discovered ?
Special wounds ? Mutilations ? "

" Only that their heads have all been chopped off.
All papers or other marks of identification have been
removed. The torsos have all been fully clothed and
no wounds or marks of violence have been found on
any of them. But the evidence left by the beheading
is conclusive ; these people have not been killed
by an axe or a butcher's knife or by any such weapon.
Their heads have been severed by a single, clean
stroke. Through Peake we had a man out here from
the French Consulate in New York. He tells us that
every one of these victims has died by a guillotine."

" A guillotine is a sizable affair. It cannot easily
be hidden."

" You are entirely correct. It cannot."

" It strikes me very forcibly," Tarrant asserted,
" that Mr. Duck's gas station is the place where
these murders are taking place. There if anywhere
along that stretch of road is cover and equipment."

Babcock said, " We have torn that place to pieces. After the second murder. For ten years it has been run by Jing Duck, a pretty spry man for a negro, and one against whom we have absolutely nothing in the way of a criminal record. Nevertheless, we searched his place thoroughly ; and when I say thoroughly, that's what I mean. We went through it with a fine comb, tore up his floors where necessary. We also tore up the portion of his new concrete flooring that had been finished—looking for the heads, you know. There was not a thing on his premises, not a drop of blood, not a sign of violence, nothing remotely like a guillotine. The only knife in the whole place is his own hunting knife, the only other cutting instruments two old saws.

" All this was done not half an hour after the second body was found. Next morning we searched the country for ten square miles or more about that station. Woods, fields, streams. Kidnapping cases in the last few years have forced us to develop an excellent technique for searching empty country. My detachments covered it completely. There is not a foot of ground anywhere near Duck where heads, for example, have been buried."

Tarrant asked : " Where does he mix his concrete for the new floor ? "

" In a shallow pit behind the gas station. He has laid planks on the bottom of this pit so that the surface dirt will not mix in with his cement. We took a pickaxe and cleaned it out right down to the planking."

My companion nodded. " And of course there is the matter of the cars. If we are reasoning correctly along these tourist lines, somewhere there are three empty automobiles. Assuming this Jing Duck to have assaulted and murdered a passing motorist, he had not only the head but the vehicle to dispose of. In this connection, Captain Babcock, I can contribute the information that there is now an

unidentified automobile on his used car line ; its
motor number has been obliterated."

For only an instant the trooper's eyes brightened.
Then he said : " A week ago, Mr. Tarrant, I should
have been much more interested in that fact. Of
course we shall report it to the Pennsylvania police,
but it cannot help us with our problem here.

" Let me tell you why not. We have checked up
on the used car situation, naturally. Jing Duck has
a brother, Lincoln Duck, who runs a second-hand
auto business in Pennsylvania ; Scranton, I think.
All the used cars on the line at the gas station come
from there."

" That being so," my companion objected, " why
couldn't Duck slip in an extra one on occasion
without it being noticed ? "

" Because we have had a man checking those
cars. Every one of the present ones has been brought
in by Lincoln Duck from Pennsylvania since the
second murder, except four of them which were there
previously. Our man didn't check the motor numbers,
true enough, but he has identified every one of the
cars there either as having been in fact recently
brought over or as having been there before the
second murder."

" Has the brother, Lincoln Duck, brought any of
these cars in at night ? "

" Yes," said Babcock, nodding his acknowledg-
ment of the point. " But there is nothing in that.
He has only done so once, on a night when no
murders took place. Moreover, one of my men on
patrol followed him through the area under guard
and saw the car actually placed on the line where it
was checked next morning. It was the following
night, when Lincoln Duck was still here, that he
constituted himself a volunteer guard about the
gas station and the murder took place under his
nose, along with those of my own men.

" I should explain," the officer went on, " how

we have put this stretch of road under observation, so you will appreciate how impossible it is that the Duck brothers should be involved.

" Aside from irregular patrols along the road itself at night, we have placed two pairs of men approximately five miles each side of the gas station, one pair to check the north-south traffic, the other to check the south-north. These pairs are in communication both by telephone and radio. Last night, as you know, there was a third body found on Route 48 and it was found between these fixed posts. But from eight o'clock in the evening, when the men took their positions, until after one in the morning when the body was discovered by a patrol, not a car passed our northern post that did not pass the southern one, not a car entered this stretch from the south that did not in turn come out at the north. Some went faster than others, of course, but in no case was there any unduly long delay in covering the ten miles, especially when we consider that some of them may have stopped for gas during their transit. These cars were checked both by body style and by licence number. In other words, at the very time the murder was being done, all the cars on the road came through without an exception."

Tarrant brought out cigarettes, offered them, lit one himself. After several slow puffs, he observed : " And you say there is no possibility these crimes are being committed some distance away and the bodies brought here ? "

" None. I am certain."

" Then this check from last night throws pretty strong doubt on your theoretical source of the victims. . . . One can scarcely stop a passing car and behead an occupant, then send the car along its way either without a driver, if he was alone, or without the other passengers mentioning the fact as soon as they are free to do so."

" I know it," groaned Captain Babcock, " you

can well believe that I know it. Those murders are committed certainly within a few miles of where the bodies are found, no one has disappeared from hereabouts and yet the tourist traffic continues to come through the road undisturbed just when the crimes are done. . . . I am at my wits' end, Mr. Tarrant. If you can suggest anything at all, I shall be more than glad to listen."

" I'm afraid there is nothing I can suggest right now," Tarrant admitted. " I should like to look over the suspected country a bit more, however. Perhaps you will supply me with a pass or even a guide ? "

" Certainly, certainly," answered the policeman, readjusting his glasses and reaching for the phone which was jangling on his desk. As we were leaving, he said : " That was a call from one of my men. Lincoln Duck has just come into the gas station with another second-hand car, brought over from Pennsylvania. . . . Not that that helps us at all."

. . . . .

" To-morrow," said Mary that evening, " you can go roll your hoop, Jerry. I'm taking Trevis around, myself."

And she did, though the day opened with a new, bitter defeat for the state troopers. Just before dawn yet another headless corpse was found on Route 48, this time several miles to the north of the gas station, whereas the others had been discovered to the south. Nevertheless Tarrant, after a hurried consultation with Captain Babcock beside the road, followed out his original programme. Accompanied by a state trooper, and with Mary in her heavy tramping boots trailing after him like a pet poodle, he set off across the country to the west of the ill-omened highway. In the details of the most recent crime which, so far as they could be ascertained, were in all respects like those of the preceding ones, he evinced little interest.

The land was alive with troopers, Mary told us

afterwards, making a frenzied search singly and in small groups as they had done before. But as before, the same result was obtained by these measures—exactly nothing. Even Tarrant, who apparently had ideas of his own, accomplished no more so far as Mary could see. They tramped for miles, up and down hills, through woods, and about two o'clock ended up actually at the Duck's station where they lunched off beer and hot dogs with which the thrifty Jing supplied the passing trade during the midday hours. Here, since no tables or chairs were provided, they stretched out on the grass near the used cars and consumed large quantities of the humble fare. All the cars of the preceding day were there, plus the newest arrival brought in the afternoon before.

Presently Tarrant got up and strolled over to the counter for another bottle of beer. When the negro presently appeared, he inquired after his brother.

" Lincoln ? He done gone back. He cain' stay long ; he got to git back to his bizness. . . . Yas, *suh*, he was heah las' night w'en it happen. But we was both sleepin' ; cain' stay up ev'ry night."

" No objection if I look around a bit ? " Tarrant asked. " You are becoming quite famous here now."

Duck waved a hand vaguely toward the house behind him. " You all look anywheres you a mind to. The police bin through heah ag'in ; ain' lef' much to see, ah guess," he chuckled. " You kin go where you please, mister." Tarrant, however, did not enter the building but merely contented himself with strolling slowly about the premises.

It was just as they were leaving that the only thing happened that seemed of any significance to Mary ; and she couldn't make much of that. They were walking back to the road from where they had been resting and Duck approached them with an empty water pail that he evidently intended to re-fill in the house. As he was passing, Tarrant said something sharply in a foreign tongue ; all Mary

could make out of it was something like, " Ousmam
alloy ? "

But the effect on the negro was obvious. He
straightened with a sudden start and looked quickly
at his questioner. In another moment he had
recovered himself and muttered : " Ah dunno what
you-all mean, mister." He passed on without
another word.

As for Tarrant, he walked slowly down the road
to where Mary had parked her car with the troopers
in the morning. It was a walk of some two or three
miles and he made it in complete silence, plainly
deep in thought. When they reached the car, however, he came out of his reverie, smiled and helped
Mary in. They drove directly to the headquarters
in Norrisville in search of Captain Babcock.

The result of this interview Mary insisted upon
keeping shrouded in the deepest mystery, much to
my annoyance. " But I promised Trevis," was all
she would say to my repeated urgings.

" And who the devil do you think he is, anyhow ? "
I demanded testily. " What if you did promise
him ? "

" Oh, he's a grand man, perfectly slick." Mary's
eyes glistened like a dead fish's and she got one of
those faraway looks on her silly face. . . . " You'll
know to-morrow night, Jerry. You're in on it,
worse luck ; I wish I was. Unless Lincoln Duck
comes back to-night. Then you'll know then."

I said, " Hell with you."

. . . . .

Evidently Lincoln Duck failed to put in an appearance, for Valerie and I spent the evening at home,
making a quiet use of the bar in the living-room without interruption. Mary, no doubt, was playing the
big hostess to Trevis at father's place a mile away.

The next noon Tarrant came over to lunch with
us and confirmed the plans for that evening. " We
ought to leave here about six o'clock, Jerry," he

informed me, standing on the terrace and twirling one of Val's excellent Martinis in his left hand. He glanced appraisingly at the sky. " That is, if the weather remains as fine as it is now." I recalled that we were still on daylight time ; it would be light at six o'clock on a clear day.

At luncheon I knew better than to waste my breath questioning him about the night ahead. But there seemed to me to be an aspect of the case that had remained unmentioned so far. I said : " Look here, Tarrant. As far as I know, everybody has been beating out his brains up to now trying to figure out the method of these crimes. But what about the motive ? Isn't that equally remarkable ? Let's grant that some one is yanking unknown tourists out of their seats and chopping their heads off—though I don't see how it's being done ; still and all, *why* should some one yank tourists out and chop off their heads ? Looks like a thoroughly screwy performance to me."

" No," he replied smiling and nearly choking over a piece of lamb in the process. He reached hastily for a glass of water. " The police have been assuming tacitly that such a series of murders is the work of a homicidal maniac ; and that is one reason for their lack of progress. Yesterday I was searching for the motive in this case rather than the means being used. I was so fortunate as to find the motive."

" But surely," Val looked up from the end of the table, " any motive that would lead people to behead a succession of perfect strangers would be a crazy one ? "

" You are sure these persons are all strangers ? "

" Pretty sure, yes."

" Well, Valerie, some would consider the present motive to be a crazy one, I admit. I am not myself entirely of their persuasion. No doubt it has been a long time since you saw the inside of a church, except for the purpose of marrying Jerry, but you will probably agree that the Christian Communion Service is not a completely insane observance. . . . That is the kind of motive we have here."

After a short silence Valerie said, " Ah."

I said nothing. To me it didn't make any sense.

" And you're *sure* that's the motive ? " she persisted. " I don't see how it can be more than a guess. It's clever, though, Trevis ; it's the only one that brings any reason into the case."

" It was a guess to begin with," he acknowledged. " But it isn't any longer. Yesterday I managed to secure some evidence for it, slight but unmistakable. It is perfectly possible," he went on, " to reconstruct theoretically the method of the murders ; but the measures employed by the police make it impossible now to obtain any evidence supporting the theory. Actually the motive is the only thing upon which a concrete clue is obtainable. But since that has been obtained, it shows that the method of reconstruction is correct, too."

I was getting fed up with all this talking around the point. " It doesn't make a picture," I objected. " If these people were guillotined—— By the way, *were* they guillotined ? "

" Yes, they were guillotined."

" Well, I understand there isn't a guillotine anywhere about."

There was a distinct twinkle in Tarrant's eye as he said, " The nature of a guillotine, Jerry, is generally considered to be two uprights between which a heavy blade is suspended in such a fashion that it drops upon the neck of the victim below. Now suppose, for example, that, instead of consisting of cut wood, the uprights in the present case were growing . . ."

" What ? " cried Valerie. " You mean something rigged up between a couple of trees ? But what about the supporting beam, or whatever it is, overhead ? "

" Those who are searching the ground seldom look

upward," Tarrant suggested. " And trees have branches, I have noticed. However, don't take it too seriously ; the guillotine we have to do with this time has been in full view all along."

" Hmm. Yes ? "

" Yes."

" And you are convinced the Duck brothers are doing the murders," Valerie continued.

" Am I ? "

" It looks so to me. You didn't pull this stunt of yours last night because Lincoln Duck hadn't got back. If you are waiting for him, he must be in it somehow. '

" From your point of view," Tarrant murmured non-committally," the conjecture would appear to be a reasonable one."

.   .   .   .   .

When we set off late that afternoon there were Tarrant, Katoh and myself in the car. He had asked me to bring along a heavy rifle and fortunately I had a large calibre that I had used in Canada hunting moose. " Babcock may be a fine shot," he had said, " but I'd rather not trust altogether to his marksmanship. Too much will depend on it."

To my surprise we did not go to Route 48. We drove nearly into Norrisville and then took a back road through the country, with which Tarrant appeared quite familiar. After bumping along it for a good nine miles or more, he indicated a halt and we drew off the road beside an ugly looking ditch. About twenty yards ahead a police car was similarly parked and Captain Babcock was walking towards us from it. It was a deserted lane at this point with not even a secluded farmhouse in sight.

Beside Babcock's car a trooper mounted guard over two objects which I soon found to be a portable police searchlight run on a strong battery, and a portable radio receiving set. " We can't send on it," the captain explained, " but we can receive the re-

ports. At least we shall not be entirely out of touch."
I saw a heavy police rifle slung over his shoulder.

Without wasting further time we set off across
the open field to our left, Katoh helping the trooper
to lift the equipment over the low stone fence.
" Lincoln Duck has not returned as yet," Babcock
remarked as we plodded forward.

Tarrant stopped short with an exclamation ; he
seemed not a little upset at the news. " You are
sure ? " he demanded.

" We have had the patrols out all day. Up to
fifteen minutes ago they had not reported him in."

We resumed our way, now up a series of wooded
slopes. Tarrant was muttering, " I don't understand it. It *can't* be put off beyond to-night." The
going was becoming harder and moreover the woods
were growing dark ; every now and then it was
necessary for me to give a hand to the trooper and
Katoh with the searchlight.

I could not help speculating upon our mission,
for Tarrant, as usual, had told me practically
nothing. It seemed that he expected something to
occur during the coming darkness ; his remark, as
well as the searchlight, made that clear. But what ?
A further murder, so closely on the heels of the last
two ? And the rifles ; apparently there was a
prospect that we might be attacked, although by
whom I could not imagine. The concern over
Lincoln Duck puzzled me, too, for I was not entirely
of Valerie's opinion that the two negroes could very
well be mixed up in the crimes, in view of the
elaborate searches and precautions of the state
troopers. And finally our destination ; where could
we be proceeding with so much difficulty ? Some
secret rendezvous deep in the woods, the actual lair
of these murderers ? It was all I could think of.

My last question was answered first. We
approached the summit of a sizable hill and Tarrant
made us halt while he crawled forward to recon-

noitre. All was satisfactory, no doubt, for he motioned us ahead and we passed over the ridge in single file, Babcock, the trooper, Katoh, and myself bringing up the rear. In the fading light of late dusk I could just make out the gas station beside the winding ribbon of Route 48; then it was hidden by a large clump of bushes behind which we passed.

Rather more than half-way down the slope Tarrant stopped and indicated that this would be our position. The spot was to the south of the gas station, above and a little behind it; a view was obtainable of most of the front, and we overlooked the rear and, of course, the south end with its dilapidated shed. In the gathering darkness the back portion of the premises appeared to be entirely deserted; there was just light enough left for me to discern the blank, empty windows and, in the yard below, the abandoned wheelbarrow that I had first seen near the tyre sign by the road.

" No smoking at any time," Tarrant cautioned us. He was struggling through the bushes that partially masked our station, pulling the large searchlight after him. At last he managed to get it set up, camouflaged by the last layer of branches. So far as I could see, he trained it upon the rear of the Ducks' establishment below; then I heard him telling the trooper to be certain the battery was firmly connected. The daylight had failed completely by this time, but suddenly there was a blaze of light beneath us; the several rows of bulbs that decorated the front of the filling station came to life. Jing Duck was evidently ready for any trade that the evening might bring his way.

Babcock meanwhile had put on the earphones and been dialling his radio. Now he took them off and observed, " The latest report, Mr. Tarrant. No sign of Lincoln Duck."

A grunt of exasperation was the only answer.

.   .   .   .   .

Quite literally we sat there for hours, for five or six of them at least. Once in a while Tarrant would make me get up, stretch and take a few steps around. He said he didn't want me to get stiff. Also he asked : " Is your gun loaded and on the safety, Jerry ? "

" Sure it is. When do we do something with it ? "

" Not yet. You'll have an opportunity . . . I think." In the darkness I could imagine the lazy smile on his face.

Below us the lights of the gas station burned brightly and the traffic on Route 48 gradually lessened as the evening advanced. Occasionally a car pulled in for gas or water and at irregular intervals a state trooper chugged by on his motor-cycle. At first I watched the cars that stopped, suspiciously, half expecting to see some one of their occupants pulled forth and attacked ; then I recollected that on the night of the third murder (and presumably on those of the others) all these cars had come through on schedule. That could hardly be what we were waiting for.

Babcock, apparently, was recalling the same matter, for I heard him saying doubtfully, " I don't know, Mr. Tarrant ; I don't see how anything can happen here."

Tarrant merely grunted. Then he added, " This part of it can be managed easily, Captain ; take my word for it. You will see, later."

" But they are guillotined."

" Easy, too. I know all about the guillotine, been on top of it, in fact. What is worrying me is Lincoln Duck's absence."

" Maybe he isn't in it, after all."

" He sure is," came in Tarrant's grimmest tone.

So the Ducks were the murderers ! They must be, considering this conversation. Yet how could they be, possibly ? I drew off a little to one side and beckoned the trooper over to me. He proved an enlightening source of information ; why hadn't I thought of him earlier ? For I soon learned from him the crux of Tarrant's plan, which was no more than to lie in wait until a trooper, disguised as a touring motorist, stopped at the filling station in the small hours of the morning. When I learned that this trick would not be played until nearly three a.m., I settled my back against a tree and prepared to go to sleep.

Shortly after midnight, just as I was dozing off, I heard Babcock's voice. The Captain was saying : " There go the lights off. The station is shut up for the night. I'm afraid, Mr. Tarrant, your plan has failed."

" It can't fail," the other rejoined. " Let me have those night glasses, Babcock ; we must watch more carefully than ever now. They may not wait for your trooper, you know . . . But after all, any one who stops will have his headlights on."

Babcock said sceptically, " Lincoln Duck hasn't come back and Jing has gone to bed. I am trying this as a last resort but it looks to me as if we were wasting our time out here."

A long silence followed, broken at last by the sound of a car approaching at high speed a mile or more down the highway. I heard the trooper's exclamation and decided there was no chance to sleep, anyhow. When I had gotten back to the clump of bushes that sheltered the others, I was surprised to see the gas station lit up. A moment later the car came round the bend in Route 48 and went down the road past the filling station without even slowing down. No sooner was it out of sight than the lights below us abruptly went out.

Captain Babcock hummed a little tune. " Now what does that show mean, I wonder ? "

Tarrant said crisply, " It means they're playing a little game of decoy, themselves. They want to be thought in bed and asleep except when they can get some one to stop. They have to trust to luck that some one will. That's why your man is necessary."

"Why do you say ' they ' ? I have had two more messages that Lincoln Duck isn't there."

" I've been thinking about that. He's there, all right ; must be. I see now how it happens he hasn't been reported."

The discussion was interrupted, this time by the approach of an unmistakable motor-cycle. Presently its light cut down the turnpike from the south ; it passed around the bend and was gone, bearing away one of Babcock's patrols. Not a glimmer had shone from the filling station.

Something must have happened to the traffic that night, for not another car passed until nearly two o'clock, although several patrols went by. The car, when it did come, rolled past the bright gas station without a glance, after which darkness descended again. Tarrant took a few steps up and down, brought the face of his wrist-watch close to his eyes. He called for Katoh.

" See if it's been moved or if it's still there. Be careful if you hear a car coming. It's a chance but we'll have to take it—you *mustn't* be seen." The little Japanese slid off into the blackness.

"My man has left Norrisville," Babcock announced from the radio.

Ten minutes may have passed and then the silence was broken by the distant sound of an automobile coming south. Tarrant's low voice came over to me : " Get your gun ready, Jerry." As I unslung it, not knowing what next step to take, " But your man down there——" began the captain.

" He'll take cover. They won't see him."

Beneath us the lights of the station came on. " Do I shoot down there ? " I demanded.

" It's between three and four hundred yards. Not too far, is it ? "

" No."

" Not until I tell you," he cautioned me. " On

no account. No matter what happens." Babcock, I saw, was bringing his gun to the ready also.

After our long wait what followed seemed to happen almost instantaneously. The car came around the bend and rolled up to a gas pump. Jing Duck came out, and, after a word or so, filled the tank. Then he came up to the front seat to receive payment. As he did so, another figure darted around the back of the car carrying what looked like a short club. He was hidden from us then, but in the dead quiet of the country night we all heard the sharp crack as he knocked out the man behind the wheel.

A moment later the two of them were pulling out the form of the unconscious trooper. And I was raising my rifle. Tarrant's voice was sharp. " Not yet ! "

Jing Duck was dragging the trooper toward the house. The other man—a negro, presumably the missing Lincoln—sprang into the empty car ; he drove out on the road again and continued to the south ! Every light in the place went out.

" What the hell ! We've missed our chance." I grounded the gun bitterly. I had no doubt that murder was even now being done in the darkness below, while we stood impotently on the hill.

Tarrant was counting aloud. " One, two, three . . ." Slowly. At thirty he snapped, " The light ! Trooper, the light ! " Dazzlingly the strong search-light played over the rear of the filling station.

As if in the centre of a stage the murder scene sprang out. The trooper's body lay partly across the wheelbarrow behind the rear wall of the building, his head resting in the hollow trough of the barrow, his neck over its edge. Jing Duck was just raising one of the sides that evidently was hinged at the wheel end ; its sharp, metal lower edge gleamed brightly in the white glare. The briefest glance told us that when that edge came down there would be another headless trunk to be put on Route 48.

Jing Duck, momentarily blinded as well as amazed, stood upright. " Jerry ! " cried Tarrant. " Fire ! "

Babcock's shot rang out a second ahead of mine. We never knew who hit him, for there was only one wound in his shoulder. He spun around and hit the ground. The trooper lay on the wheelbarrow, its deadly side still upright.

And then Duck pulled himself to his feet. He hadn't been badly hit ; he knew he was caught and he had plainly decided to take his last victim with him. He groped towards his hinged guillotine, staggering a little but well able still to operate it. Neither Babcock nor I had reloaded. I stared horror-struck at the scene below, grabbing in panic for another cartridge.

So closely were all our eyes focused that no one saw Katoh springing across the yard. He struck the negro just in time, they went down together. The Japanese, even in falling, made two arm movements, almost too quick to be seen. Duck's head bent far back ; his neck snapped.

Then we were all down there, lifting Katoh to his feet, shaking his hand. " Damn it," ground Tarrant, " that was a close thing. You should have held your fire, Babcock ; I wanted Jerry to shoot first." He turned to his valet. " You might have been hit coming across the yard, Katoh."

The latter was still puffing after his hard run. " Hear—two shots," he gasped. " Not to *re*load in time maybe."

Babcock was busy trying to revive his trooper, who responded by falling out of the wheelbarrow and sipping dizzily from a flask of brandy. Presently the captain rose and came over to us.

" You see what happened to the cars," Tarrant addressed him. " Lincoln Duck got in them and drove them over to Pennsylvania. Sometimes he probably waited long enough to take the torso with him and drop it off along the road, inside your picket lines, of course. Anyhow, that's how the traffic came through all right while the murders were being done. Once in Scranton, there was no possibility of connecting one of his used cars with these crimes. I wouldn't be surprised if he had actually brought some of them back here lately, using his own dealer's licences. . . . To-day he must have come back by train and walked out, avoiding your patrols. They were getting suspicious of me and they had one more murder to do. I felt sure they would do it as soon as they could, and in case we were getting on to their method, they didn't want us to know Lincoln was here. Your men will have him by now ? "

" They will," said Babcock. " The car part is all right, but what about the heads ? Not a single one has been found."

Without a word Tarrant led us across the yard to the shallow pit for concrete mixing. At its bottom the bare planks, encrusted with past cement, lay uncovered. Taking Babcock's rifle, he struck at them with its butt, loosening them. Finally he managed to pull one up. Underneath the centre of the depression appeared a further, smaller pit filled with a whitish substance.

" You had better be careful how you clean that out," he cautioned. " It's quicklime. When that bucket of water there is thrown into it, enough heat will be generated to do away with a dozen heads. Still, you may be able to find some evidence here to-morrow."

The State policeman could not conceal his surprise. " But how could you know about this ? " he demanded. " You could never have found an opportunity to examine underneath those planks while Duck was around."

" No," Tarrant conceded, " of course not. . . . I didn't need to examine it. I worked the rest of it

out and then I knew that somehow the heads had
to be disposed of right here, and quickly. Your own
searches showed me that underneath these planks
was the *only* place available. . . . When there is
only one possibility, it can't be wrong."

· · · · ·

It was some time later when we were finally taken
around in a police car to the spot where we had left
our own. For most of the way home we rode in
silence, let down after the past excitement. Then I
remembered my own point at luncheon.

" But the motive ? " I said suddenly.

" Voodoo," murmured Tarrant. " As soon as I
saw Duck, I thought of the West Indies and he
obliged me by saying he had been born in Hayti. It
went well with beheadings ; there are many blood
sacrifice rites in that religion. The blood from those
torsos was used, Jerry—well, it isn't a pretty
picture.

" The second time I visited the station, I tried a
little experiment. The priests of that cult are called
pappaloi and the priestesses *mammaloi*. I asked
Duck, *ou es mammaloi ?*—' where is the priestess ? '
He gave himself away ; and that settled it. . . .
I knew he would work fast when he found himself
suspected ; even so small a hint would make him
hurry to finish the rite. The final murder would take
place as soon as Lincoln Duck could get back from
Scranton. . . . For cult reasons there had to be
five victims—and only four had been killed up to
yesterday."

At the end of the drive the lights were lit in Mary's
house. She and Val would probably have sat up
all night waiting for us. At the sound of the car
Mary came to the door herself. " Come in," she
called. " Val's mixing drinks. You're going to tell
us all about it."

Tired as I was I couldn't help seeing that she was
wearing a pretty snappy négligée.

THE EPISODE OF THE VANISHING HARP

Characters of the Episode

JERRY PHELAN, the narrator
DONATELLI DABEN, wealthy, cultured Irishman
MOLLA DABEN, his wife
FREDERICK STUART, his secretary
JOHN BRINKERSTALL, a man of finance
DR. TORPINGTON, a family physician
TREVIS TARRANT, interested in disappearances

THE EPISODE OF THE VANISHING HARP

I REMEMBER being asked, once, about Trevis Tarrant —who he was, how he came to be involved as a participant in such a succession of extraordinary happenings ; what qualifications he possessed as a " detective " that permitted him to emerge, time after time, with a neat and satisfactory explanation of these occurrences.

It was not so easy a question as it appeared. For Tarrant is not a detective in any sense of the word as usually accepted ; nor is he connected with the police. True, he knows a policeman, but then, so do I ; the same policeman, in fact ; a chap named Peake, who is an Inspector in the New York Department and whom we met through an unnamed friend of Tarrant's on the occasion of a particularly gruesome murder a number of floors above Tarrant's apartment. He, that is, Tarrant, has co-operated with the police at other times, notably with the New Jersey Troopers on the " Headless Horrors " case, but that was directly traceable to Peake himself, not to any official or semi-official connection with the forces of order. For Tarrant is simply not interested in ordinary police work, which he asserts to be chiefly a routine and drudging attack upon criminals who, for their part, have little to offer beyond brute force and a diseased attitude towards their fellows. Such " action dramas " leave his curious and questing intellect with small nourishment.

Moreover, at the time the question was posed, I had known Tarrant only a short while and his background was still more or less nebulous to me. That he was of independent means, even wealthy, was apparent from the expensive, comfortable furnishings of his apartment in the East Thirties, in conjunction with the fact that he was employed with no commercial undertaking nor any of the common professions. Where he had come from, I had no idea—one does not usually catechise one's acquaintances concerning their early life and, as our friendship grew, it never occurred to me to inquire.

But, my questioner persisted, what sort of man is he, what does he do with his time, what pursuits— the fellow actually said " pursuits "—does he follow ? Here again I was at a loss for, frankly, I didn't know how he spent his time. Not that there was anything mysterious about it ; it was merely that whenever I had chanced to be with him, he had been engaged upon a case, or as he preferred to call it, an episode, " case " being too formal an expression for his activities.

I threw myself back upon memories of conversations with him and at once I realised that his interests were wide. At one time or another he had mentioned psychoanalysis (for which he had no use), folklore and archeology, with which he appeared profoundly acquainted, wines, philosophy and literature. While driving with me from New York to Norristown, to the assistance of Valerie, whom I was lucky enough to marry soon afterwards, he had remarked that America had so far produced only a single writer of any real depth, Booth Tarkington. Not caring much about literature or writers, not caring a damn about them just then, I neglected to ask why he thought so.

Then there was physics. He certainly knew plenty about physics. The advanced, theoretical kind, I guess. He had lectured me more than once, in our brief friendship, about the Law of Causation, the contradictory " nonsense " embodied in the Second Law of Thermodynamics and the traitorous, scientific heresies of Eddington and Jeans who, he told me, " were trying their best to get an enfeebled Jahveh through the laboratory back door." I gathered that he admired Max Planck.

It was his conviction of the immutability of the Law of Causation that kept him at many of his problems when any one more easily discouraged would have admitted a final impasse. " Causation may be a mirage," he would repeat, " but if so, it is not a mirage of nature but of deep, human subjectivity. Therefore, it will remain consistent. Somewhere there is a logically satisfying, causative answer to our puzzle." To find these answers, and demonstrate them, in the strange and peculiar happenings of life that occur, perhaps, more frequently than we realise, was a passion with him.

Such a man was not interested at all in murder *per se* but only in those occasional murders that really offered an enigma either of means or of motive. The most diverse questions caught his fancy. I have known him, in the course of half an hour, to turn his attention and his keen speculation upon the nature of sub-electronic substance, the original purpose of the Birth House of Horus, still preserved at Denderah, the problem of persons recently guillotined in the absence of a guillotine, and the organisation of the galactic universe. It was under those circumstances, I believe, that I made the only remark to which he had ever paid much attention. I had said, " You know, Tarrant, you range so far and wide for mysteries that I think you must hope some day to find a really insoluble one." He had stopped and regarded me closely, with a quick widening of the eyes. " You may be right, Jerry," he had said after a moment.

My questioner interrupted me abruptly. " That," he announced, " is the very man I'm looking for. Can you get him to join us for dinner ? "

. . . . .

So that was the way in which Donatelli Daben met Tarrant, for the latter was free and we all had dinner at my club.

Daben was a couple of years older than myself, had been two years ahead of me at the same college. I had known him there and ran into him infrequently in New York or at a football game. His father, dead these many years, had been an Irish gentleman with an authentic coat-of-arms and I shall always remember his mother as, I think, the most beautiful woman I have ever seen. Before her marriage she had been an Italian countess, making a parental combination that endowed Donatelli, named after his mother's family, with Gaelic mysticism and the intricate personality of the southern peoples. His mother had died the year of our graduation, leaving him a handsome fortune ; and not long afterwards he himself had married a Molla Mallory, a typical blue-eyed, dark-haired Irish beauty whom I had met only once, at her wedding. So far as my rather casual acquaintance went, Daben was wealthy, cultured and possessed of an attractive wife—in brief, on an enviable spot.

That something had gone wrong, however, his questions of the afternoon had implied plainly enough. And after dinner, when we had adjourned to the tap-room and grouped ourselves about a table with our choices in the glasses before us, he went to the point of his difficulties.

" I understand, Mr. Tarrant," he began, " that you interest yourself in—what shall I say ?—mysterious affairs ; with your permission I should like to have your advice about a matter of that kind that has been forced upon me. Well, to tell you the truth immediately, I should like to have you investigate the thing. Of course, I shall be glad, in respect of a fee——"

" I never accept fees," said Tarrant, with a smile. " Try to keep my amateur standing. I don't want ' cases ' brought to me, as would happen if I set up professionally."

" But you do engage in this sort of work, I've been told."

" Oh, yes. But only upon such things as actually interest me. I select my own cases, the basic qualifications being that they must involve an apparently inexplicable problem, the more inexplicable the better. I keep myself free of any obligation, either to the person who brings me the problem or, as sometimes happens in the case of a crime, to the police authorities. I am not amused by crime as such. In these matters I serve only the truth. For example, if you should happen to have a question sufficiently intriguing, my fee would consist in complete freedom of action during and at the conclusion of the episode. I mean that in the investigation of your problem, I must be free to follow the evidence and the proof *wherever* they may lead."

Daben looked a little puzzled. " Of course. The point is precisely to find out where they do lead. They don't lead me to anything that I can credit."

" With that understood," Tarrant pointed out, " I must remind you that as yet I have no idea what your trouble is."

" In order to tell you," continued Deban, " I

shall have to speak of my family. In this democratic time heredity is almost taboo but my family have a very long and traditional history, and my present worries are connected with it. About the period 700-1000 B.C. prehistoric Ireland was invaded by the so-called Milesians, a people supposed to have come from Scythia, sojourned for some time in Egypt, returned to Scythia again, and finally arrived in Ireland via Spain. The eight sons of the leader-in-chief, one Miled, set out to conquer the island and eventually made a pretty good job of it. It was from the branch of Breogan, one of these sons, that my own family stems. In the course of time and tribal differentiation the name passed through such stages as Dabheoin and many others and has now taken the Americanised form of Daben. The name, Brogan, of course, belongs to another sub-branch of the same original family.

" My own line from the most remote age were harpists, which meant that they did much more than play upon the instrument ; they were the composers also and especially the historians and guardians of the clan's traditions. The profession with its secrets as well as its instruments was hereditary, passed down from father to son. There is a mis-conception among many persons that the Irish harpist was no more than a hired musician attached to the court. This is nonsense, of course ; in ancient times only those of high noble rank, originally of royal rank, were permitted the privilege."

A note of pride had crept into the speaker's voice and Tarrant remarked, " I am well aware that what you say is true, Mr. Daben."

" Ah. . . . Then perhaps you will also know that the earliest authenticated record of an Irish harp exists upon an early monument, the harp upon the cross of the ancient church of Ullard near Kilkenny. E. Bunting, A. J. Hipkins, Kathleen Schlesinger and other authorities place the date of this as certainly not later than 830 A.D. The workmanship of the carving is crude, but the reproduction in Bunting's book, as well as the original stone, shows without doubt that the instrument possesses no front pillar, thus differing fundamentally from the later *clairseach* of native Irish invention or modification. The instrument I speak of, although played in a diagonal position rather than horizontally, bears the closest resemblance to the primitive Egyptian *nanga* which was made with a boat-shaped sounding board, only a few strings, and was played on the shoulder. I have compared it with the three or four *nangas* preserved in the British Museum and with the exception that the Irish instrument is better made and has more strings, they are all undoubtedly the same."

Daben paused and was almost obviously awaiting incredulous criticism. Tarrant, however, smiled broadly. " The timidity of academic archeologists is one of the bad jokes of present science. I do not share their dis-ease."

" I am relieved," declared the other. " I see that I have indeed come to a man of understanding. For that harp, at the time of the Kilkenny sculpture already a venerated relic, was of course never used but was preserved and jealously guarded in the possession of my own branch of the Breogan line. Tradition says that it was the harp brought to Ireland from Egypt by the original Breogan who, from those remote times, may be said to have been the founder of the whole profession in Ireland, whose legends form a good part of Ireland's most glorious history. And if tradition lies, it remains difficult to explain how an Egyptian *nanga* came to furnish objective evidence of a link between the two countries.

" But that is not all, Mr. Tarrant. That harp, the very instrument which in 830 A.D. was believed by my family to have come from Egypt 1000 to 1200 years previously, still exists, preserved by every aid of modern chemistry. It was brought to this country by my grandfather shortly after 1800 and it stands in the library of my estate in Connecticut."

" Well," Tarrant contributed, " that *is* remarkable. I am glad that we have met if for no other reason than that I may have an opportunity to see this relic. But I judge, from the details you have given me, that your troubles have arisen in connection with this inherited responsibility of yours ? "

Daben rejoined grimly, " That is quite true. Back in the twelfth century a prophecy was made about the harp. The Normans had come to Ireland then and they were great hands at composing prophecies in doggerel verse. The original document, almost illegible, must now be kept in darkness, but I can show you a copy. And I can tell you what it said without the necessity of mis-spelling all of the words. It ran partly like this :

' Once but not twice Dabheoin and Malorye
May wed without danger of traveillie ;
If again—the harpe in peril stande.
When Breogan Harpe thrice shall elude
The guardian that to harpe be trowed,
Then shall the race of Dabheoin eande.' "

He paused, then after a moment added, " That's all of it that matters just now."

The voice stopped and Tarrant sat regarding the haze of smoke from his cigarette. Presently he asked, " And has the harp ever eluded its proper guardian, Mr. Daben ? "

" No," answered the latter. " Through all the centuries there has never been a recorded instance when the harp has been out of the physical possession of the head of the Daben family."

" And you are uneasy on the score of this 800-year-old prophecy written in doggerel English ? "

" I most certainly am."

Tarrant's eyebrows were raised, ever so slightly.

" You see," said Daben, " three weeks ago, out of my apparently impregnable library, Breogan's harp vanished."

.   .   .   .   .

" Taking your legend quite seriously, I should say, in the first place, that you are bound to recover the harp eventually, and in the second, in view of that phrase about its third disappearance, that it will probably be your grandson who will find himself under the gravest apprehension in the matter."

It was Tarrant who was speaking, it was the following afternoon, and he and Daben were lounging in the club car of a Boston Limited, bound for Daben's estate outside Hartford. I was not present during the remainder of the episode, but Tarrant told me about it later and I am able to relate it from the copious and complete notes I then made.

In the club car Daben shook his head, frowning dubiously. " It is not simply the prophecy, which appears to threaten some form of extinction ; aside from that, the disappearance of the relic, my sacred responsibility, concerns me deeply. Don't you realise that this is the first time, the first time in centuries if not in its entire history, that its rightful custodian has ever lost possession of the Breogan symbol ? It is nothing that I cannot take lightly. I *must* make every effort to regain it, but I have no idea even where to begin to search."

" No doubt it is an ordinary theft. You have been to the police, of course ? "

" The police ? " Daben's eyebrows shot up almost vertically. " This is not a matter for the peasantry. I have been nowhere near them. Especially as the harp cannot possibly have been stolen. In any ordinary way."

Tarrant, still smiling at the novel characterisation of the uniformed forces, remarked, " But if it is gone, it must have been taken by some one. It can scarcely have walked away under its own power. You do not, I take it, credit any possibility of its having assumed invisibility."

"God knows," groaned Daben. "But theft is out of the question. You will see for yourself. . . . I have spent considerable time and money in *making* my library impregnable ; the room was constructed with a view to housing the relic. The walls, floor and ceiling are of reinforced concrete which can be penetrated only by blasting or heavy shell-fire. It is ventilated by the air conditioning system of the house, through slits in the concrete, too small to admit a mouse. The only door, though camouflaged, is of steel and armour plate. It has no knob, no lock ; it is opened both from without and within by an electrical device, the means for operating which are concealed and known only to myself and the builders. Mindful of the fact that this left undesirable knowledge in the possession of others, I myself later installed a cut-out switch for the electrical mechanism, whose existence and location are known to nobody except me. . . . It was out of that locked room that the harp disappeared sometime during the night, a few weeks ago."

"A nice problem," Tarrant acknowledged. "We can only suppose that, despite your precautions, some one *has* discovered the secret of entry."

"In that case," observed the other, "no less than two systems of alarm gongs would have gone off ; one when the door was opened, the other when the cabinet in which the harp rested was tampered with. But they did not function."

"Hmm. Well, let us not speculate prematurely. We shall see what conclusions arise when I have been over the ground at first hand." Tarrant shrugged, dismissing the subject for the time being.

They were met at the station by a Rolls Royce and whirled through the rather attractive outskirts of the city. Daben's estate was some eight miles beyond the limits. Turning off the highway, they sped between two tall gates and began· mounting a winding incline, over a perfectly gravelled surface ; to each side were thickly growing trees, miniature forests already dimming in the dusk, between which they drove up and up and up. The ascent was probably shorter than it seemed for the first time ; abruptly they emerged into an esplanade before the mansion proper and into the final brilliance of the sunset. The house, sizable, almost palatial, with its formal gardens stretching away from the side opposite the roadway's entrance, was built of grey stone and occupied the exact summit of the hill. In the distance below, the lights of Hartford were already twinkling and other lights, more widely spaced but legion in number, began to answer them from the surrounding country.

In the broad hallway, a massive fireplace taking up most of one side, Tarrant stood alert for a first impression. A servant had carried his bags in from the car.

Daben, divesting himself of coat, hat and gloves, which he handed to another footman, seemed suddenly nervous within his own walls. He said, " Seven o'clock. We dine at eight, and dress. Black tie. Plenty of time. Cocktails won't be until ten minutes before. John will show you your quarters." He turned away with a nod and walked down the big hall towards its farther end.

The servant with the bags began mounting the stairs. Tarrant lingered momentarily, watching his host. The latter had stopped before a panel at the far end of the hall and appeared to be running his hands lightly over the carving in the wood at both sides. The panel opened, to a humming so low that Tarrant could scarcely hear it at that distance, and without a glance about, Daben went in. The door swung shut. Tarrant followed the servant upstairs.

  · · · · · ·

His apartments were perfect, even including a little balcony outside one of the windows, from which a magnificent view spread out. A shower, a shave—when he stepped back into the bedroom, his clothes were neatly laid out, from underwear to tie.

It was as he was fastening the studs of his stiff shirt that Daben burst into the room. The man was excited and out of breath ; he was still in his travelling clothes. " It's back ! " cried Daben. " The harp is back in the cabinet ! We must have a drink on this. You must join me." He pressed a button beside the bed, kept his hand pushing on it unnecessarily long.

Tarrant had turned and was regarding him quizzically, continuing to fasten his studs.

There was a knock at the door. " Come," Daben cried. " Bring us some cocktails, John. Anything. Bacardi. Bring the shaker with you." John closed the door.

" I congratulate you, Mr. Daben," Tarrant began ; but the other hurried on.

" I went into the library before coming up to dress. Everything was as usual so far as getting in. Everything was the same inside. But the harp stood in the cabinet, just as it always has ! I could not believe my eyes for some minutes. When I had somewhat recovered, I hurried up to tell you about it."

Tarrant repeated, " I congratulate you sincerely. Am I to understand, then, that your trouble is over and the affair ended ? "

Here the footman returned with the cocktails. The two men pledged the Breogan harp, each other, and the owner's sudden good fortune, before the latter returned to Tarrant's question.

" Of course the harp is back, that is the main thing. I have recovered possession of what I have sworn to guard. But I do not know how I have done so, how it disappeared or how it was returned. It is necessary to discover this. Reluctant as I am to admit it—and I will especially ask you not to repeat this to Mrs. Daben—it appears that part of that old prophecy is true. In some way ' the harpe in peril stande.' We must find out whence this peril comes, so that I can prevent any repetition. That much of our task remains and it is as important as ever. . . . And, my word, it is twenty minutes of eight ! I must get along and dress. You will excuse me ; I'll see you below."

" You may count on me," replied Tarrant, as the other left, " to help you try to discover what has happened." He stood for a few moments in silence beside the cocktail tray after his host's departure, then turned and stepped out on to the little balcony. He had been in the house shortly more than half an hour. In that period the vanished harp, the purpose of his visit, had reappeared. He lit a cigarette.

Or had it reappeared within that time ? According to Daben, he had entered the library and seen the relic in its accustomed place almost immediately. But Daben had entered the library as soon as he had taken off his coat ; Tarrant felt certain that the door, so peculiarly opened, must have been the one in question. Then the harp must have returned during Daben's absence.

However, he continued, there are elements about this situation reminiscent of a very old gag. Many a lady of fashion has been known to stage a fake theft and subsequent recovery of her pearl necklace for no other reason than to effect a substitution of a replica for the original, upon which it has become necessary to realise. Could Daben himself, the only person known to have access to the library, have been repeating such a stratagem ? Could he have smuggled the original down to New York and smuggled a substitute back again ? As to the first item, one could not say, except that it seemed unlikely in the case of a man who made so much of his family line and its heritage, and who obviously had many other resources at his disposal. As to smuggling something back, he had certainly not had it on the train and he had certainly been empty-handed when, under Tarrant's observation, he had gone through that door. A harp of any size at all cannot be concealed under one's coat.

"I think," murmured Tarrant, "that I shall inspect the harp and likewise the other residents here, before I indulge in further phantasies." He threw away his cigarette and prepared to make his way below.

But before he had fully carried out this intention, a singular occurrence turned his attention sharply to these very residents. The broad corridor upon which his door opened, led directly to the head of the stairway, but beyond where the stairs debouched, the corridor turned at right angles and was cut off by an inner wall which met the balustrade extending for some fifteen feet along Tarrant's portion of the corridor. As he proceeded soundlessly over the thick carpet towards the head of the stairs, it became apparent that some one was just around the corner where the corridor turned.

He heard a murmur, then a woman's voice; a voice of lovely clarity—and broken. "Oh, Frederick, don't, please. . . . I can't. . . . Oh, I do. But I can't now. Please, please. . . . Not while he is in this trouble. My place is with him, I must help him in this crisis—I—I——" A sob ended the uneven words.

Tarrant, whose step had not faltered a fraction during his passage, turned on to the velour of the steps and passed downward. His expression, before he smoothed it out, evidenced his appreciation that a new element had entered the problem.

.   .   .   .   .

The drawing-room was large, well supplied with floor lamps; there was also some form of indirect lighting and, as Tarrant stepped across the threshold, he noticed, first, that as yet he held solitary possession and, second, that the room was most luxuriously furnished. A kind of combination of modern living-room and the " parlour " of his youth.

He turned as a step sounded at the entrance. He had purposely passed to the other side of the room in order better to observe the next comer ; now, without the appearance of staring, he made a close inspection of the girl who was advancing towards him.

She was not large—medium height even for a girl ; she was slender, with coal black hair and lips of a red that exactly matched her veneered finger-nails. As she came closer he saw that her eyes were a deep blue. A face piquant by contour but not now piquant by animation. She looked tired and even her anticipatory smile held worry. Her make-up did not quite succeed in concealing the darkness under her eyes. He judged her to be not over thirty and to be entitled to congratulations upon her choice of a dinner dress.

They met midway of the floor and she held out a gracious hand. " Mr. Tarrant, I am sure. Donatelli sent me a wire. I'm Mrs. Daben, sorry I couldn't welcome you when you arrived." She stepped closer and said in a low voice, " I do so hope you will be able to help us. It is really—really serious. I understand you know——"

" My dear lady," Tarrant interrupted, " I can see that you do not know. I beg you not to distress yourself needlessly any longer. The harp is safe and sound in the library once more."

" Oh ! " He was surprised, even a little shocked, to notice the intensity of relief that spread over her face. " Oh. But when, but how——"

This time she interrupted herself. Two men, both of them unknown to Tarrant, were entering. The girl made the introductions quickly. " This is Mr.

Tarrant, a friend of Donatelli's. Mr. Brinkerstall, formerly my guardian, now my financial adviser; and Mr. Stuart, my husband's secretary. Oh, Frederick," she hurried on, " the harp has been found. It's been recovered, it's in the library ! "

While they were exclaiming over the news, Tarrant found a brief moment to observe them. Brinkerstall must have been sixty, a grizzled man, not ill-looking in his dinner jacket. The secretary was much younger—possibly thirty-four or five— far from handsome but a nice enough appearing young man. So this was the " Frederick " of the corridor above. And Molla Daben had been the other party to that rather foolhardy, rather compromising exchange. No one, least of all Tarrant, could have mistaken the clear beauty of her voice, even heard around a corner ; he had recognised her with her first word of greeting. Were these two in love with each other, carrying on an intrigue under the husband's nose ? If so, they had themselves well in hand now ; their expressions, their glances were no more than those of good friends. Stuart was plainly delighted with the news and made no effort to conceal it. The older man received the information more calmly ; his felicitations were perfunctory and he gave the impression of considering the importance of the matter exaggerated.

Then Daben came hurrying in and the exclamations were repeated. Momentarily, Tarrant thought, he looked displeased that the harp's return was known ; perhaps he had wished to break the news himself. However, it was only for an instant. Then he turned to the cocktail service and insisted upon himself pouring every one a portion for the toast he immediately proposed. For his part Tarrant was thankful that dinner was announced before there had been time for more than two cocktails. John, the genius of the aperitif, made a stiff drink, he found.

The dinner was a conventional meal, served by two footmen whom the butler supervised from the background. The wines were good and Daben, with the advent of the main course, ordered a Great Burgundy uncorked in honour of the occasion. Conversation was general and, try as he would, Tarrant could detect no undertones of significance. Every one took part, with the exception of Brinkerstall who was silent the greater portion of the time ; but that may have been accounted for by his age, a full generation beyond that of the others. Also he was obviously enjoying the excellent fare. Molla Daben, relieved of her anxiety, made a sparkling hostess, impartially throwing the conversational ball from one to the other about her table. From the only sustained contribution he made, it was obvious that Brinkerstall, as a financial man, was not in sympathy with the policies of the current administration.

It was fully an hour later when Daben appeared in the drawing-room doorway to ask if they would care to see Breogan's harp back in its proper resting-place. He had already opened the library door and they all trooped through, into the long, narrow room with its book-lined walls, heavy Chinese rugs, its four big chairs and, looming beyond the desk, a large globe-map of the world.

In the centre of the floor, facing the doorway, stood a glass-enclosed cabinet. The host pressed a switch beneath it and a concealed light played brightly upon the harp lying upon a plush cushion within. Tarrant, who had intended to ask that it be removed so that he could examine it at close quarters, found this unnecessary. Interested and experienced in archeological finds, his first glance told him that here was no replica, however skilfully copied. The ancient wood, curved in a graceful bow, the loose strings filling the segment within, the crude but effective tuning mechanism unused for hundreds of years, all bespoke a legitimate antiquity. It was an Egyptian harp, an original, at which he was looking. But what was that little hole, through the centre of the frame ? An idiosyncrasy, perhaps, of this particular specimen.

As the others were leaving, he made his request. " If it's all right," he said, " I'd like to spend half an hour in here, alone, looking about. As I cannot operate the door, perhaps you would close it for me from the outside and come back to get me in about thirty minutes ? "

Daben acquiesced immediately. " By all means. Anything you suggest. But don't waste your time looking for secret entrances in here. I was present while this room was being constructed, and I can tell you they are out of the question. Searching for that sort of thing would be a waste."

Tarrant, when he found himself alone, did indeed waste little energy on possible tricks of architecture. He quickly assured himself that the entire floor was of concrete, precluding any traps ; he inspected the ceiling from where he stood, clear enough in the room's lighting, but did not even make a superficial examination of the walls. Any exit through them, he felt, could more easily be discovered from outside.

He strolled slowly about the room, counting the books ranged in case after case. His curiosity extended so far as to cause him to push back at least a few of them on each and every shelf, but in no instance did he find they could be moved farther inwards ; the shelves, evidently, had been made to order of such dimensions that the books just filled them.

He sat down at the desk and began to write : " First row, south—Encyclopedia Britannica, 14th Edition ; Dictionary of Famous Men ; Second row— Works of Bulwer, Lord Lytton. . . ." He wrote rapidly, but by the time he had finished, more than half of his thirty minutes had elapsed. Above the books a cornice ran round three sides of the room, reached, of course, by the three library ladders on rollers that permitted access to the top shelf. Upon the cornice stood as fine a collection of ship models as he had ever seen gathered in one place. South sea proas followed in the wake of Yankee clipper ships, Greek biremes and triremes jostled modern Mediterranean fishing smacks bright with their lateen sails, a fighting frigate of Elizabethan times stood between a model of a P. & O. liner and and American half-brig of the nineteenth century. Altogether there were eighteen boats. Once more Tarrant sauntered around the room, sat down and wrote.

Again he got up and this time approached the cabinet in the centre of the library. It consisted of a supporting stand, topped by a box of clear glass set in a steel framework. Somewhere, of course, there was a concealed lock but he did not attempt to locate it. Sighting through the glass with his fountain pen, he took the dimensions of the harp, which, together with its colour and other character-istics, followed into his notebook the data he had already collected. Then he brought out his handker-chief and carefully wiped the whole surface of the cabinet.

A low humming behind his back told him his time was up. Slipping the notebook into a pocket, he turned to meet his host's smile from the doorway. " Any progress ? " Daben asked. " Have you found any clue at all to this extraordinary disappearance and return ? "

" I'm afraid not as yet. Just getting a first acquaintance with the scene of the affair. . . . By the way, that's a fine collection of boats you have ; did you construct those models yourself ? "

The other was plainly pleased. He said, " No, not all of them. I bought the P. & O. boat and the frigate, too. But most of the others I made myself.

As a matter of fact several of them need a little attention now ; I've been meaning to get at it lately but haven't managed somehow." He mounted one of the ladders and came down with a fair-sized brigantine in one hand. " I've never fathomed the mystery of how these things wear out." He pointed to a miniature block, hanging from a broken thread. " They do, though ; all of them ought to be gone over periodically. I'm going to take the opportunity to repair this one to-night, if you won't think me too inhospitable. I heard the others mentioning a table of contract ; but I'm not fond of the game especially and I thought perhaps you might care to play. Or don't you ? "

" I should be delighted," Tarrant admitted. " What sort of game shall I be up against ? "

" Well, Molla and Fred Stuart are fair, that's all. Brinkerstall's very good. Been an expert all his life ; whist, auction bridge, now contract." The door closed behind them and they were at the lower end of the hall. " Humph, I see Molla's had the table set up already ; rather taking you for granted, I'm afraid.

" She wanted to play in the hall to-night, by the fireplace," Daben added. " This hall, you see, is a correct reproduction of the chief hall of a castle in Leinster, the family seat of my line for a long period. I believe she wants to spend the evening here, rather in celebration of the harp's recovery. . . . I wish to heaven *she* wouldn't take my responsibility so seriously."

Daben sighed, nodded, turned towards the main staircase, the brigantine under his arm. Tarrant strolled towards the still empty table.

.   .   .   .   .

It was the following afternoon before he found an opportunity to have any private conversation with his hostess. He had spent part of the morning in a further examination of the library, this time from the outside. Combining two purposes, he had gotten hold of Stuart after breakfast to serve as guide, hoping to improve his acquaintance with the secretary and possibly to draw him out upon the matter of the relic.

The first part of the programme had been a complete success, the survey of the room's exterior. It occupied a corner of the house and thus two of its walls were likewise those of the building itself. There were no windows ; and also there was no possibility of any other exit on these two sides, no matter how contrived. He and Stuart approached immediately to the walls and no doubt was left in Tarrant's mind.

The third wall of the library formed one side of the main staircase well. The entire expanse was visible from all over the hall, from the stairs and even from part of the drawing-room ; a more conspicuous location for a secret entrance could scarcely be found. That left only the fourth wall, in which the legitimate doorway already stood. Aside from the fact that this position was also conspicuous, Tarrent found it difficult to imagine what function a secret entrance practically beside the acknowledged one could serve. Should one wish to gain access to the room, the proper door would do as well ; any one entering the library would be under observation, or the absence of it, equally in both cases. Unless such a person could be supposed to have been unable to discover the mechanism by which the original door was operated.

But that was out of the question, too. An additional entrance through the solid concrete of the walls argued extensive alterations, which could not possibly have been undertaken and completed without Daben's knowledge. He realised, fully and finally, that the only one who could have procured another means of admission was Daben himself. And to suspect him further was ridiculous. The harp now in the cabinet *was* the original, and Daben was unquestionably its legal owner from every aspect. What possible motive could he have for secreting his own property, only to restore it at the earliest available moment? Furthermore, it was now established that no possibility existed of a second entrance unknown to the members of the household or to Daben himself. Tarrant decided that it was merely his love of paradox that had led him to make Daben his first suspect and that it was high time to give serious consideration to others.

In this connection his second objective, of drawing out the secretary, did not prosper so well. The young man was courteous but reserved. Very plainly he did not desire to enter into any further discussion with Tarrant than was necessary as a minimum.

" I suppose," ventured the latter, in an attempt to surprise him into saying something, " that the harp really *did* disappear ? "

The suggestion certainly surprised Stuart ; he stared at his questioner before replying, " Well, of course. I should say it did. It was only about ten-thirty one evening when Daben raised the alarm. Mrs. Daben and I ran to the library. Dr. Torpington, the physician, was here and came along, too. All four of us searched the room thoroughly, we simply could not believe our eyes. But I can assure you there was not a trace of the harp in the place."

" And no doubt the rest of the house was also searched ? "

" Extensively."

" And what," pursued Tarrant, " is your opinion of your employer ? "

" I beg your pardon ? " The secretary's tone conveyed an almost theatrical rebuff.

" Well, well, of Mrs. Daben, then ? Come, man, you must realise that I am trying to investigate what seems a most peculiar occurrence. It is essential that I be able to form some estimate of the background, of the people here, their characters and mutual relations."

" I am afraid you will have to apply elsewhere," retorted Stuart shortly. " I see nothing unusual about the background or the people. It is true that Mrs. Daben has been greatly upset over the disappearance of the harp, for which none of us can offer an explanation. In my opinion, unnecessarily upset. If that harp ever had any real importance, it was very long ago and nowadays it is no more and no less valuable than any other museum piece. But she is high-strung and she——"

He caught himself up abruptly. " Frankly, I will not discuss her further. That is all I intend to say."

Discovering that this was the truth, Tarrant presently took his leave and spent the remainder of the sunny morning wandering about the hilltop outside. He met no one until lunch-time when the entire party gathered in the dining-room.

It was during luncheon that Molla Daben proposed a canter for the afternoon. " Sorry," said Daben, " but I have some work to be done and I shall want Stuart with me." Brinkerstall, apparently, did not ride.

" I will join you with pleasure, Mrs. Daben," Tarrent volunteered. " I'm fond of horses. If you'll let me substitute for the others ? "

" Surely. The ridge extends about half a mile. I can't offer you much exercise, but a little, anyhow. And we have a pretty fair slide down the northern slope."

Stuart looked plainly disappointed, Brinkerstall grunted ; he wondered whether Daben, also, were not concealing a slight disgruntlement. Interesting, if true, although he could not imagine the cause.

Out on the bridle paths there was not much chance

for conversation until he made it, by dismounting where a meadow touched the edge of the hill, on the pretence of the view and a rest for his horse. With the bridle loosely looped over an arm he sat down on the long grass and the girl had no choice but to join him. She let her mount wander, told him to do the same.

Tarrant lost no time in generalities. "You will forgive my being personal," he began, "but you seem a new woman since the return of the harp."

She had been smiling but her face clouded instantly. "Oh, what can have happened to it? Of course it is vitally important to have it back again, but I don't understand even how that came about. And, so long as we don't know, it may happen again! I am not as worried now as I was, naturally; but I have been half sick about it. Dr. Torpington—that's our physician—has been urging me to go on a cruise with him and his family, he said I must get away and recover my health or I should have a complete breakdown. But of course I couldn't—I can't now, as long as this uncertainty continues."

"Ah," said Tarrant. "When does Dr. Torpington set sail?"

"In two weeks. No, about ten days now. But you must see it is impossible."

"Why, really, Mrs. Daben, I can't say that I do. Isn't it possible you are taking the whole matter far too seriously? After all, though it is disconcerting to lose such a valuable heirloom, it does not seem an especially dangerous experience. And it is back again, safe and sound."

"For the time being."

"Well, let us suppose the worst. Let us suppose that it vanishes again. If so, we should have some reason now, I think, to expect another return. And how could that injure you?"

"Not me. Donatelli, Mr. Daben."

" You are thinking about that old prophecy of the harp's disappearing thrice ? "

" Yes. Don't you see ? If some one, some *thing*, can get into our locked library, to take the harp and to bring it back, what measures or what vigilance can keep it from attacking my husband after a triple warning ? I am Irish, Mr. Tarrant. Oh, I know the upper classes have never taken the banshees very seriously, but what *can* it be that is doing this ? "

" My dear lady," said Tarrant soothingly, " there are no banshees. Whatever reality the ' mound people ' ever had, ceased when belief in them ceased. You *are* overwrought about this, truly."

The girl looked at him. Her voice was nearly a wail as she cried, " But it's all my fault. Don't you know it's all my fault ? "

" What ? " For a moment Tarrant had a sudden suspicion that he was about to hear confession. Some plot to make use of the ancient legend for a modern purpose ? Frederick ?

She was speaking rapidly. " So he didn't tell you all of it ? I thought you knew, but it's like him to leave this out. It's a code, part of his code. . . .

" I'll tell you. Way back, about 1156, there was a man Dermod, King of Leinster. He lost his throne and had to flee to Henry the Second for aid. Later he came back with Pembroke, Richard de Clare ; and Henry himself came to Ireland soon after. It was the beginning of the Anglo-Norman invasion. I won't bother you with the complicated politics but presently a betrothal was arranged, and a marriage followed, between Donatelli's great-great-great-great-grandfather, the head of the Daben line and custodian of the harp at that time, and Beren de Maleore or Malorye or Malloire—no one spelled the same then—who was a very important young Norman noblewoman. Of course it's forgotten now, but then it affected the destiny of both Ireland and England ; the Irish *ardri*, the chief king, didn't

have as much standing as the head of the house
that had descended from the great Breogan, and
possessed his harp to prove the succession.

"That was when the Norman soothsayers
composed the prophecy, for the marriage celebration
of Brian Dabheoin and Beren de Maleore. And of
course it hinged on the harp which was the very
symbol of the bargain. I can remember every word
of it."

Tarrant said nothing and she went on, a low voice
now, repeating the old words.

"' Once but not twice Dabheoin and Malorye
May wed without danger of traveillie ;
If again—the harpe in peril stande.
When Breogan Harpe thrice shall elude
The guardian that to harpe be trowed,
Then shall the race of Dabheoin eande.'

Well, but that rhyme affects us. Donatelli is the
present guardian of the harp. Beren de Malorye's
younger brother also made an Irish marriage in
1172. And I am his direct descendant," finished the
former Molla Mallory simply.

"But the relationship is far from close," was
Tarrant's puzzled comment. "Or do you mean that
you only discovered the prophecy after your
marriage ? "

"It is not a question of the degree of our relationship," explained Molla patiently. "The point is that
this is the second time ' Dabheoin and Malorye have
wed.' Oh, we knew about it ; I knew and so did
Donatelli. We thought—— I don't know why I
tell you all this, Mr. Tarrant, except that I must tell
some one and I'm sure you are a gentleman, in the
older sense. I may as well tell it all, now. I won't
pretend I have ever been fully in love with Donatelli ;
our marriage was made for—dynastic reasons. Not
political, of course ; we were the surviving heads of

two old lines and, as such, he had inherited control of a considerable fortune, while mine is even larger. We wanted to perpetuate the lines, we wanted to unite the fortunes ; in a democracy finance has taken over many of the prerogatives of aristocracy.

" We had both, we had the lineage and also the corresponding financial power. Please don't think it was a distasteful *mariage de convenance*. I have always liked Donatelli and admired him ; I have reason to believe that, just as a man, he is very fond of me. And contrary to democratic dogma, I have always thought that a marriage based upon practical as well as emotional reasons is likely to turn out as well as any, if only for the fact that it is founded on two good grounds rather than merely one. . . . I am not defending our action, I am explaining it. But we thought the prophecy was just old words ; we thought that in 1934 we could chance that part of it without much danger."

Tarrant said, " And you still think the bargain you made a good one ? "

" My marriage ? Yes, I do. I should do it over again. But the prophecy——"

" Is just old words, Mrs. Daben, I assure you."

" Oh, how can you say that ? The harp has never been lost by the Daben line, never in combat, never by theft, *never* ! And this *is* the second occurrence of just the marriage that was mentioned. How can you explain such a coincidence ? What other explanation can there be ? "

He had been racking his brains for an answer to that very question. Now he said slowly, " I can think of several. The Malorye family possessed political importance in the twelfth century, I take it. I doubt if the English, though willing to give away one of them for value received, looked with favour upon the emigration of any others. Common sense, Mrs. Daben, tells us that this rhyme was made for reasons that were cogent at the time of its composing ; we must agree that there were no wizards at Henry's court capable of foreseeing the events of 1930."

" But then it would have been made against the Irish, not the Dabheoin family."

" And," Tarrant went on, struck by an idea, " I should make a shrewd guess that the prophecy was made for the very purpose of discouraging your own ancestor, Beren's brother, from adding to the Irish influence the Maloryes could wield in London. English influence in Ireland was one thing, Irish influence in England another."

" No," Molla Daben spoke with a hopeless conviction. " Beren's brother married an O'Neill, not a Dabheoin. . . . And common sense should go the whole way, not stop short in the middle. I tells me that no modern person stole Breogan's harp ; no modern person could, as it is safeguarded. What kind of being, what sort of power can pluck the harp from behind concrete walls through the door that I do not myself know how to open ? Until that is explained, I am not likely to forget a prophecy that is already two-fifths verified. . . . Can you explain it—by common sense ? "

Tarrant said, " No, Mrs. Daben, I cannot. Yet.'

. . . . .

As he went up the broad staircase, still in his riding kit, Daben was coming down.

His host drew him to one side. " I hope you did not discuss the harp with Mrs. Daben this afternoon. I have been worried about her attitude towards the affair. Very worried."

" I'm afraid I mentioned it," Tarrant admitted. " I did my best to reassure her. I don't know how far I succeeded."

" Tsck ! "

" And by the way, are you positive no one except yourself knows how to operate the library panel. We must get that straight. Is there any possibility ?"

"There is," Daben assured him, "none at all. . . . I know."

   .   .   .   .   .

Tarrant showered and changed with fair speed, but none the less, when he came down again, Molla Daben was already in the drawing-room. The heavy rugs in the hall were responsible for the slight contretemps—if it was one—that marked his entrance, for they deadened his footsteps until he reached the doorway.

Across the room Brinkerstall was talking to the girl, seriously. His voice, raised in emphasis, carried plainly. "Molla, it is not necessary. I am opposed to it absolutely. If you do go, there is no reason at all to execute——" He caught sight of Tarrant and stopped abruptly.

The latter said at once, "I'm afraid I'm interrupting you people. Sorry. I'll take a turn——"

"Not a bit of it," Molla Daben smiled across to him. "I'm glad you rescued me. It's just something about finances ; Snooky is still the heavy guardian, so zealous. . . . Come over here, Mr. Tarrant, and I'll show you how to mix a brand new cocktail."

Tarrant came over, grinning inwardly. "Snooky"; what a name for the dignified John Brinkerstall, Esq. ! Still, a girl as pretty as Molla could probably make 'em like whatever tags she picked. He had a distinct impression that the financier was hrmp-hrmping a very flattered disapproval.

The others came in while Tarrant was still vigorously jingling the ice in the shaker. No doubt it was John's day off. The dinner that followed was a repetition of that of the previous evening ; and afterwards the game of contract was reconstituted. Although no special orders had been given this time, they found the table again set up in the great hall.

Molla remarked, "I must tell them we don't want to play here every evening. But we may as well not move now." It was a decision that Tarrant was later to find a fortunate one.

Just as they were sitting down Daben came out of the library, another boat under his arm. This time it was a far eastern craft, a long war canoe of some kind with a single mast. As he passed the table, Tarrant called casually, " All quiet in the fortress ? "

" How ? . . . Oh, I see. Yes, the harp is there all right. When I was looking at it just now, I could scarcely believe it had ever been away. It really *can't* be gotten out of that room." He passed on his way up the staircase.

The card play seemed to Tarrant rather ragged that evening. He cut with Brinkerstall, then cut with him again. That left Stuart with Molla and, although the stakes were small enough, the secretary seemed to have been seized with an intense desire to win. Against Brinkerstall, who placed every card in the pack with uncanny accuracy, it led to disaster. Molla let him down once with an unjustified redouble, but for the most part it was the other way around. Pressing can do as much damage to a hand of contract as to a drive from the tee ; and Stuart pressed. The previous evening, when he had had Tarrant for a partner, he had played a sound, conservative game. Tarrant noted the difference silently and filed it away, first in his memory, later in his notebook.

It was all of one o'clock when the debacle had been completed. Molla and Stuart were off 9000 points, $45. They settled immediately, Molla with a cheque, the secretary from a roll of bills he produced from a pocket. It was Tarrant who received the cheque and, as he folded it away, saw with surprise that his hostess dealt with the same New York bank that had his own account.

Stuart was saying ruefully, looking up at Daben who had returned and had stood watching the play for the past half-hour, " I let her down pretty badly.

Though I guess she can stand it better than I can. If I do this often, I shall have to have a raise in salary."

Deben laughed. " In that case I shall play more frequently myself. Against you. I haven't any objection to paying you fifty dollars each morning, provided I win it back again the same night." He turned to Tarrant. " I suppose," he said, half-seriously, " there has been no disturbance from the library while I was up in my workshop."

" I can guarantee that the room has remained closed." The other spoke lightly, leaning back and stretching out his long legs beside the table. " We cut to keep seats and partners. I have been facing the door the entire evening."

" Let's look," Molla proposed suddenly, getting up from her chair so that the men had to come to their feet also. She smiled as she said it, in no way nervously ; despite her protests Tarrant's talk of the afternoon seemed to have confirmed the return of her spirits.

" Don't be silly, darling," her husband spoke. " If Mr. Tarrant has had his eye on the door all the time, nothing can have happened."

" Oh, well, let's anyhow. We can sleep better after seeing it. I know I can."

Daben shrugged, then yielded gracefully. " I can't imagine anything more foolish, but very well." He led the way down the hall, followed by all except Brinkerstall who lingered to light a cigar. His hands, as they swept over the carved panelling, were deft and too swift to disclose just what he did. The door hummed open and he pressed the light-switch beside it.

" Oh ! " cried Molla. " Oh." The cabinet was plainly empty, the harp had vanished ! The colour drained out of the girl's face, leaving it dead white, and Tarrant put out an arm to steady her as she swayed beside him.

His own expression was surprised, almost in-credulous. " Don't go in there, anybody ! I think," he added quietly, " that I shall spend another half-hour here. Alone."

.   .   .   .   .

As the door closed, shutting him in, his notebook was already half out of his pocket. First he went to his knees, squinting along the thick pile of the rug ; but it was resilient and, if any tracks had been made since Daben's visit just after dinner, they had had time to disappear.

He went about his task methodically. " First row, south—Encyclopedia Britannica, 14th Edition, check ; Dictionary of Famous Men, check ; Second row—Works of Bulwer, Lord Lytton, check . . . check . . . check. . . ." He continued about the room, noting the position of each piece of furniture, as recorded in the notebook. The eighteen boats ; yes, they were there on the cornice. Everything, in fact, was exactly as it had been on his other visit, with the exception of the relic in the centre of the room. He climbed on to one of the ladders, climbed off again.

He approached the cabinet, producing from his coat a small can no larger than those that hold shaving powder. He smiled as he dusted the tiny grey grains over the metal framework and over the glass sides and top of the harp's resting-place. He did use part of a regular detective's equipment, but beyond the fingerprint powder and an automatic it would have been hard to find among his possessions those numerous and intricate gadgets he was always reading about.

As he continued his careful dusting he reflected that they had all been under his observation when this had happened. Even Daben himself, for all practical purposes, since he had certainly not re-entered the library. The obvious conclusion was that some one else, some one outside the small party he had met, must have gained access to the room by another means than the door. The servants? But there was no other entrance, that was the rub.

Now he leaned over and blew at the powder, gently. Of course, if Daben's prints were there, they would be there rightfully, although it was doubtful if he had unlocked the cabinet since Tarrant had wiped it clear. But if any one else's stood out, he would know who the thief was, no matter how mysterious the thief's coming and going remained. With an amateur it was always likely that finger-prints would be overlooked.

He finished blowing and stood looking down at the cabinet. There was not a print, not a smudge, not a mark of any kind on it.

" Now that," he murmured, " is either clever . . . or it is very damned queer."

Daben let him out and sat down beside the deserted bridge table, on whose top he commenced to drum nervously. He said, " They've gone to bed. Molla's very upset ; she's had a regular relapse and Torpington's up with her now. What the devil could you make out of it, Tarrant ? From the doorway the place looked exactly as I had left it when I came out after dinner."

" Yes," agreed Tarrant. He spoke rather absently. " It was just the same. Everything, except your harp. . . . That's the trouble. . . ." The silence continued until finally he added, " There were no fingerprints on the cabinet."

" Was the cabinet closed ? I thought so, from the glimpse I had."

" I don't know whether it was or not. I don't know how you lock it."

" It locks automatically when it is closed. Unless it was open, it was locked."

" It certainly wasn't open. Therefore it must have been locked."

Daben barked a short nervous laugh. " I'm not a superstitious man. I hope I'm not. But the room was locked and closed, and you yourself could see the only door all the time. The cabinet was locked. We went in and the cabinet was still locked. I gather that you found no signs of any tampering at all. And yet the harp is gone. Long ago there were powers in Ireland ; and their fame still lingers in banshee legends——"

Tarrant said wearily, " Need I remind you that the *ban sith*, ' the woman of the fairies,' the banshee if you like, was never a harp-thief ? It was her keening in the night that announced an impending death among those she visited. There has been no mention of keening, nor have I heard any."

" No-o," said Daben uncertainly.

The hall was high ; with only the two bridge lamps and the dying fire for light the beams above looked distant and shadowy. Tarrant's host gave a slight start as a log collapsed in the carven fireplace behind him. Tarrant blew a thin spiral of cigarette smoke towards the dimness over their heads.

He said ruminatively, " In the old days, I believe, only families of pure Milesian descent were ever attended by a banshee. That was one of the privileges Brian Dabheoin lost when he married Beren de Malorye. No doubt we should have agreed with his choice."

The other looked up. " I see that Mrs. Daben has been telling you about Brian and Beren de Malorye. I'm sorry you discussed it with her. She works herself up into an absurd belief that she is somehow responsible for this trouble. I had rather she didn't even think about it."

" But of course that is scarcely possible. She is as concerned about her own heritage and its responsibilities as you are about yours."

" I suppose so. Yes, of course, you're right. I am reluctant to connect these disappearances with our old prophecy but can there be a more 'ordinary' explanation ? "

Tarrant nodded slightly, looking over at his companion. " Yes," he said, " there can."

" What ! Do you, can you——"

" Oh, just an idea, nothing more as yet. I shouldn't think of sketching it out for you until I have some more tangible evidence."

" And you say your solution is straightforward, commonplace ? "

" My dear man, it is not a solution now ; when it becomes one, there will be evidence to support it. And I haven't any evidence yet. . . . You must be prepared for a shock, Daben. I still hold to my *carte blanche.*"

" Naturally," said the other a little stiffly. " It was in our bargain. I do not intend to back down. But how can you dismiss——"

" I do not," Tarrant pointed out, " invent solutions, I discover them. It is not my fault that they usually turn out to be what you would call ' ordinary.' If I succeed here, I venture to say that there will be no ghosts, or banshees, involved. And by the way, I must get back to New York for a day or so."

" What, you mean on this matter ? But it takes place here. Surely there will be no clue in New York to a mystery in Hartford."

" There are other matters that demand my attention," Tarrant returned vaguely. " I came up with you a bit unexpectedly. Of course I may find an opportunity to check one or two details on your affair. I'd not be surprised to find relevant details in New York. I'll be back, say, within three days. I have a notion to go down with Brinkerstall ; I think he leaves to-morrow."

His host appeared somewhat doubtful. " Well, of course, just as you say. I'd rather you stayed here for the time being. But very well. . . . It's

late, you know. Shall we go on up ? " He rose to
his feet and pulled an enormous fender across the
fireplace.

"You go ahead," Tarrant adjured him. " I shall
stay a few minutes and smoke another cigarette.
There are a few things I want to get straight in my
mind. No, really, don't wait for me."

Daben hesitated, then saw the other did not mind
his leaving. " All right. Good-night, then. I'll see
you in the morning before you leave." He mounted
the stairs and disappeared in the corridor above.

Tarrant got up, took another, more comfortable
chair, and prepared to wait. The silence in the house
had deepened ; it was so still that he could
distinguish a kind of undertone, a steady, nearly
imperceptible throbbing. That must be the air
conditioning system. He lit a cigarette.

There was another sound, too, almost as low as the
whisper from the ventilators. It was so regular that
for some time Tarrant did not recognise it. Then,
when he did, he jumped out of his chair and looked
searchingly around the dim reaches of the hall.
Yes, far up in the shadows near the main entrance,
a man sprawled in a big davenport.

Tarrant tiptoed across the rugs until he stood
beside him. He listened intently ; to all appearances
the man was sound asleep. Tarrant reached out and
shook him gently.

John Brinkerstall stirred. " Ugh. Agh." He
shook himself awake. " Uh, Tarrant, uh. I sat down
to finish my cigar. Must have fallen asleep. What
time is it ? "

" About two-thirty." Tarrant observed the half-
burned cigar in the other's fingers, the ash droppings
on the floor below his knee.

" I must get to bed. I can't imagine how I did it."

" I'm going back to New York to-morrow, for a
day or so. I thought we might take the same train,
if you won't mind my company. There are

some questions I would like to put to you."

Brinkerstall cleared his throat. " I'll be glad of your company. As to the questions—hrmp—we'll see. Good-night, Tarrant." He followed Daben, lumbering up the stairs. As he turned at the top, a small man, dapper and quick, passed him on the way down.

Tarrant stepped forward and accosted the new-comer. " You're Dr. Torpington? I've been waiting to see you. How is your patient ? "

" Good as can be expected. Shock, worry. May I ask who you are, sir ? "

Tarrant made haste to explain his identity and his presence in the house. " I know it's late, I'll only keep you a moment. Mrs. Daben's, ah, illness is entirely due to the matter of the harp ? "

" Harp, harp," snapped the doctor. " No doubt. Illness due to worry that upsets central nervous system ; disturbance jangles down through the sympathetic and affects all the ordinary functions. Digestion, elimination, bad upset. Reciprocal action back on the sympathetic. Of course. Get away from the harp. New faces, new scenes. Another relapse like this and I shall insist on it. Insist."

" When do you leave on your cruise, doctor ? "

" Next week. Friday, next week."

" But can she go ? Her accommodations, on a cruise, at the last moment——"

" Spoke to Daben long ago. Authorised me get her accommodations if warranted in my judg-ment. Have 'em. Have everything except her consent."

" And can you get that ? "

Dr. Torpington stared at him. " Certainly. If necessary. My patient. Insist."

" Of course the harp is back of it all," Tarrant observed. " What is your opinion about the harp ? "

" Don't know the details. Don't want to. Some fol-de-rol about curse or prophecy or something.

That's the stimulus but it's gone beyond stimulus now. Completely run down. I'm responsible for my patient's health. Get away, get health back, then she can come home and face her problem with resource. No organic trouble, purely functional."

" And are you going to insist, Dr. Torpington ? "

" If she improves, I can't. If she gets another shock, insist. Told Daben so just now. Must be getting along."

" Just a minute." Tarrant walked over to the card table, tore off a blank score and began to write. " Maybe I can reassure your patient somewhat. Will you give her this note when you stop to see her to-morrow ? I won't be here," he explained.

The doctor looked rather surprised. " Certainly. If it's all right. Have to read it myself."

Tarrant folded the paper, extended it. Torpington took it, and read :

" MRS. DABEN.—I must be away for the next two days. Please accept my assurance that the harp will have returned by the time I do.
TREVIS TARRANT.

" Know what you're talking about ? " the doctor demanded.

Tarrant smiled. " Usually," he admitted.

This time he was right, at any rate. When he got back, driving out from Hartford in the Rolls through afternoon flurries of snow, the harp's return was the first news with which Daben greeted him in the great hallway.

Tarrant had had a busy two days. The trip down to New York had been taken up with adroit questioning of Brinkerstall. Most of the questions the financier had answered, though not all of them. He had, however, evaded rather than flatly refused on those occasions. He would not commit himself to the amount of the combined fortunes of Daben and Molla, maintaining that he was not familiar with the former's affairs, and Tarrant did not press him as to the extent of the wife's means. Brinkerstall believed that in case anything happened to Daben, he had left everything to his wife ; he knew this to be true vice versa.

" See here, young man," he had interjected at this point, " these are serious questions. You don't think anything might happen to Daben, do you ? "

" I should not be entirely surprised if something happened to him."

" Nonsense—hrmp—nonsense." The other's tone had been half-way between a snort and a chuckle. " I never heard such absurd gravity over a piece of paper written by medieval dunces. I don't know what monkeyshines are going on with that old stick of a harp, but no one has been hurt, or is going to be."

In view of the conference in the drawing-room that he had inadvertently interrupted, Tarrant wanted to reassure himself that Molla's money was still safe despite the depression and the financier assured him that this was emphatically the case. It was just because her investments were so sound that her adviser had been urging upon her a course which he went on to explain could only be to her advantage. Tarrant admitted the incorrectness of his first conclusion. Nevertheless, when he left his companion at Grand Central, he felt well satisfied with the outcome of the trip. Even more so, perhaps, because of what Brinkerstall had *not* said.

He had visited his banker and broker—he really had private business in town—from both of whom he had made discreet inquiries. He had found out little from either, although the wealth of the Dabens naturally put them in the position of being subject to the continual rumours that waft about Wall Street. What little he did discover, however, was acceptable. He had also spent an hour with a certain wholesale supply house that dealt in everything from chemical supplies to hospital equipment. Then, feeling that he had done everything he could, he took a train back to Hartford.

On the journey there had been time for reflection. Among other things he had noted down the following table :

OCCASION	TIME	PRESENT
First disappearance -	Night - -	Daben, Molla Daben, Stuart, Torpington
First reappearance -	Aft'noon (?)	Molla Daben, Stuart, Brinkerstall
Second disappearance	Night - -	Daben, Molla Daben, Stuart, Brinkerstall

He had considered the listing for a time, then turned back through the pages of his notes. Torpington's attitude regarding his patient, his preparedness to take her away with him ; well, that fitted. Stuart had played very bad bridge the evening of the second disappearance. And that conversation between Molla and Stuart overheard in the corridor upstairs. Of course, there was a real controversy about the girl's going away ; could it be that the speeches he had heard were far more innocent than they appeared, were really no more than the secretary's appeal to Molla to be sensible and to take the trip for her health ? Were Molla and Stuart in love with each other, that was the question. He recalled Molla's assurance that she would repeat her marriage, he recalled her " dynastic " reasons. She had been sincere about both these matters, he felt sure ; but were they quite the same ? He glanced through his notes again and smiled openly as the answer to his question stood plainly before him.

He had closed the notebook with a snap just

as the train ground into the Hartford station.

. . . . .

Now he stood talking with Daben.

" I rather thought your relic would precede me,"
he acknowledged. " However, I'm glad it has. Oh,
before I forget it : Brinkerstall asked me to tell you
he'll be up again to-morrow. No, just over night.
There's some further business he has to take up with
Mrs. Daben and he wants to see her personally
rather than writing. She is better than when I left,
I trust ? "

" Well, better, yes. Not herself though, by any
means. . . . We shall be quite a party to-morrow
evening. Dr. Torpington and his wife are coming
for dinner and will spend the night. They're great
contract players ; it's quite a fixture. I do hope
nothing further happens to disturb Molla."

" I am rather afraid," said Tarrant slowly, " that
it will."

" My God, man ! You mean you expect Breogan's
harp to vanish for the *third* time ? "

" Just that."

" But we can't allow that to happen. I shall post
guards in the hall ! "

" I was on guard in your hall myself last time.
It didn't seem to help much. . . . No, here is what
I suggest. I propose to spend the next few nights
in your library, inside instead of outside. It has
always disappeared at night, hasn't it ? "

" It returned in the daytime yesterday ; some
time between noon and six p.m. But it has always
disappeared at night. If you are going to do that, I
shall keep you company. God knows what happens,
but whatever it is, we shall take it on together."

" I'd rather be alone," said Tarrant. " Really."

" No, no. I wouldn't think of it. It is my difficulty,
my place is there with you."

Tarrant capitulated. " As you will. All right.
Let us begin with to-night."

But though they did, nothing occurred. In the closed and quiet library Tarrant spent the long hours in reading composedly. Daben for the most part paced up and down, back and forth around the cabinet where the harp lay motionless and undisturbed under the glowing lights. At seven they emerged and breakfasted. And went wearily up the stairs to bed.

.   .   .   .   .

It was late in the afternoon when Tarrant descended, to find his fellow guests gathered in the drawing-room at tea. Every one was present. Daben and Molla and Stuart, of course ; also Brinkerstall, who greeted him cordially. Dr. Torpington and his wife sat together beyond the tea table. She was a large woman, a nondescript blonde, her hair just a little straggly around the edges ; a motherly type of person whose chief characteristic, one could tell at a glance, was placidity. Tarrant, watching them as tea progressed, felt convinced that the doctor, staccato and dapper, was her actual slave, little as he might sometimes suspect it. At other times no doubt he not only suspected it but loved it.

After dinner Tarrant drew his host to one side. " You have your guests," he pointed out. " And I've no objection to doing the vigil alone ; in fact, I prefer it. I've had enough bridge for the time being. So if you will let me into the library in a few minutes, I'll begin."

" I don't know," Daben began doubtfully. Molla and Stuart were passing and he detained them to explain the proposal. " If I'm not there, how will you get out, if you should want to ? " he asked Tarrant.

" But I don't want to. If you will come for me at seven or seven-thirty, that will be all that's necessary."

Daben still hesitated. " I would really rather not disclose the mechanism, even to you. But perhaps under the circum——"

"Not at all. It is quite unnecessary. Nothing would persuade me to leave, were the door wide open. I am quite serious."

"Oh, please be careful, Mr. Tarrant," Molla begged him. "I know you won't believe the prophecy has anything to do with it. But how can you tell?" She was pale and uncomfortable beneath her rôle of hostess and it was plain for a moment what effort it cost her to play it.

Her husband strove to combat her anxiety. "Nothing at all happened last night," he remarked. "I don't believe that anything will, so long as one of us is there." He came to a decision quickly, possibly for Molla's benefit. "All right, Tarrant, we shall do as you say. I'll let you in now."

"Just a minute. I have a portfolio upstairs that I shall want. Might as well get a little of my own work done during the night." Not very much more than a minute later he met Daben before the library door and was admitted. There was a slight clink as he dropped the portfolio casually upon an easy-chair but by that time the door had closed again and he was alone.

His first concern was to check the inventory he had made on his first visit to the room; more or less familiar with it by now, he completed the checking well within fifteen minutes. On the present occasion everything, he found, was accounted for, including the harp reposing innocently on its cushion. As he closed his notebook and put it away he experienced the strangest conviction that at some time during the coming night the harp would vanish for the third time.

Of course, that was what he was counting on; it would be strictly in accord with his deductions. But the feeling he had was not logical, it was not the conclusion of a syllogism, it was an immediacy of emotional perception as distinct as a visual or tactile one. Everything about the room was the same as always, *except the room itself.* His impression, queer, and for a minute or so overwhelming, was that the room was shocked ; it was the room as a whole, the room as an entity, that was talking to him. And what it said, very definitely, was that what had gone before had been minor, in a way harmless, but that what it now foresaw and was bracing itself to witness would be dangerous. Very dangerous and very evil.

Tarrant gave himself a tentative shake and murmured " Bosh." Rooms do not talk to one, assuredly they do not share their apprehensions as to the future with those who chance to sit down in them. He recalled the unctuousness with which sentimental lady novelists endowed rooms, and even pieces of furniture, with personalities, making them whisper their reminiscences of dead romances and dead crimes and dead this and that. It was anthropomorphism with a vengeance. No, rooms were rooms ; they might be the scenes of all sorts of things, but unless definite clues were left behind, they told no tales. It was on quite other grounds that he expected the harp to vanish to-night. There would be a certain amount of danger naturally.

On an impulse he opened his portfolio and spread out its contents for a final check. He might have neglected something on that hurried visit to his apartments, or something might have been tampered with.

The objects he placed under the light on the desk were curious. There were two sealed cans, not large but rather heavy. There was something that looked a little like a money belt, very thin and very strong and hard to the touch ; it ended in a pair of tapes, now untied. The next object resembled a football player's noseguard. A high-powered electric torch and a loaded automatic completed the equipment.

Those were his weapons, both of defence and offence. Upon those few diverse particulars he would have to rely not only for a solution of the

mystery of the harp that vanished ; quite possibly
he would have to rely upon them for his own life.
He checked them over carefully, and found them
properly ready. " Gadgets," smiled Tarrant as he
put them away again.

He looked at his watch. Ten o'clock. He took
from the portfolio its single other burden, a book—
Emotions of Normal People, W. M. Marston, Harcourt
Brace & Company. Some one had called it to his
attention the week before ; it spoke well of his nerves
that he could give himself up to its complexities at
the present moment. He opened it at the beginning
and became absorbed in the text. He was still
reading it, carefully and attentively, at one o'clock
when the library door hummed open and Daben
stood on the threshold.

" I thought I'd look in," Daben said, " and see
how you were making out. I cut out this rubber
but it's the last they're going to play. An early
evening. They want to get to bed because of that
show at the Country Club to-morrow morning."

" Ah. I didn't know about that."

" Yes. A horse show. Late in the season, but it's
the first one out here and they couldn't get a better
date. . . ." Daben paused, then went on, " You
know, old man, I'd forgotten all about this show,
but I really ought to put in an appearance. Two of
Molla's horses in the morning. I'd rather meant to
keep you company, but I think, if you don't mind,
I'll turn in. After last night I have no doubt nothing
will happen here. . . . Sure you won't call it off
yourself ? "

" No, I'll stick. I have, well, call it a hunch, that
the harp will disappear again to-night." He looked
meaningly at Daben. " You might watch yourself
to-night, here or anywhere else. Lock your door."

The other laughed. " I ? Lock my door ? Come
on, you're taking this more seriously than I am.
You'll be as bad as Molla presently. We spent the

whole night in here last evening and nothing happened at all. We might better have been in our
beds. Nothing will happen ; it's hopeless to attack
it this way."

"And don't unlock it till morning," said Tarrant
quietly. "Maybe—I'm not sure—but maybe nothing
will happen then."

Daben said : "I don't know what you're talking
about. But I'm going to bed. I'd really rather you
gave it up this time. . . . Well, good-night. And
good hunting. I'll come for you by seven-thirty."

"Good-night."

The door closed, with a click of finality. Tarrant
shrugged, sat staring at it for some little time.
Unless some one else had discovered his host's
secrets, that was the last human face he would see,
the last voice he would hear and the last chance of
escape he would possess until after the attempt—
and the danger—had come and passed. He was
alone, as securely shut away as if prisoned in a bank
vault with the time lock set for seven-thirty a.m.

He smiled, a bit grimly. Yes, in many respects
the room was like a bank vault. He really had not
discovered how the one door was opened either from
the inside or from without. For that omission he had
had his reasons. It would be amusing if this room
came to resemble a bank vault in *all* respects.

For the best part of half an hour he sat considering
the situation ; and toward the end of it a little doubt,
that grew, began edging its way into his mind. It
was dead quiet, just that tiny whisper of the ventilators that he had noticed for the first time out in the
entrance hall a number of nights before.

What if he were wrong ? There were a lot of un-
confirmed steps in the process by which he had come
to the conclusion on which he was now staking his
success. It was a surprising conclusion and he had
to admit that it was based on something uncomfort-
ably like surmise. His deductions only differed

from surmise in the strict and rigid logic by which one proceeded from another. Well, that was what he believed in, that was the way Causation worked and the sure way in which it could be understood— sometimes anticipated. It had never failed him yet.

Still—— There were too many factors missing for certainty. It was scarcely a week since he had first heard of the Legend of the Harp and there might be a score of factors unknown to him, maybe merely because no one had chanced to mention them as yet. Any one of these unknowns might conceivably invalidate the train of reasoning that had set the present stage. He had planned against a definite form of procedure, a definite kind of attack, by putting himself in his theoretical adversary's place. But facts remained the same whether they were taken into consideration or not ; what if some fact had escaped inclusion in his reasoning and the attack, when it came, arose from an unexpected quarter, one against which he had failed to guard ?

Curiously enough, although he was doubting his own concrete predictions, he felt strangely certain that this night the harp would vanish again. That conviction seemed to come, not from logic, but from some other vague region of perception. Could there, coldly considered, be anything in the old tales that clustered about the relic ? There, before his eyes, lay the harp. It, at any rate, had spanned some thousands of years, to be present in physical actuality in this room. . . . Banshees, of course were out ; the entire situation was outside that tradition. But who had been the " mound people " ? Of all legendary beings they were the vaguest ; their reports had come down far more fragmentarily than those of Horus or Set or the gods of the Aztecs. Who really knew anything about them, or about what they were once believed to have been ? The *ban sith* was one of them, yes ; but what other creatures had they comprised, with what other different attributes ?

He glanced at his watch, shook himself back out the dim past of Ireland. A stray thought lingered before fading ; the remarkable tie-up, through the harp, with Egypt. There if anywhere in the old times had been real knowledge rather than priestly superstition. . . . One-thirty-five. . . . More than one threat out of the ancient world he had investigated, more than one legendary menace before which very modern people had trembled. All of those threats had been empty. And at the back of his head wandered a peculiar impression about this one.

He went back to his book. If he were right in his view of this case, he knew what to expect ; and there would be warning of a kind he couldn't miss. If not, he might as well be engaging his attention upon something important as fussing about the unknown. He had reached a point in the volume where a preliminary discussion of the appetitive type was undertaken.

This type of personality, the text stated, was one in which the love response mechanisms of the higher centres were subordinated to the self-seeking mechanisms originally based upon hunger drive. The love mechanisms were responsible not only for what was generally considered love behaviour but also for those forms of response upon which social intercourse and fair dealing with one's fellow men were founded. Thus the criminal was the example *par excellence* of the appetitive personality type. And when the correlation centres of the head brain (whose operation determined mental functioning) were highly organised, this meant that the criminal person, in his or her activities, could draw upon much imagination and ingenuity. Such a person would employ deceit to unexpected lengths, even continuing a rôle of innocence when alone and unobserved——

It was just one-forty-four when the library was plunged abruptly into darkness.

. . . . .

Tarrant closed his book, switched on his flashlight and looked at the time. He was not disturbed ; this was what he had expected. It was confirmation of sorts ; but it was nothing he could rely upon. The next move might still be quite outside his calculations.

There was absolute silence now, not a sound of any kind. He played the light around the room from his position at the desk ; its bright beam threw the lined books, the ships and the chairs into sharp relief and made the library look longer and narrower than it was. Also larger ; he realised, making the necessary corrections for the perspectives revealed by the flash, that the room was really rather small.

For more than an hour he sat thus, sometimes in darkness, sometimes throwing the light about the room. Nothing happened, Always he strained his ears for the slightest noise. There was no sound at all, there was no movement of any kind in the chamber. Only time, with its silent regularity, flowed through the room.

Suddenly he realised that he was getting drowsy ; he had actually been nodding when he caught himself. He sat up straight and pinched his leg, gave a prodigious yawn and pressed the flashlight. Nothing had moved, everything was the same, the harp lay in the cabinet untouched. He was frightfully sleepy. He yawned again.

The next time Tarrant lit the torch he was so dizzy that the wall at the library's end played tricks of receding then advancing again in the wavering glare. It was four-twenty-six. . . . And there was a low humming somewhere. Groggily he reached for the automatic and nearly dropped it. Then he was covering the door. A moment later he had dropped the gun into his pocket and was resting his head on his hands. He had realised that the humming came from no part of the room ; it was the blood pounding in his own ears that he heard.

He staggered to his feet and stumbled across the floor, noting painfully as he passed that the relic in the cabinet was still undisturbed. Three times he gasped out Daben's name as loudly as he could, and was beating with his fists on the panel he did not know how to open. The blows were feeble ; he wondered if they could be heard even by any one in the hall outside.

He swayed once. He swayed again and fell backwards in a sprawled, untidy heap to the right of the closed doorway.

.   .   .   .   .

The lights came on at five-fifteen.

But there was no movement in the room. None from the door, none about the walls, or floor, or ceiling. None from the quiet figure lying beside the entrance. It was five-thirty-five before the preliminary buzz announced the opening of the panel-doorway.

A figure stood there, muffled in a robe ; stood for some seconds sniffing, then slipped through as the panel swung shut. It bent over Tarrant, felt for his heart ; felt stillness.

The figure nodded to itself and made straightway for the cabinet. Presently that was open and the harp was lifted out. The cabinet was closed again. The figure went then about its further business.

Later it crossed the room, stopping once more beside Tarrant's body, just to make sure.

The panel swung open, the figure passed through, the panel swung shut.

The lights burned down into the library ; and there was no movement of any kind.

.   .   .   .   .

At seven-twenty-five the doorway hummed again and Daben walked through without hesitation. He looked in bewilderment at the empty desk and the empty chairs. It was a matter of seconds before his glance fell upon the man almost at his feet.

" Tarrant ! " he cried. He, too, knelt down and felt for his guest's heart.

" My God ! " gasped Daben. He stood uncertainly, and hesitated. Then the patter of his feet sped through the open entrance and down the great hall. As he ran up the stairs his shout came dwindling back.

" Torpington ! . . . Torpington ! . . ."

.   .   .   .   .

The footsteps were coming back. They jarred down the velour-covered stairs, clattered across a bare spot on the flooring of the hall.

The two men turned into the library. They found themselves covered by a very steady automatic. From the seat behind the desk Tarrant spoke in a grimly level voice.

" Come in. And leave that door open."

The amazement on the two faces was surely sincere. Torpington plainly could make nothing of his sudden experience and Daben, if anything, was even more greatly astonished. But then, Daben had seen Tarrant's lifeless body only a few minutes before.

" I—but—— " he stuttered. " You—I—— What are you threatening us for ? "

" I am not necessarily threatening you," Tarrant returned. " But it has been an eventful night. There has been, among other things, an attempted murder. And you will notice that the harp has gone."

Daben stared at the empty cabinet, his face paling to a sickly white.

" I intend," continued Tarrant, " to settle this whole matter here and now. By force, if necessary. You will summon the rest of your party, Mr. Daben. And you, Dr. Torpington, will stand by that door and see that it does not close."

" But I—— But you can't do that. You will give every one a frightful turn. Mrs. Daben—no, I won't have her shocked this way ! " Under the force of his protest the host's colour returned to his cheeks.

Tarrant did not raise his voice. " I am perfectly capable of calling the police. I shall do so within ten minutes. Unless my demands are followed immediately."

" But the scandal, the notoriety——"

" Make up your mind ! " snapped Tarrant, rising from his chair. The automatic did not move at all.

That did it. Daben, still protesting futilely, made a reluctant exit to arouse the others and Tarrant took a place close to Torpington beside the door to await their arrival. " You need not summon Mrs. Torpington," he called as an afterthought to the departing man. " Everybody else. And don't delay too long."

They arrived separately, Molla Daben surprisingly first of all. She had not dressed but had thrown a tea gown over her nightdress and slipped her feet into a pair of mules. It is remarkable what different effects feminine attire produce ; in riding habit she had looked a robust, hearty young woman ; now she appeared fragile and astonishingly dainty.

Evidently she had not been apprised of many details, for when she saw the cabinet empty of its treasure she gasped and clutched the tea gown instinctively to her throat.

" Oh," she moaned. " It's gone ; it's gone for the third time."

" Come over here, Mrs. Daben." Tarrant put her in one of the large chairs and, standing so he could continue to observe Torpington, addressed her steadily. " Your husband is not the only one in this house whose ancestry is long and honourable. Your own line, unless I am mistaken, bears the same distinctions. You talk about our modern democracy, you look down upon it, and in many fundamentals I agree with you.

"You are going to face a series of shocks in this room," he continued, "and you are going to face them very soon. The first shock will not be the end of them and the final one will be as severe as any that life will ever give you. One of your party is a criminal ; and there is no one here to whom you are not bound by ties of affection and loyalty. Also, when I say one of this party is a criminal "— he gave her a direct and searching glance—" I include you in the party. . . . Let us see if you can take this crisis as a Malorye should."

With careful accuracy he had selected the one appeal to pull the girl together. Why had he done it, he wondered fleetingly ; because she was lovely, because she was highly-bred, because her femininity seemed defenceless and appealing in contrast to her masculine companions ?

She flushed a little under his gaze. She spoke in that low, clear voice, firmly. " Whatever is coming, I shall take."

While he had been talking to her, the others had arrived. An occasional " hrmp " evidenced Brinkerstall's position at one side of the room against the book shelves ; his eyes were protruding slightly, giving him a somewhat froggy appearance. Stuart had drawn a chair to the vicinity of his employer's wife ; Torpington still stood in the doorway.

" You are the master of this house, Mr. Daben," Tarrant said abruptly. " You will sit at the desk, if you please. Torpington, take a chair if you wish to. I shall stay at the door myself.

" Now," he went on, when these instructions had been complied with, " you all know the general outlines of what I intend to call the episode of Mr. Daben's harp. It is a relic of very great value, of which he is the legitimate custodian, and it has recently suffered a series of inexplicable disappearances. There is an ancient rune or prophecy that appears to have foretold these occurrences and even to include a threat against his safety.

" When the matter was brought to me, I came up here to investigate, as I think all of you have been well aware. I do not happen to believe in the efficacy of thousand-year-old threats ; but I can easily understand some one unearthing them and using them to his or her own advantage. That is exactly what has been done. One of you, in this room now, has employed the Norman prophecy as a cover under which to gain criminal ends, and has not scrupled to plan a murder when the opportunity arose. That person, together with the details of the plot, is going to be disclosed and is going to pay the just penalty."

He paused and let the silence endure. They were all looking at him and at the automatic in his hand. Observation could pick out no guilty expression.

Tarrant's words came again. " The harp disappeared for the second time while I was here. I knew then, or immediately afterwards, what happened to it and who was engineering the disappearances. But I did not then know why. I hinted my discoveries rather broadly and set about seeking the motive. I had to go down to New York at that time on business of my own, but when I returned I deliberately put myself into the criminal's hands. I intended that to be thought and it was thought. I knew that the first night thereafter that I spent in this room alone I would be attacked. The opportunity not only to make the harp vanish but to leave behind a dead body as evidence of the threat's power was too good to be missed."

Brinkerstall cleared his throat loudly. " How could you be attacked, sir, if you were here alone ? "

" Oh, not directly. How would *you* attack a man

in this room ? That is what I put to myself. There is a simple and certain way, one that leaves no traces because it does not necessitate the criminal's presence. It is only required, when the whole household is in bed and asleep, to pull the main switch controlling the house current. That shuts off the light—and the air conditioning system, too. There are no windows or other openings here ; the place is a sealed box. Sooner or later, when the air in the room and that in the small flues leading to it is exhausted, suffocation is inevitable. This happens to be a system in which the blowers operate like valves, making a little rumbling and whispering when they are on. . . . I think there is no one present who has not known that I, in fact purposely, remained in ignorance of how to effect an exit from the library.

"But I had no intention of dying so meekly, obviously. I provided myself with the essential safeguards—two small cans of oxygen sealed under high pressure, and an inhalator in the convenient form of a noseguard with a heavy valve attachment for feeding small quantities from the cans. I went through the expected manœuvres of calling out in a strangled voice and beating not too strongly on the door, in case the criminal waited outside to observe his success. And I took the precaution of tying around my body and over my heart a tight band of material through which it would not be possible to feel any heartbeat when the criminal came in later to accomplish the rest of the task. For of course the harp had to vanish also."

"I see it has," said Dr. Torpington calmly. "Where has it been taken ? "

"It has not been taken anywhere. It is right here in the library." Tarrant watched their glances go to the cabinet, then around the room. But no one saw the harp.

"Stuart," he said, "you have never, I believe,

thought highly of the harp's own powers. Neither have I. You may bring it down. It is at the top of the ladder beside Brinkerstall."

The secretary, as if in a daze, got up and mounted the ladder. At the top he stood stupidly, his head just above the level of the cornice.

"The boat," Tarrant cried. "That long war canoe with the single mast right in front of your nose!"

Stuart grasped it suddenly and stumbled down the library ladder. Over the side of the hull dangled a whole series of strings, still fastened to the wood at the stern. He placed it on top of the cabinet in the centre of the room and went back to his seat without a word.

Tarrant explained the obvious. "The main support of the harp is boat-shaped," he stated, "and it possesses no front pillar. It is only necessary to re-attach the strings, hidden behind the frame when it was on the cornice, to the forward end of the frame. And, of course, to remove the mast. I noticed that small hole on the inside of the framework when I first saw the harp. And it puzzled me. I am familiar with the Egyptian *nanga*, of which this is certainly an example, and I had never seen one with such an aperture. It looked new too."

"I was puzzled by it until the evening of the second disappearance. For I had taken an inventory of this room when I first arrived and there were eighteen boats on the cornice, when the harp was in its cabinet. But on that evening one of the boats was taken from the library; I saw it done. Yet, with the harp gone, there were still eighteen boats in the room, as I immediately ascertained. One less harp, one extra boat. A trip up the ladder showed what had happened.

"That fact itself did not reveal the criminal. You have perhaps sought to remember who has been present on the occasions of these happenings. At one point I constructed such a list and I can recite it to you from memory :

First disappearance	- -	Daben, Molla Daben, Stuart, Torpington
First reappearance	- -	Molla Daben, Stuart, Brinkerstall
Second disappearance	- -	Daben, Molla Daben, Stuart, Brinkerstall
Second reappearance	- -	Daben, Molla Daben, Stuart
Third disappearance	- -	Daben, Molla Daben, Stuart, Brinkerstall, Torpington, Mrs. Torpington

" You will observe that two names occur in every instance, those of Molla Daben and Stuart." He stopped as Stuart half rose in his chair with an inarticulate cry. " Sit down ! " he commanded sharply. The secretary collapsed again in his seat.

" But even supposing one of them to have fathomed the means of opening this door," Tarrant's voice continued, " *neither of them could have been responsible.* On the evening of the second vanishing both of them sat at a bridge table with me from the time Daben came out of this room and told us the harp was still here until the moment when, with them, I discovered it had gone. As to this occasion I realised of my own knowledge that they were innocent ; there was no need or reason to suspect them on the other occasions. Brinkerstall was in the same position, Torpington was not here at all then."

His voice ceased and he stood watching the expressions in the room. For the moment they were all blank with the attention of following his reasoning. Then gradually the inevitable conclusion commenced to twist them. Brinkerstall, jerking round toward the desk, began to rasp : " Why, of——" And caught himself sharply. Tarrant's tone, as he took up again, was edged with contempt.

" Yes, Daben is the man who has been desecrating his own inheritance, that priceless relic that is his legitimate property ! By means of this juggling he has been playing upon the traditions his wife cherishes and fears, attempting to cause her breakdown, trying to get her out of the country. And he nearly succeeded. The third disappearance alone, even unaccompanied by my death in this room at the same time, would have been sufficient. Dr. Torpington would have insisted. With my own murder in addition, there could have been no question.

" I know, you see, what instrument Mr. Brinkerstall has been opposing Molla's signing. It was a power of attorney made out to her husband for use during her absence. And he didn't really need it, there was no excuse at all ; his own fortune is more or less intact, as I found out. I am afraid he has just that appetitive personality type, based on hunger and later transferred to money, of which I have read quite recently. He is so excellent an example, in fact, that he plays his deceptive rôles even when he believes himself unobserved."

He had been watching Daben who, during these words, had sat perfectly still, his expression unchanged.

Now Daben spoke. He said quietly, " Tarrant, you're crazy. I could have accomplished these disappearances no more than the others. Once, according to your own list, I wasn't even here. All you have done is to clear us all, and we are right back at the inexplicable."

" Stop it," answered Tarrant. " Stop hoping. You forget that I was fully conscious when you came in here at half-past five this morning and did your trick again. I watched you, but it only confirmed what I already knew.

" Don't think there is an alternative for any of the other occasions ; there is no possibility except you. The first reappearance was the first time I was here. What you did was to enter the library alone, take the harp from the cornice, restring it and put it in the cabinet. You then got one of the boats from your workshop and took it to the library. You had time ; it was a full half-hour between your first entrance to this room, which I saw, and your arrival at my room. You weren't spending all that time lost in astonishment before the cabinet. That lapse of time turned my attention to you immediately, but I admit I dismissed you for a bit afterwards. The harp reappeared *after* your arrival home, not, as you pretended, while you were away.

" When it vanished a second time, you dismantled it before you came out of the library with your boat, knowing that no one could get in until you returned and knowing we would accept your statement that the harp was intact when you had left. Later you made an opening for the suggestion of a final inspection, which you opposed only enough to escape suspicion. And when you finally opened the door, you feigned the same bewilderment as the others.

" As to its subsequent reappearance, I went away and left you with all the opportunity you wanted, to get it back in the cabinet and ready for the final act, to be played on my return. Naturally, despite your proposal of keeping me company, I knew you would find some excuse, sooner or later, for leaving me to watch alone. So I helped you with the excuse, that's all. We know what happened then.

" Why did you ask me here in the first place ? That is simple, surely. You wanted the testimony of an independent investigator who would be as baffled as your wife ; or better yet, who would furnish a corpse for the vengeance of the ' banshees,' if he turned out to be clever enough to see through your tricks.

" And I think that is all."

The voice that came from the girl's chair was low and firm. And utterly hopeless. " Oh," she said. " Oh, my God."

It just reached Tarrant's ears and suddenly he

felt an overwhelming pity for her, with not only the man but with all that he stood for crumbling beneath her.

He called "Molla!" abruptly. "You have taken it well. *Your* traditions are still unsmirched. Don't forget now who you are! . . . You will not be entirely alone," he added, less sharply. "No young man, ordinarily unruffled at the bridge table, can play so fatuously as your partner without giving his feelings away pretty completely." For an instant Stuart failed to perceive the implication; when he did, even in that room at that moment his answer was the confirmation of a furious blush.

And still Daben sat staring stonily before him. When the silence had grown almost unbearable, he said : " I realise that you can prove your charges. I shall not commit the final cowardice of denying them further. But I beg you not to spread my name, the name of my family, across the common pages of this country's yellow journals. To be read and gloated over by every tabloid monger in the subways, by every yokel at the crossroads. If you are a gentle-man yourself, I beg you to leave me the honourable way."

He looked at Tarrant as calmly as if he had just invited the latter to dinner. Or made any other ordinary pronouncement.

And Tarrant answered him equally calmly. " I suppose you still consider yourself a gentleman. . . . It is not because of your family, which you have brought to disgrace, that I will entertain your suggestion. It is simply because I myself have a certain attachment to the principles which your wife honours and which your own actions, if not your speech, have belied. I have no objection to cheating the herd of its dish of scandal ; but I recognise, as you have not, that my attitude carries with it the strictest of obligations. *You* are not better than the commonest of men ; by your betrayal

of your own position you are inestimably worse.
. . . You will recall that from the beginning of this
episode I have insisted upon my freedom of choice
throughout. At its end I am my own master and
can choose. . . . You will find what you need where
I left it for you, in the first drawer at your right
hand."

The little pellet which Donatelli Daben lifted,
between forefinger and thumb of a hand that was
steady, looked absurdly small. Nobody made a
motion or seemed to draw a breath as he put it into
his mouth. Irrelevantly a jingle was running
through Tarrant's brain :

> " When Breogan Harpe thrice shall elude
> The guardian that to harpe be trowed,
> Then shall the race of Dabheoin eande."

Daben stiffened and slumped heavily over the
desk.

And Molla was on her feet, swaying. She said
dreamily, " The prophecy. It *has* come true."

Stuart was just in time to catch her as she crumpled
forward.

THE EPISODE OF
THE MAN WITH THREE EYES

Characters of the Episode

JERRY PHELAN, the narrator
VALERIE PHELAN, his wife
OLGA MARKOVA, maybe a spy !
SAM GINSBERG, *alias* Kuprovitch
JOSE, a waiter
MONSIEUR HOR, an extraordinary person
DEPUTY-INSPECTOR PEAKE, of the New York
    Police Department
TREVIS TARRANT, interested in spite of himself
KATOH, his butler-valet

THE EPISODE OF THE MAN WITH THREE EYES

" ANOTHER ? "

" Thanks," said Valerie, " I will. You ought to mix them oftener, Trevis. I really believe you turn out a better cocktail than Katoh."

We had been in New York that day, Val and I, and had dropped in to see Tarrant late in the afternoon, before driving out to Norrisville. Whereupon he had invited us to dine with him. " Yes, certainly," said Val. (It's funny how soft both Val and Mary, my sister, are about that man ; anything he wants.)

So here we were having cocktails, very good cocktails, in Tarrant's sunken living-room while a darkening drizzle dampened the casement windows outside and our host turned on a lamp or so in his luxurious but entirely masculine apartment. Across the room, under the soft little light on the cellarette, a fat, jade Buddha, recently acquired through one of his friends at the Museum, dozed somnolently.

Tarrant was saying, " Do you like *borsch* ? The real thing ? Every so often I get ravenous for it. Then I have to take the trouble of going downtown, but it's worth it. That is, if you like the dish as much as I do."

" Where do you go ? "

" Place called the Food Club. An awful name ; rather awful place, for that matter. It's on a back street in the Village, and filled mostly with second-rate communists and bad artists. There is usually a sprinkling of others, nondescripts, unplaceables ; even a few White Russians. The food is chiefly Russian, and nothing to celebrate except for the *borsch*; they have a man there who can prepare *borsch* as I have never found it anywhere else in this country."

" Let's go there," said Valerie. " I'd like to see it. Let's, Trevis."

" We're not dressing, so that's all right. Surely, I'll be glad to take you. I'll have to take you somewhere anyhow, for Katoh isn't here to-day."

" So that paragon butler-valet of yours does get a day off now and then ? He always gives the impression of being able to appear instantly, anywhere, if you clap a hand. Where do you suppose he goes, Trevis, when he's off ? Out to compare pressing-irons and steak grills with other Japs ? "

Tarrant chuckled. " He's out spying. He's not a servant, you know ; not in that class at all. He's an an honest-to-God professional man, doctor ; this butling job is only a cover. I try to keep him as busy as possible so he won't find out too much too soon ; I'm hoping the supply of secrets will hold out long enough to keep him here permanently."

" If he buttles as well as this, just as a side issue," it seemed to me, " he probably knows just what the Americans plan before it even occurs to any one in Washington."

" Is he really a spy ? " Valerie asked. " I thought it was only some kind of joke you had together."

Tarrant shook his head with another chuckle. "Oh, no," he assured her. "Katoh is the real thing. He passes on devious information through obscure channels in the most desperate way. Quite solemnly. I shall never forget his consternation when I had worked out his true occupation and casually mentioned it to him one day at breakfast. He didn't want to attack me and yet for a few minutes he felt sure I had had the apartment surrounded with counter-espionage agents. . . . Fortunately I was able to reassure him that I took his butling more seriously than his fell designs on the country.

"But my word," Tarrant added suddenly, "what are we doing, standing here gossiping about Katoh ? The *borsch* will be spoiling down below. We must be on our way."

.   .   .   .   .

It was on a back street, all right. A dingy place and not too clean. The Food Club occupied an ancient brown-stone mansion, a survival from the residential days of the Greenwich section. The proprietor, no doubt, had his own quarters above, but on the ground floor, as we found, no less than three separate rooms served as restaurant, with the kitchens in the basement.

Crossing the wet pavement from the car, we mounted the front steps and found ourselves in a small hallway. A closet had been knocked away to one side, forming an alcove where we left our coats and hats. Opposite the house entrance, at the end of the hallway and a couple of steps down, was the main dining-hall, a sizable room with small booths around its sides, tables on the floor and in the centre a small, cleared space for dancing.

The whole place was in gloom, very dimly lit by small purple bulbs which were supposed to be artistic or bohemian or something. On most of the tables a single candle gave just about enough light to see one's food.

As we hesitated at the top of the steps, peering into the cavern, a stair at our right led to a tiny balcony above. Evidently a spotlight had been installed there, one of those things that throws coloured lights on the dancers, for even now it was jerking spasmodically about the room ; but the coloured discs had been removed and it gave forth a beam of fairly strong, white light. It flitted about over the tables, then steadied and came to rest for a moment, illuminating a booth across the room ; by chance it was the only booth into which, from our position, a clear view was possible.

Thus emphasised in the dimness, the occupants of the booth stood out sharply. They were two men and a strikingly handsome woman in a low-necked dinner dress.

" Trevis," cried Valerie. " One of those men, isn't one of those men Katoh ? "

" Looks like it," Tarrant admitted negligently. " One of his famous conferences, perhaps. . . . What interests me is the booth just beyond. You know, Jerry, I think that's that Hor man in the farther booth, the chap who helped me out so opportunely when our friends of the City of Evil nearly got me on Thirty-eighth Street. I told you there were unusual characters here. . . . I can't quite see him. Maybe if the light shifted a little . . ."

The light didn't shift. It went out. And for an instant or so, by contrast, the place seemed black. Some moments passed and we were just beginning to grope our way down the two steps before us, when the show started. From somewhere in the room came a high, piercing scream that bubbled out ! Almost on top of it a man came scrambling down the stairs to our right in frantic haste. He was a swarthy man, dressed as a waiter ; he ran through the short hall-way and out the door to the street before I had more than time to think, " My God, has he shot some one and made a getaway ? "

There was a babbling of voices from the restaurant, the noise of chairs scraping on the floor as some of the diners jumped to their feet, a great deal of confused pushing about in the semi-darkness. Then two things happened at once. The swarthy waiter opened the front door and walked in quickly, followed by two policemen ; Katoh bounded up the steps past us and came to a halt, suddenly, in the hallway.

The policemen and the waiter stopped also and stood looking at him suspiciously.

But before there was a chance for them to say anything, I heard Valerie's voice from just behind me, clear, imperious, annoyed. I could scarcely believe my ears. She said, " Katoh, this is the second time you have forgotten to keep the umbrella in the car. You will go back to the apartment and fetch one at once ! "

He mumbled something and started for the door. The policemen hesitated and he was gone. Valerie drew her coat about her haughtily and added : " We shall have to wait until he comes back. So stupid. Then we shall go somewhere else. There seems to be some sort of brawl."

" What goes on here, you ? " demanded one of the policemen, addressing all of us.

Tarrant answered : " I'm afraid we don't know, officer. We have just this minute come in, as the check-room girl can tell you. We have not even stepped inside the restaurant. There was a scream and the place is in confusion. You had better see to it, I think."

The three stepped past us, down into the noise of the room below. The waiter gave us a distinctly appraising scowl.

. . . . .

We had dinner at the Food Club, after all. In one of the other rooms, entirely separate from the large restaurant in which the police were busy.

Tarrant first saw the girl who guarded our coats

and made sure of our alibi; I glimpsed something that looked very much like a five dollar bill passing into her complaisant hand. Then he descended into the restaurant and in the first period of confusion succeed in bringing out Monsieur Hor. He had been correct in his recognition just before the excitement.

They had been able to make their escape just in time, too. Hardly had we procured our table in the other room than rumours of " murder " began circulating, and the large restaurant below was securely bottled by the police. But by that time we were all on the innocent side of the fence.

And incredible as it may seem, Monsieur Hor's presence with us made the furor at our elbows dwindle into no more than an evanescent hubbub. I have tried to describe him before, with his voice pitched so low as to be scarcely audible, his uncannily healthy, grey complexion, his strange attribute (in so heavy a man) of physical grace, his wise eyes. It is almost impossible to suggest the atmosphere he brought with him. He was not a special kind of man or a peculiar kind ; he was, in the most literal sense, extraordinary. It was this *intensification* of the ordinary, I suppose, that constituted a peculiarity in itself.*

He had ordered vodka and was saying, " I have

---

* We had met Monsieur Hor only a little time before, during our embroilment with the ' City of Evil,' as strange a band of criminals as I have ever heard of. For various reasons I have thought it best not to recount that episode at present. Needless to say, Monsieur Hor was not connected with this gang of ruffians ; and in fact, to this day, it remains a complete mystery to me who his associates may be, if indeed he has any.

He is a most remarkable man. He moves like a tiger, and his eyes are very calm and dark and clear. But when all of his physical attributes have been put together, the essence of his impression is still left out ; an intangible something felt, something you are just about to name but never can quite name. It is an uncanny impression but totally without that slight inspiring of fear that accompanies the unknown ; an impression as if the commonplace and ordinary had been raised to a degree of vividness that transformed them into quite other characteristics. That seems to be about as close as I can get to it.

to thank you for bringing me out of that room. I am not familiar with your police work ; they will detain every one so unfortunate as to be there now ? They will detain them with questions, for hours perhaps ? "

Tarrant smiled. " Yes. And they will catch up with you, too, probably. I noticed that it happened in the booth next to you. If it was a serious crime, they will trace every one in the vicinity eventually."

" It was a crime, yes. Some one has died. Agh, it does not matter ; all your history is crimes, either for people or for nations. This one they will perhaps solve now before I am bothered." He looked away and applied himself to lighting a long, Russian cigarette.

Just then the *borsch* was brought, that soup that had been the innocent cause of our arrival. For some minutes we were busy appreciating its excellence. Tarrant had not exaggerated it, for it was delicious. Monsieur Hor had ordered another vodka and sat sipping it.

Then he turned again to Tarrant. " Crime," he said, " is below interest, if only because it is so general. But pardon ; you amuse yourself with these matters, my friend, I believe ? You are now upon the scene ; it is no doubt a welcome opportunity."

" Not this time," Tarrant returned. " If Katoh has gotten himself involved, I shall keep hands off." Lowering his voice, he explained our meeting with his butler-valet and his knowledge that the latter had been in the booth at the crucial time.

" Ah," said Hor. " Your servant. . . ." He paused, and a moment later shifted the subject. " When you do interest yourself in your hobby, much depends upon what you are able to observe, upon observation, no ? "

" Indeed yes. I should say that four-fifths of success, if not more, depended upon observation, upon noticing and remembering a series of little details that finally add up into a big fact. Yes, I agree."

" But, my friend,"—the other spoke, as usual, in so low a tone that I had to lean forward to hear him at all—" you do not observe nearly enough."

" I note as much as I can," Tarrant replied. " No doubt I miss some things. Or perhaps I do not take your meaning."

" You do not," Monsieur Hor assured him. " All your observation is external ; it is at outside things, outside persons, that you look. But it is very necessary to employ inside observation. How do you suppose that I was able to recognise, never having seen you or them before, that you were in danger from those men on the street ? "

I thought I saw what he meant. I said, " But how could you look inside them unless you had X-ray eyes ? You can't tell a person's intentions just by looking at him."

" It is not X-ray eyes one needs ; it is three eyes. Here "—he touched his eyelids—" I have two eyes ; but also I have another eye, that does not look out, but in. . . . I did not look at those men, Mr. Phelan ; I looked at myself."

Well, that didn't ring any bell in me ; I went back to the *borsch*.

" You see," Monsieur Hor continued to Tarrant, " there are a great many things registered in your body which you miss, not because it is impossible to observe them but because you never look. This is not an easy kind of observation ; it is much more difficult than to note what you call outside happenings ; it is unaccustomed ; it takes very much energy."

From there they went on into " voluntary " and " involuntary " functions, some business about neurology. I lost interest, and since Valerie seemed fascinated by the obscure discussion, ate the rest of my meal in silence. But just as we were about finishing and commencing to plan an unobtrusive departure, something more practical came up.

Monsieur Hor remarked, " This kind of observation we discuss, I have employed it to-night. You say you do not interest yourself in the crime here, but perhaps you find later that you will have to be interested. Just a moment."

He fumbled in his pockets and brought forth an empty envelope. He tore off the blank half of one of the restaurant cheques on the table, wrote on it, placed it in the envelope which he then sealed. He held it out to Tarrant, saying, " I do not give you my address and you will not see me for a little time. But soon, in a few weeks, a month perhaps, you will need me and then you will see me again. It will be what you call—a coincidence."

Tarrant took the envelope and put it away. " But what," he asked, " is in this ? "

" Ah. Do not open it at all, please, unless you need it. It is something important that I have observed to-night. With my third eye."

.　　.　　.　　.　　.

When we got back to Tarrant's apartment it was fairly late. The weather was abominable and he had persuaded us to change our plans and spend the night. We turned the car over to the doorman and went up.

At his apartment door there was no answer to the bell. Katoh had not yet come in, then. Tarrant reached for his key and opened the door. It was I who went into the living-room first and was startled to see a stranger sitting quietly in one of the best chairs.

Then he got up and it wasn't a stranger at all. It was our friend, Deputy-Inspector Peake, the man we had first met during the penthouse murder, the one who had given Tarrant his credentials to the New Jersey police at the time of the headless horrors episode. It seemed to me he looked a little stern, and at the same time uneasy, as Tarrant came into the room.

The latter presented him to Valerie, and there was an uncomfortable pause.

"We have your man," Peake said baldly.

Tarrant appeared unastonished. "Indeed?" he remarked. "What for?"

"Material witness, accessory, possibly principal in a murder."

"Interesting," Tarrant admitted. "H'm. You know, I *thought* we got away from the Food Club almost too easily."

"I arranged it; after all, I am under certain obligations to you," said Peake grimly. "I was there for a time this evening. I checked you up with the coat-girl and had you passed out. . . . I had to come up here anyhow. For your man. And I thought your party would rather be questioned here."

"Very decent of you, Peake. We appreciate it. But what questions? What can we tell you?"

"You might begin by telling me just why you smuggled your man out of that place immediately after the commission of a major crime."

"Tut, tut," admonished Tarrant. "'Smuggled him out?' My dear Peake. It is true, of course, that we saw him in the hall for a moment and had a few words with him. After which he left, without even a remonstrance on the part of your minions. I detect no flavour of 'smuggling' there. And, as a matter of fact, none of us even know the details of what really happened. We have had no opportunity to find out."

"That's true enough," grunted the inspector.

"Well, will you tell us? Here, let me get us some drinks. Since you have taken Katoh, I'll have to do it myself." Tarrant busied himself with the cellarette and presently set highballs before us. "How about those details?" he repeated.

Peake considered, and finally spoke. "All right. I don't suspect you or your own party of having been mixed up in this; don't see how you could have been. Well, three people had dinner in that booth across from the entrance. First, there was Olga Markova. She was a Russian refugee who came to New York about fifteen years ago and remained. She is something of a character in the village, poses as an artist but is certainly an unsuccessful one. Although she has never been known to have much money, she has always been in funds to a certain amount and no one knows the source of this income. It is possible that she was an agent for some foreign government.

"The only reason I have for thinking so is that the second person in the booth was Kuprovitch and he is an agent of the Soviets. His real name is Sam Ginsberg, but he went to Russia for a few years following the revolution and then came back with the Amtorg outfit, a new Russian name and a steady job for the first time in his life. There is no doubt that he is a bolshevik political agent. He busies himself with trying to stir up labour troubles and creating political dissatisfaction during strikes.

"The third person in the booth was your man, Katoh. He is a Jap, and for all I know is a Jap spy. How about it?"

Tarrant's expression was blandly innocent as he smiled, "My word, Peake, do you go in for this spy stuff?"

"I don't know the first thing about spy stuff," the policeman admitted. "My job is to apprehend criminals who break the peace. Olga Markova was murdered, stabbed with a steel knife belonging to the restaurant service, and that's about as wide open as the peace can be broken. There were two other people in that booth, Ginsberg and Katoh; one of them did it. No doubt spies cut each other up during their operations. I don't care much what the motive

was. After the boys get through with them down at
headquarters, they'll talk ; and when they talk,
we'll find out which one it is."

" Suppose each of them accuses the other ? "

" They may begin that way but they won't end
that way. We'll sweat the truth out of them."

" Well, it's a stupid means," said Tarrant, " of
trying to solve a crime, but what am I supposed to
do about it ? "

" I thought perhaps you could tell me something
of the people involved, of your own man, anyhow.
Did he know both the others, or only one of them ?
If he had only met Markova for the first time
to-night, it would be more unlikely that he was the
one to stab her. I've no doubt you'd like to get your
valet back as soon as possible, if he *is* innocent ? "
Peake suggested.

" I certainly would. It's damned annoying, you
know, Peake ; and with guests here, too. . . .
No, I can't tell you anything about the others ; I
have never heard of the Markova woman before, or
Ginsberg, either. I don't know who Katoh's friends
are, no idea. He is a first-class valet and butler, and
that's all I can tell you about him.

" But I can tell you this : that your hypothesis of
the crime looks pretty fishy to me. You're assuming
a spy murder. Probably spies do murder each other
occasionally, but I doubt very much if they pick
a public restaurant, commit the crime in full view
of the patrons and then run away. A dark alley
would be a good deal more likely. The whole
picture is wrong. It much more suggests an
impulsive, private murder than a political
one."

" Wait a minute," said Peake, " wait a minute.
You're wrong if you think that booth was a public
place ; it was as private as you'd want. The walls
are high, you can't see over them. And the fact is
about that particular booth that no one could see

into it from any other part of the restaurant. I know
that because I examined the point for myself."

" Just the same, all of us looked into it about a
minute before the murder."

" From the entrance, yes. Those entrance steps
are the only place in the entire restaurant from which
the interior of the booth can be seen. During the
evening there is seldom any one there. It's private
enough."

Tarrant shrugged. " If you must stick to your
idea, it occurs to me that there are still a number
of points in Katoh's favour. What do you have ?
You have a bolshevik, a Japanese and a White
Russian. The White Russians are the enemies of
the bolsheviks and so are the Japanese ; there can
hardly be any doubt that war between the bolsheviks
and Japan is an eventual certainty. But that makes
Katoh and Markova allies and, by the same token,
establishes Ginsberg as her enemy and Katoh as her
friend."

" It's a point," Peake conceded. " We have been
told that Olga Markova was a Russian aristocrat and
an extremely haughty one. For a while she was
called the village snob. For example, she has lived
with one or two men down there, but only those
whom she considered eligible. Others, who have
tried to flirt with her, she has snubbed in no un-
certain way. And she certainly hated the bolshies,
from all accounts. It seems peculiar that she was
eating with Ginsberg at all. But that will all come
out when we discover whether he or Katoh killed
her."

" By the way," asked Tarrant, " how did Katoh
act when you arrested him ? Did he try to get
away ? "

" No. He didn't. Said he was waiting for me,
as a matter of fact. He denied attacking the woman
himself, but said he didn't know who had. That's a
phoney, because, if he didn't do it, he was sitting

right next the man who did and couldn't help knowing it."

"Maybe your men have got a confession by this time. Why not phone down and see ?"

"I will, if you want the information. Then I shall have to get down there. I've been here too long as it is. I rather hoped you could give me some help."

The inspector turned to the telephone and dialed Centre Street. After a considerable interval he managed to get the man he wanted. He talked for several minutes, then returned the instrument to its cradle and turned back to us.

"Too bad," he announced. "Ginsberg says Katoh is the criminal and your man persists that he doesn't know who did it. Of course, that's impossible. It looks as if he were the one all right."

Valerie walked over and put her glass on the table. She said, "Trevis, oughtn't you to get a lawyer for him ? We must help him. I don't believe he's lying at all."

Peake grunted and Tarrant smiled his agreement. "I shall in the morning, of course, if it's necessary. It certainly looks now as if I should have to take a hand in this myself, after all."

He stopped, apparently struck by a sudden thought ; then continued, "As a matter of fact, I have the answer right here in my pocket." He reached within his coat and brought out the envelope Monsieur Hor had given him. He glanced at it and handed it over to Peake.

This is what they read :

"No murderer in booth next me to-night."

.   .   .   .   .

"It's impossible," snapped Peake. "A few words on a piece of paper don't change the facts. Who is this man ? I want to talk to him."

"I don't know his address, but probably you can find him, if it is necessary. I don't believe, though,

that he can tell you a thing more than he has
written. He couldn't see into the booth, I'm sure.
He reached his conclusion by means of making
certain observations of his *own* body. Call it a
feeling, if you like."

"A feeling?" The policeman looked incredulously at Tarrant. "He had a feeling that there was
no murderer in the booth? Well, his feeling was
wrong, then. Maybe he had a feeling that there
wasn't any murder, too."

"That isn't what he said."

"What difference does it make what he says?
The woman was stabbed at the base of the throat.
There were only two people near enough to her,
physically, to do it and they were in the booth with
her, naturally. You'd need an arm as long as a
giraffe's neck to reach around those walls ; and even
then you'd have to get your head around, too, to
see what you were doing. There would have been
fifty witnesses to any such proceeding. . . . No,
that's out. One of the men in the booth killed her.
I'm going to get down to Centre Street now and
find out which one."

Tarrant was on his feet, walking up and down the
room. He said, "Now, Peake, you've been here
long enough already ; you can spare fifteen minutes
more. I ask you as a favour to give me fifteen
minutes to think about this."

"What do you want to think about?"

"I was there, man. So far as any one could be,
I was a witness to the murder. I know what the
conditions were in the place and at the time it
occurred. It can't have been very complicated.
There must be an answer."

"Of course there's an answer, and a very simple
one. One of the men in the booth stabbed her."

"I'm assuming that neither of them did."

Peake sighed with exasperation. "Oh, well . . .
All right, I'll give you fifteen minutes ; that's what

you stipulated. Then I'm off." He brought out his watch and placed it ostentatiously on the arm of his chair, while Tarrant continued his pacing, silently now, his forehead drawn into a frown of concentration. . . .

.   .   .   .   .

" I'm certainly letting you run me around to-night," grunted Peake. We were all of us jammed into a small police car with him, on the way downtown again. But not to Centre Street ; we were going back to the Food Club.

Tarrant chuckled. " I'm going to give you a solution that will stick, because it will be correct. All you've got now is a wrong one that won't stick. Whom are you holding ? "

" Ginsberg and Katoh."

" And both of them innocent. You haven't even arrested the real criminal."

" That's not what Ginsberg says."

" Oh, that." There was something very like contempt in Tarrant's tone. " You don't believe him yourself, Peake."

" I don't, for a fact," the other admitted. " In my opinion he's a yellow little rat who would tell any lie he could think of to save his dirty skin. But one of them must have done it."

" Nonsense. There are several alternatives. Have you thought of suicide yet ? "

" Suicide ! " In the gleam of a passing light the inspector's eyes opened widely. " Why should the woman go to dinner and commit suicide ? "

" A great many people have thought there were good reasons for suicide. Probably nearly as many as have considered murder."

" And left no fingerprints on the knife ? It's impossible ! "

" Not quite impossible," Tarrant corrected. " I think myself that the explanation of that will turn out to be simple ; my own idea is that there were no fingerprints on the knife because no fingers had held it. Well, we shall soon see which of the possible alternatives is the right one."

We were already drawing up to the Food Club and lost no time in getting into its hallway and out of the rain. The lights were still on but the place was deserted now by all except a few of Peake's men and the proprietor, who evidently was loath to retire and leave his premises in the unwatched hands of the law.

When all of our party had gathered in the entrance hall, Tarrant announced, " I am going to try the venerable business of reconstructing the scene of the crime. But first I want some information about this establishment and I don't want it from him." He nodded towards the owner of the place who was sleepily expostulating with an officer just beyond the steps of the main restaurant. " Where is the man who summoned the police in the first place ? He will do."

It soon appeared that this man, employed as a waiter, slept on the premises ; in the basement, in fact. " Have him brought up," Tarrant requested. " I want to speak to him alone. I'll take him into one of the empty dining-rooms."

When the man presently appeared, tucking a very dirty shirt into an equally soiled pair of trousers, I recognised him at once as the swarthy servant who had run out for help just after Markova's dying cry. If he had looked surly then, he looked even more so at having been pulled out of his bed now and I thought, as I watched him being pushed along by a policeman, that he would probably give Tarrant very little willing assistance. However, he let himself be shoved into one of the rooms and, as Tarrant followed him, closing the door, I heard my friend's voice beginning, " About the way it is customary to set the table service. How many knives——"

We stood in the hallway and could hear only a murmur of voices from behind the door. Then suddenly the waiter's voice was raised in a scream of rage. He was a foreigner of some sort, possibly a Mexican, for I think the proprietor had referred to him as Jose; his shrill jabbering and chattering continued for some minutes but not clearly enough for us to distinguish any words. He calmed down presently, however, for when Tarrant opened the door and stepped out, he came after him and stood silently glaring at every one within sight.

Tarrant said, "Let us proceed. I want all your men out of the main restaurant, Peake, if you please. No, not in the hallway here, either. Let them go into that room I have just left. And shut the door."

"What for?" demanded the inspector. "This is very unusual."

"I have a good reason. For one thing there weren't any police here earlier this evening when the murder took place," was all Tarrant would say. He waited until his peculiar request had been complied with.

"Now," he continued, "I am going to reconstruct the scene as closely as possible. We can't fill the main room with diners again, but that will be a help rather than a hindrance.

"I want the owner to sit at one of the tables out there on the floor. Any table." He waited again while the man selected a chair and sat down in it.

Then he said, "Now, Valerie," for she had insisted upon coming with us, "I want you to stand at the foot of the steps against the wall. And don't you move away from that wall, whatever happens. Jerry will stand at the head of the steps, just where we were when we first came in here to-night.

"I am going to sit in the booth where the murdered woman was eating; in fact, I am going to sit just where she did. And I want you, Peake, to take some position on the open floor from which you can see the owner, Valerie, Jerry and myself. It is important that you be able to have a clear view of all of us. Every one."

The inspector, still grumbling over the exclusion of his men, stalked out on the floor and Tarrant turned to the Mexican. " Now get up there, Jose, and you do everything exactly as you were doing just before the murder. Don't forget it and don't omit anything."

The man started to climb the stairs, when Tarrant suddenly called after him, " Have you forgotten anything ? "

The other gave an inarticulate snarl and disappeared above. Tarrant smiled slightly and walked away to the booth in which he proposed to take his place.

Peake called across to him, " I don't see what this absurd stunt is going to prove. You don't imagine any one is going to attack *you*. Under these conditions. Anyhow, where is the criminal ? "

" Your notion is that you have him at Centre Street," Tarrant replied.

" Oh, I see. No doubt you are going to commit suicide for our benefit ? "

" Stop worrying about what I'm going to do." Tarrant had reached the booth and carefully selecting his seat, looked about the room. " You can see every one down here. You watch us, all of us, carefully."

Peake subsided with a grunt and the restaurant was silent. From where I stood everything was as much like our first view as it could be. The lighting in the restaurant was dim, there were even a few of the candles still burning on the tables ; and the white beam of the spotlight was jerking around haphazardly over the tables.

Tarrant sat quietly in the booth where Valerie had recognised Katoh, watching the play of the light. I could not imagine what he had in mind, yet the tension grew as I stood peering into the room, waiting for something. How could anything occur now that would provide a clue to the previous murder ? It seemed impossible, yet——

The light suddenly came to rest on Tarrant. For only a few seconds his figure stood out sharply, illuminated at the expense of the rest of the room. Then the light winked out.

In the contrast, just as before, I saw nothing. But I heard a kind of swish, followed by a plainly definite thud. And that waiter was coming scrambling down the stairs again in a mad rush.

"Grab him ! " yelled Tarrant. " Jerry, grab him ! "

For an instant I didn't understand ; then I saw the fellow's face. It was contorted with desperate rage and with an expression of desperate flight. Quite without any instructions, it was plain that he was guilty of something.

He had just turned into the hall to dash for the door. I took a dive at his legs and we crashed down together. He was cursing and spitting and he would probably have gotten his hands around my neck to some purpose if Tarrant had not come leaping up the steps from the restaurant at the same time that the police, aroused by the sounds of combat, came bursting out of their place of confinement. They threw us apart in short order and some one clapped handcuffs on the raging Mexican.

Back in the restaurant Valerie was dusting me off with a napkin and Tarrant was pointing to the knife firmly impaled in the back wall of the booth. " I thought that man might be stupid enough to throw it again," he told Peake. " It was my best chance to convince you quickly and get my valet back to-night. There is the knife and, if you were watching every one in this room as I asked you to, you know none of them threw it. That leaves only the waiter, even if he hadn't given himself away by flight.

" He had to use the spotlight to get a good aim. Then, as soon as he turned it off he threw. Naturally I ducked down on the floor as soon as it went out. The best knife-throwing, by the way, is done from the palm ; that's why there were no fingerprints. He knew I was going to denounce him ; I let him get that clearly. But he thought that by going through my farce he might get a crack at me and a chance to escape, himself. That's why I got your men out of the way. He is stupid, you see, very stupid."

Peake said, " I'm damned. It certainly looks as if you were right about this. But why should that waiter, of all people, have wanted to kill Markova ? Did he know her ? Is he some species of spy, too ? "

" Oh, there's no spying at all in this ; that's all in your fervid imagination, Peake. And he didn't know her ; he very much didn't know her. Although I was going to leave the motive for you to find out, I happened to stumble on it when I was talking with him alone for the purpose of sizing him up. This is a pretty democratic place down here and it seems that at some artist's ball or other he ran up against her drunk and made what is called an indecent proposal. As I gathered it, Markova not only snubbed him, she gave him a verbal lashing in public, called him a varlet, a serf and doubtless various worse things. . . . This Jose is a low type of latin, you know. They're vengeful and violent ; live, and die, on crimes of passion just like this. . . . And I'm afraid he had been inoculated with our doctrine that all men are equal ; equal, at any rate, in their rights to abuse women."

.   .   .   .   .

" How you work this out ? " asked Katoh. We were all back at the apartment and, aside from his own black eye, little the worse for our night's experience. " One minute we talk about affairs ; next, there is knife in Markova throat. I know not done by any one in booth. Seem quite impossible."

"Sit down, doctor," said Tarrant. "Have a drink with us; you need it. . . . Of course, I had more information than you; I was at the door and had been watching the spotlight perform. Later, I was told there had been no murderer in your booth and I accepted it without being able to check it. On that assumption it was either suicide or the knife had been thrown. There was no chance of any one entering the booth and killing her without being observed.

"Aside from the general improbability of suicide, the fact that you had not seen her kill herself, ruled that out. No matter how quick she might have been, you couldn't have missed it.

"So it was knife-throwing. But that brought up a serious difficulty. Knives cannot be thrown around corners and, furthermore, the thrower has to be able to see his target. But the only place in the entire room from which the interior of your booth can be seen is the entrance steps and I was there myself! No one was with me except Valerie and Jerry, and I knew they hadn't done it. I was stumped until it suddenly occurred to me that light follows as straight a line as a thrown knife. If the spotlight could play into that booth, then there was a second place from which the attack could be made. That gave me both the means and the criminal, no matter what the motive might have been. I only ran across the motive by chance and maybe I haven't got the real one, at that. It doesn't matter."

He paused and lit a cigarette, then stepped over to the cellarette to replenish the glasses. As he did so, he inquired over his shoulder, "Why were you such a fool as to run away, Katoh? You must have known the police would surely get you."

"I only run from police temporarily," Katoh grinned. "We talk about affairs in booth and I have new information on some affairs that must be sent at once. I not have time to wait all night while police make questions about who, why, what. Misster Ginsberg wait. Misster Ginsberg information now quite late. Also wrong ; I see to that, too."

Katoh jumped to his feet. " I get breakfast now," he announced. " I very grateful to you, Misster Tarrant. And I even more grateful, perhaps, to very honourable Miss Valerie. She permit to get news to Garcia, like rum old American expression."

THE EPISODE OF THE FINAL BARGAIN

Characters of the Episode

JERRY PHELAN, the narrator
VALERIE PHELAN, his wife
MARY PHELAN, his sister
MORTON BAKER, an eminent brain specialist
MONSIEUR HOR, an extraordinary person
TREVIS TARRANT, interested in Mary
KATOH, his butler-valet

THE EPISODE OF THE FINAL BARGAIN

OF the whole sequence of episodes through which
I had the privilege of accompanying Trevis Tarrant
it is the last of all which, I admit inconsistently,
brings back to me most clearly my recollection of
him. It has been almost six years now since I have
seen Tarrant. Sometimes I find myself wondering
whether I shall ever see him again, and on such
occasions I recognise one thing, at least, clearly ;
it is certain that something over another year must
pass before that possibility can arise.

Sometimes, also, I wonder what sort of meeting we
should have, were he to return. If at parting, the
gap opening between us was already too wide for
me to leap, what sort of relationship would be
possible seven years after he had commenced his
extraordinary quest ? Should we be strangers ?
Not superficially, of course ; but underneath
appearances, down where the fundamental premises
lie on which rest one's thoughts, assumptions and
the basic ability of mutual understanding, in those
realms would there be that void, rather than
barrier, between us ? Would I meet Tarrant now as

blindly and uncomprehendingly as I have always had to meet Monsieur Hor ?

When I think of the five years during which he was my intimate friend, and on the same footing with Valerie and with my sister, Mary, I cannot believe that we should ever meet as strangers, underneath. Why, without his help, I don't believe I should have succeeded in marrying Valerie in the first place ; and when I recall the terrors of the City of Evil, the suddenness with which we stepped into the mystery on sunny Winnespequam, the horror we found within the artist's sealed studio above Tarrant's own apartment—well, if I contributed little to the solutions of these and other problems, at least I shared the anxieties and some of the dangers.

Nor have I set down all, or even most, of the cases in which I watched Tarrant at work ; in those five years there were many more calls upon his abilities than the half-dozen or so I have related, and in most of them I had some part. There was the water-death case in Bermuda (one of the few I wasn't in on), which brought him so much unsought publicity, there was the matter of the Submarine Transmission, and the strange business about the old-fashioned ice-wagon, and the case of the sinister inventor who never invented, and that most peculiar and frightening affair at Maverick Mansion. And others. No doubt the episodes I have related throw as much light upon my own unconscious processes of selection as upon the qualities of Tarrant.

Naturally, his name isn't Tarrant, nor have I disclosed his real address during the time I knew him ; even with his permission (which I have yet to obtain, by the way) there seem to me to be a few details that are his own business. Still, almost from the first moment I saw him, as the lights came on in the little room where I guarded the ancient Codex in vain, to that last minute when he held out his hand to me in the bare corridor of the Polyclinic Hospital, I knew him well. I knew him quite well enough to understand to what he would object and to what he wouldn't.

And so I propose to set down the final episode. Not to illustrate Tarrant's own qualities, his keenly analytical mind, his dogged persistence to successful solutions despite all obstacles ; not even in order to tell a mystery story, complete with the answer. For there is no answer this time ; there is no mystery story in the usual sense. Or perhaps it would be more accurate to say that the mystery is of a kind to which neat, wrapped up and paid for solutions don't exist.

What is here is the end of adventures and the beginning of an Adventure, if that means anything. Probably it doesn't. At any rate, there are no heroes and no villains. Again—in the usual sense. Maybe you will think you see a villain, a hero too, maybe. But although it has not always seemed so to me, it seems now that these labels become singularly meaningless under the sort of circumstances that brought my association with Tarrant to a close.

Maybe he went nuts, cuckoo, hoppy, crazy. I shall think I'm a touch looney myself before I finish writing this one. What other people—the few who are acquainted with the affair—think of Tarrant I don't know. Except for one other person. I'm afraid I know what Mary thinks. She is twenty-nine now and in the past six years has declined twelve proposals, two a year on the average. Mary can't forget Tarrant. And neither can I. That's that.

.   .   .   .   .

It all began so casually. For one thing it was a balmy, spring day, one of those precociously warm days that brings you the first realisation winter is over and makes you stretch your body and snort, rather. Relaxing, too, strangely enough ; not-acloud-on-the-horizon sort of thing. It wasn't late, only about one-thirty in the afternoon. We had had an early luncheon at the Plaza and gone down to see the old man off on the *Aquitania*.

Afterwards we walked off the pier and got into our cars, Val and I into the sedan, Mary and Tarrant into the roadster. She was going to drop him at his apartment uptown, while we were driving straight out to Norrisville from the dock.

Val waved to them and I yelled to Mary, " Snap into it, stupid. We'll see you at the club."

She swung her car out from under the Elevated Highway north and we followed, to take the ramp. That was the last we saw of them for the time being, but every word of what happened next was carefully repeated later.

As they turned into 23rd Street, Tarrant remarked, " Your father is a very handsome man, Mary. I see now where you get part of your good looks."

" Why, Trevis." I know just how the girl giggles on such occasions. " If you really think I'm good-looking, you don't do much about it. Why not give me a little action ? "

" Hey, none of that," said Tarrant hastily. " I know you're beautiful because I'm not blind. It doesn't mean I have designs on you."

" I'll say it doesn't." She spoke grimly. " I have some of my own, though. If you won't make me an honourable proposal one of these days, I'm going to get out at your apartment, and just settle down and live there. I like you, Trevis."

The traffic at 11th Avenue saved further argument for the moment. And when they had gotten across, the silence continued a little longer. They were just about in the middle of the block between 10th and 11th when it happened. Tarrant was on the verge of being drawn into the absurdity of defending his position ; he was actually turning in his seat to begin talking when Mary's whole body relaxed.

As she spoke, her voice went down scale until he could scarcely hear it. " Trevis, turn off the—ignition—key. I—can't——"

His astonishment at first attributed the performance to some flirtatious nonsense. I should have had the same notion, I confess. Then he saw the unfeigned look of surprise that held her features for a moment before fading into blankness as the facial muscles relaxed. The car was commencing to wobble ; Mary's hands fell limply from the wheel. He grasped it, guided the roadster towards the curb, snapped off the ignition at the dashboard. They came to a stop fairly close to the side of the street, in a space that fortunately was empty.

Tarrant turned to look at her more closely. She had slumped down in the seat, her head resting at an angle against the back. But she hadn't fainted ; her eyes were open and they still expressed astonishment.

" My God, Mary," he cried, " what's the matter ! " Her face remained blank, her lips motionless ; only her eyes showed that she was trying to answer, to explain. He was convinced now that something was seriously wrong ; no doubt was left. He reached for her wrist, caught the pulse. It was weak and slow ; even as he held it, it slowed further.

She was lucky to have been with Tarrant then. When action is called for, he is on the ball quicker than any one I have ever met. Now he did several things at once. He lifted Mary out of her seat and into his ; he noted the position of the car and memorised, almost unconsciously, the numbers of the houses opposite which they had stopped ; he climbed into the driver's seat and started the motor. Then he shot the car forward, slipped around a trolley in the middle of the street and turned left into 10th Avenue against a red light.

Pursued by the embittered shrilling of police whistles, he really let the roadster out and wove a

scudding way northward. He made the Polyclinic
Hospital in a little under six minutes. Five more,
and Mary had been wheeled into a private room on
the sixth floor ; a doctor and a nurse began
undressing her.

Tarrant averted modest eyes and stepped back into
the corridor. He approached the nurse in charge of
the floor at her desk by the elevators. " Is Morton
Baker in the hospital ? " he asked.

" Dr. Baker ? Do you mean the gynecologist or
the brain surgeon ? "

" Morton Baker. Yes, he's a brain specialist."

After a few moments at the phone she turned back
to him. " Dr. Baker is in the staff-room. He has
just finished an operation. Do you wish to speak
to him ? "

" Tell him my name is Trevis Tarrant. I should
like to have him come up to this ward as soon as he
can."

Tarrant blessed his luck when, well within ten
minutes, the surgeon stepped from an elevator. He
had discarded his operating gown and gloves but,
despite post-operative scrubbing, an evanescent
odour of ether still wafted about him. He wore a
white hospital coat.

" Well, well," boomed Baker in a hearty voice.
" How are you, Tarrant ? I haven't seen you since
that water case of yours. Must be a year. I hope
nothing serious brings you into my jungle."

" I don't know," Tarrant answered, wasting little
time on greetings. " I'm worried." He briefly
described what had happened and Mary's symptoms
so far as he had been able to observe them. " It's
possible, of course, that she was wounded," he
finished. " I took a note of the place where it
happened. There seems to be a complete failure of
the voluntary muscles. Looks like a matter of the
brain to me. Will you take the case, Baker ? "

" H'm. The facial muscles, too, you say. Not

anterior *poliomyelitis. Hemiplegia,* double *hemiplegia.* Could it be possible ? I've never heard of so sudden an incidence, either. Yes, I'll take the case, if you want me to. Let us see what we can find."

The surgeon escorted Tarrant to the visitor's room at the far end of the corridor, then left him and disappeared through the door behind which Mary was being examined. For some time he stood regarding the actions of the doctor already in attendance, without offering either advice or interference. At length the latter straightened up with a dubious shake of his head. For the first time he saw Baker ; and he saw him with obvious relief. His expression, hidden from the patient, said as plainly as if he had spoken the words—" I'm stumped."

Without remark the surgeon stepped forward. His own examination was lengthy and meticulous. First he went over Mary's entire body with the utmost care ; he found no wound, no bruise, not even a tiny puncture such as might have been made by a hypodermic needle, for which he was particularly searching. He took the feeble pulse, the blood pressure, listened for and noted down the breathing ratio, examined various reflexes, paying especial attention to the contraction of the eye pupils under different intensities of light ; he even went so far as to take specimens from the membranes of nose and mouth, and no less than two blood specimens, one for analysis, the other for blood count.

When all these things had been done and the samples dispatched to the laboratory, he leaned over the bed and patted Mary reassuringly on the shoulder. " Don't worry," he said quietly ; " we'll have you around again before long." She was unable to answer, but her eyes followed him as he left the room.

To Tarrant the wait of more than an hour had been interminable. After telephoning a message out to the

Norrisville Country Club for Valerie and me, he had had nothing to do except sit and smoke, one cigarette after another. He had used the interval to consider the possibilities of the situation. Although possessing a general acquaintance with physiology he had ended with the forced admission that he was out of his depth here ; the affair was plainly a matter for a specialist. His first feeling of concern, however, had only deepened ; he was convinced from the beginning that the matter was serious.

And when Baker finally came back to him, his feeling was not lessened. The surgeon's attitude had lost the bland assurance he exhibited to his patient. He knew Tarrant and considered that he could be frank.

" This is very nearly the most curious case I have met with," he admitted. " There is a complete paralysis of the voluntary musculature, or perhaps I should say of the contractors. So far, I have been unable to establish any cause ; of course, I could make a number of guesses, but when I can find no support for any of them, I am still at sea. When the laboratory tests are done, we shall know more, I hope. For the moment there is nothing to be done except to give the patient the best possible care. I have given instructions for three nurses ; I thought you would——"

" Right," said Tarrant briefly.

" Yes. Well, there is no immediate cause for worry. Of course, if the paralysis should spread to the involuntary systems, the blood vessels would relax, the blood would lake into the visceral organs, and cerebral anæmia and unconsciousness, possibly coma, would supervene."

" Do you foresee that, Baker ? "

The physician shrugged expressively. " I don't know—frankly. I don't recognise the condition, that's the fact of it. It hasn't happened yet ; the blood pressure remains satisfactory and the girl is certainly conscious even though she can neither speak nor move. Of course we meet with peculiar conditions more often than you would suppose. As I say, there is nothing to worry about right now. The best of care. And presently I shall have the laboratory report ; that may indicate something. Either I myself or my assistant will be in constant observation, at least until a diagnosis is made and treatment indicated. . . . Yes ? "

The floor nurse had appeared in the doorway. " A telephone call for Mr. Tarrant, doctor."

Tarrant ground out a cigarette. " You have done everything, Baker ? "

" Everything. She has had a complete examination, even the stomach pump. She seems to be in the most excellent physical condition, except for this mysterious attack."

" I shall have to take this call. It will be Jerry Phelan, her brother. I shall be back here when I've finished. I expect to stay until you have something definite for me."

He followed the floor nurse down the corridor.

.   .   .   .   .

It was late in the afternoon when Val and I reached the hospital ; we had been held up in a jam in the Tunnels. Tarrant was still in the sixth-floor visitors' room, still smoking. Valerie went in to see Mary, while I stayed with Tarrant and he told me everything that had happened since we had left him at the pier. Valerie was not gone long ; she came back with Dr. Baker on her heels. She looked distinctly shocked.

" Whatever has happened ? She can't speak or move. She gives me the queerest feeling, Trevis, as if she were—stripped. Not undressed, I don't mean anything like that ; naturally she's undressed in bed. But this is as if—as if her skin had been taken off. Of course it hasn't ; that's not what I mean exactly, either. I don't know what I mean—it's a horrible feeling. And she's scared. I'm scared myself somehow. Can't we *do* something ? "

Baker said, " Do not distress yourself, young lady," in his most paternal voice. Then he went on to tell us, first, that there was no change in Mary's condition, and subsequently to ask us a number of questions, most of which I was in a position to answer. I told him that, so far as I knew, there was no history of such attacks in our family, that both Mary and I had been so healthy ever since childhood that, with the exception of colds and an infrequent siege of grippe, we scarcely consulted a doctor from one year's end to another's ; we just didn't have a medical history. As to Mary's recent movements, and so on, they were clear and the opposite of illuminating for Baker's purposes. She had just returned from San Francisco, whither she had journeyed by by train to meet father on his arrival from the Far East. They had reached San Francisco the same day, met and at once taken a plane for New York. He was making a hurried trip to London on some government business. It was for this reason, since he had not been home for over a year and would not now have time to come out to Norrisville, that she had accompanied him across continent.

Thus for the past ten days she had been among total strangers ; she had seen no friends or even acquaintances, which still further removed the improbable idea that her condition was the result of some poison administered to her. She and father had arrived at Newark Airport only yesterday afternoon and had proceeded at once, with us, to the Plaza. Only this noon he had sailed.

When I had finished, the surgeon shook his head and looked about at the others. No one could add anything except confirmation. He said, " There is certainly nothing there to help me. . . . Well, as I told you, her condition remains without change. Most of the test results are in ; they only show what you have told us, Mr. Phelan, and what my own examination indicated, that your sister is in excellent health. We can find no evidences of bacterial attack; the X-rays——"

" Have you taken X-rays ? " It was Tarrant who broke in.

" Of the brain. I have taken every test that has even a remote chance of being of value. So far as I can discover, there are no lesions ; we have found nothing whatsoever to account for the condition. The voluntary system is paralysed and from various indications I believe it to be paralysed from the thalamic or subthalamic regions. I couldn't prove it and I am not assuming it to the exclusion of other causes.

" I have been frank with you ; I have told you all I know myself about this case at present. You can do nothing here ; I do not want the patient disturbed by visits now and my sincere advice is that you go home and return in the morning. I am extremely interested in the case. I have a double mastoid at nine in the morning but I shall stay here all night in observation and, while I am getting some sleep, my assistant, Slaten, will be in constant attendance." He hesitated. " I should like to call Sir Roger Britt into consultation this evening, if you approve. He is perhaps the foremost brain man in England and is in New York just now. It is possible he may be able to make some suggestion."

Tarrant said, " Have him in by all means, Baker. You're to take *all* steps you think worth while, every step."

Valerie didn't want to leave ; the surgeon looked at her, then addressed her directly. " There is nothing you can do here, Mrs. Phelan. The case is very interesting from a professional point of view, but really you have no cause for serious alarm. I anticipate no change and, even if we never discover the answer to this riddle, we shall have every reason to expect a gradual retreat of the paralysis and eventual recovery. That is the usual outcome of paralysis in any one so young and healthy as Miss Phelan, under proper care. . . . It will be better if you leave, and I shall see you here in the morning, say about ten o'clock."

We left. We took the cars over on the East Side and garaged them. We all returned to Tarrant's apartment where Katoh, although our entrance was his first intimation of our overnight visit, evinced his customary absence of surprise at the contingencies confronting him. Val and Tarrant were unusually quiet. In view of the doctor's assurances, I could not quite see why.

. . . . .

The following afternoon I saw why. Well, I didn't see why exactly, but I did see that their apprehensions had been justified. We sat in Tarrant's living-room, having constituted a sort of council of war. Katoh sat with us ; Tarrant had summoned him by addressing him as " doctor," a form which he habitually used to indicate that his unusual valet was to be present in the guise of adviser rather than servant. On these occasions Katoh invariably helped himself to Tarrant's Dimitrinoes, perched himself on the long divan and solemnly contributed his knowledge and experience to his friend's problems.

Our problem now was serious enough. During the previous night Mary had gone into a coma. Baker had called us early ; we had reached the hospital around eight o'clock and had been permitted to see her. She lay in bed, pale, her face composed, eyes closed, completely unconscious. When I first saw her, I thought she was dead. It gave me something of a kick in the pants. Only a few hours before she had been plenty alive and hopping around. She's only a red-headed gal, true enough ; but after all she's my sister and, although I can never see how any one could get very overheated about her, I didn't want anything to happen to her. I remembered suddenly a good deal about our lives together, quite a number of times when she had helped me out about one thing or another ; in fact I got a damned mushy feeling all at once.

So did Valerie and Tarrant, apparently. Tarrant was white around the lips when we left, after giving instructions that we should be called immediately if any further change occurred and asserting our intention of returning in a few hours. I was a bit surprised at Tarrant's attitude ; Mary isn't his sister or anything else, for that matter. I wondered briefly about it, then forgot it. Tarrant wanted to discuss the situation in his own surroundings ; he wanted Katoh in on the discussion.

Now he was summing up the state of affairs with his usual neatness. " Here's where we are," he said decisively. " Mary has gotten worse, and very rapidly worse. She may get better at any moment ; she may even recover ; also, she may die. We don't know what will happen ; we don't know what has caused this, and we don't know what to do about it. Neither do the doctors.

" There's the rub ; the doctors don't know. I don't say this because he's a friend of mine, but I happen to know that Morton Baker is the finest man on brain ailments in America. He has had his British confrere for consultation and they are both in a fog. The plain truth is that they don't know what is the trouble or what to do about it any more than we do, and both being big men, they admit it. The point is that there is no one better for us to go to. The point is that every resource of medical science has been employed already and that it is inadequate. Except for continued nursing, nothing more is available. Nursing won't solve the problem.

" What are we going to do, then ? Are we going to let her die while these men, competent as they

undoubtedly are, look on in ' observation,' unable to
do anything but note down what they can see, for
later use in a medical brochure ? If we are going
to do anything else, what can we do that will hold
out any promise of assistance ? "

He stopped and looked at us. He had formulated
what we were up against, but if he hadn't an answer
to his questions himself, I didn't see how he could
expect one from us. Katoh drew his feet up on the
divan and sat regarding the end of his burning
cigarette, as he spoke.

" Please repeat all symptoms from beginning."

Tarrant went through the whole thing again,
slowly ; the sudden weakness, the paralysis, the
business about the blood vessels and the resulting
coma ; the measures taken for care and feeding, and
so on, and the lack of other measures due to the
absence of diagnostic information.

After he had finished Katoh still sat watching the
cigarette burn away. He sat in silence for so long that
I thought he had given up any idea of replying.
When he finally spoke, it was plain that he did so
with reluctance.

" I am doctor in my own country," he said slowly.
" You know. Still here I study research pamphlets
and medical literature. I not know on medical
grounds what cause this malady any more than
famous doctors which already search. . . ."

Again I thought he had completed his contribution, when his voice resumed, in a curiously dreamy
tone.

" In my country, in Nippon, we are still young in
matter of scientific background ; we learn quick, we
have laboratories and research as fine as anywhere
else, but we closer to old things, old religion for
Shinto, old belief. Perhaps we not so much—
hypnotise, by all-scientific viewpoint. . . . Fifty
year ago what happen to this lady be called magh-ic
in my country. This happen here now in western

land and is not called magh-ic—but it is not called anything else, either."

He stopped. And he did not continue.

Tarrant stirred and asked him perfectly seriously, " Are you suggesting, doctor, that we have to do with magic in this case ? "

" Is magh-ic. This I tell once before, when strange thing occur in Miss Valerie house. Not it is magh-ic then, as I say. But magh-ic is."

" H'm. Well, let's get this straight. You are suggesting, then, that something or somebody is attacking Miss Phelan by magical means. You think of some such thing as the casting of a ' spell ' ? I'm afraid I don't know much about ' spells ' or what to do about them, how to counteract them. Something like hypnotism ? Could it be hypnotism, by the way ? "

" Hypnotism I study. For hypnotism necessary almost always that subject be willing ; very difficult for hypnotism for reluctant person. And must be that hypnotist is present, that subject know about this and even co-operate. Not see how could this be hypnotism."

" Post-hypnotic suggestion ? "

" For God's sake, Tarrant." Even I could see that Katoh must be right about the hypnotism. " Mary can't have been doing any tricks like that for the last ten days. She would surely have mentioned it, and so would father. People don't go in for vaudeville shows on the transcontinental trains or in airplanes. Of course she hasn't been hypnotised."

" I didn't think she had, Jerry. But magic. I'm willing to consider anything at the present pass, but I don't see that that is going to help us. It's only a label, anyhow. Unless some specific form of—of attack upon her is suspected, and we have some notion as to who does it or how, what can we do in opposition ? Have you anything definite in mind, doctor ? "

" I am doctor for science. Science I know but not magh-ic. Magh-ic is above science, is like ju-jitsu, is mental ju-jitsu. Like ju-jitsu man can disable ordinary wrestler, so can magh-ic be for science superior. . . . Not I can help, myself. But you have friend who know magh-ic. Only once I see this man, when you have case about City of Evil. He is here for small time only, but that man, I certain, know for magh-ic more than I know for science. Must get this man ; this man which call himself Monsieur Hor. Could help, I think."

" Good heavens, Trevis, of course ! " Valerie cried. " I'm sure I don't know whether he's an adept at magic or not, but he is strange enough to know about all sorts of things. We're up against it, even your friend, Dr. Baker. And you said yourself that Monsieur Hor helped you on the Meganaut. It can't do any harm ; get him."

Tarrant had risen from his chair and was pacing up and down the room. He muttered, " I've thought of him. I'd get him if I could. But he would never give me his address ; I don't know how to reach him." He sat down rather abruptly, and continued in a tone that more than suggested soliloquy, " Of course, I don't believe in this magic of Katoh's. I've investigated a good deal of so-called magic, some of it venerable enough, but I've never found anything in it more supernatural than a criminal's tool or a modern racket."

" The Codex," I interjected. " Daben's harp, for that matter."

Tarrant said, " Yes. . . . On the other hand, I hope I've as much self-respect as Morton Baker ; enough to admit when I need advice, anyhow. I certainly need it now. And I'll stake my opinion that Hor, for all his peculiarities, is a wise man.

" All right," he went on, as if a decision had crystallised. " I believe he is in New York somewhere. We know his name ; let's get busy. Jerry, you take the classified directory and begin calling all the hotels and apartments listed. I'm off to Centre Street to see if I can get hold of Inspector Peake. Katoh, let's see ; no, I'll leave you to take any steps you can think of. We have to find Monsieur Hor and we have to find him as quickly as possible."

Well, it was something to do, action at any rate ; it was better than just sitting there, waiting. I was already over at the telephone cabinet and Tarrant was picking up his gloves and stick from the end of the divan where he had thrown them, when the bell sounded in the hallway.

Katoh pattered out to answer it. Whoever this visitor is, I thought, he'll receive short shrift. We heard a murmur at the outer door.

With his tiger-like tread Monsieur Hor walked into the room.

.   .   .   .   .

For some absurd reason we were all too astonished to say a word. After all, Monsieur Hor knew Tarrant ; there was no miracle in his stepping in. It was just that he had stepped in at this particular moment—so opportunely——. For the third time— this was only the third time I had seen Monsieur Hor—I found myself again experiencing the curious sense of strangeness that surrounded him, an atmosphere not of the bizarre or the unusual *per se*, but an atmosphere of the ordinary raised to such an intensity that it became the completely extraordinary. Perhaps you have seen hysterical people quivering, hands clenched, eyes burning. Monsieur Hor's hands were not clenched and his eyes, when he looked at you, were deeply calm. Yet there remained the feeling of this intense energy burning, in back of his movements, behind his voice when he spoke ; the strength of hysteria, calmly directed by deliberate purpose.

I know it's a contradiction. I have tried to describe Monsieur Hor before and I realise that I can't. There is nothing definite to put a finger on. Perhaps that is the secret of his impression.

He was smiling slightly as he gave his hat and gloves to Katoh, who had followed him, and his voice, as always, was so low that we had to strain our ears to hear him. His bow to Valerie held a hint of mocking exaggeration. But his words were sober enough.

" You are in much trouble. Have I come in time ? "

Usually I am almost tongue-tied before Monsieur Hor. Maybe because of my worry I now burst forth, " How do you know we're in trouble ? "

His glance flickered towards me. He said, " As soon as I came into the room, I perceived vibrations, emotional vibrations, very chaotic."

" Are you psychic ? "

For a moment it seemed that he would disregard me ; then he turned back and pronounced patiently, " There is nothing ' psychic ' in the whole, great universe. There are certain people on this planet, having a specific disease whose symptoms are confused with abilities ; these symptoms are ignorantly labelled ' psychic.' Actually psychic there is nothing."

" But how——"

" When I speak—to you—I speak literally. Vibrations are vibrations, a physical matter. Even you believe when you see me that it is a question of vibrations striking your eyes ; you do not know it but you believe it because some children with spectroscopes have told you so. Emotional disturbances transmit another kind of vibrations which it is perfectly normal to be able to receive. Although you do not know it, you also possess the necessary sense organ but have not developed it. I have. . . ."

Monsieur Hor turned to Tarrant. " This is a waste of time. What is the trouble ? "

The latter had discarded his own gloves and stick

during the exchange and was standing, waiting for
his visitor to select a seat. Now he said, " I wonder
if you already know ? "

" Even if I did, I should still wish to hear your
description of it."

Tarrant indicated a chair and, taking one himself,
embarked without more ado upon a repetition of the
circumstances of Mary's peculiar illness and the
serious situation in which she now lay. Monsieur
Hor heard him through with but a single interruption ; that was to inquire the exact time when
the paralysis had intensified during the night.
Because Baker had lost all his sleep, having been in
observation the entire time, Tarrant was able to
tell him. " These physicians," he finished, " are in
fact the two best men in America and England.
But they have been unable to help. They can tell us
nothing."

" Ah." Monsieur Hor calmly removed from his
lips one of the long Russian cigarettes he affected.
" Your physicians. The average is a plain ignor-
amus ; the best of them are conscientious children.
Of serious matters they know nothing."

" Do you know ? " Tarrant demanded bluntly.

" I know something of serious matters. Yes."
The other spoke with a complete lack of emphasis ;
he spoke as one speaks of a town or of a country that
one has visited and that others have not visited,
rather than as of a superior accomplishment.

Tarrant leaned forward. " Monsieur Hor, if you
know, if you have any inkling, of what is the matter
with Miss Phelan, for God's sake tell us ! I am afraid
she is dying."

" If left to her own resources, she will surely die."

No one said anything. We looked at Monsieur
Hor. And I had a distinct impression, for a moment,
of the superiority of expression over words as a means
of communication. Our acceptance of his statement,
our questions, our appeals for his advice in the

emergency, were summed up concisely and unmistakably in our faces.

" There are several possibilities in this case." He might have been speaking of a chemical experiment. " But one of them is far more probable than the others. Of this you know nothing. I shall not tell you what it is, for you do not have the data to enable you to understand it, or even to believe it." His eyes turned again towards Tarrant. " How much control have you over the case ? " the low voice went on.

" Complete."

" That is well. It will be necessary for you to have a photograph of your friend's etheric body made immediately. I could observe the condition of the body at a glance, should I go to the hospital, but it may be well to convince you about it. You cannot see the etheric body. A photograph will serve."

I said, " The etheric body ! " incredulously.

Tarrant's expression was somewhat different. " Do you really believe that etheric bodies exist ? What the old Egyptians called the ' *Khu* ' ? "

" This is not an esoteric matter, or even one of folklore," replied Monsieur Hor in a tone that asserted the subject to be beneath argument. "The Egyptians named it differently but they were aware of it, naturally. It is known, even to some of your own medical profession. An Englishman named Kilner made the first ' scientific ' observations of the etheric body, employing dicyanin screens, about 1920, I believe. There has been progress since ; it can now be photographed through filters upon a special film. . . . The physician you employ is doubtless curious about the case he does not understand ? "

Tarrant nodded. In fact, there could be little doubt about Baker's interest.

" He will not object, then, even if he does not know the process. There will be no harm in allowing him

to have a photograph. He will not know what it
means. He will suppose its significance purely—
diagnostic."

Tarrant considered briefly. " But I scarcely know
where to begin," he admitted. " I did not even know
such measures were used."

" It does not matter." Monsieur Hor gave every
evidence of being willing to dismiss the entire
subject. " You are in one of the world capitals. You
have money, and friends ; where you do not have
friends, you have influence, on this level. . . .
If your report of the condition is correct, speed is
essential. You must have the photograph here early
this evening. . . . I shall return, if you wish me."

Monsieur Hor got up.

Tarrant got up, decisively.

    .   .   .   .   .

The photographs had been obtained. They lay on
the table in Tarrant's living-room in a little pile
under the reading lamp. With some luck he had
managed to locate a certain Dr. Bardolyi, an
Austrian who made a speciality of these things and
claimed to have the finest equipment for such work
on the American continent. Although engaged at the
time upon an exciting pinochle game, the latter had
yielded to the temptation of a high fee and consented
to the transport of his apparatus to the hospital.
Here he had set to work with only the delay
necessary to convince Morton Baker that no un-
certain rays were to be directed upon his patient.
As a matter of fact, it was a question of quite
ordinary photography, although against a special
background, employing special filters and a peculiarly
sensitised plate. The development of these plates,
in the hospital's dark room, took no longer than in
the case of any other photographs.

With Viennese thoroughness, following a short
lecture delivered to Tarrant and Baker upon the
diagnostic uses of his speciality, Dr. Bardolyi had

left a collection of photographs of other subjects for comparison. They were the pictures of men and of women, sometimes against black backgrounds, sometimes against white. The peculiarity of the photographs consisted of various bands surrounding the bodies pictured, labelled by means of arrows and notations on the plates as " etheric body," " inner aura " and " outer aura." In a few cases there was still another nebula outside all the above, named the " ultra-outer aura." Some examples were much more clearly marked than others, but once one knew what to look for, the various envelopes, as it were, could be distinguished in all the pictures.

The demonstration, I must admit, was impressive. I saw the reason for Monsieur Hor's insistence on the photographs, for with the evidence right before one's eyes it was impossible to doubt that there was something perfectly real that corresponded to what he called the etheric body.

Naturally we inspected the part thus labelled most closely. In the case of the subjects marked "healthy" it was a very narrow dark band completely and very closely surrounding the physical body ; in instances of disease it might be broader, and sometimes was twice as broad on one side, while disappearing entirely on the other side. In such cases the auras appeared considerably distorted.

When I finally reached the pictures of Mary, which Tarrant told me to inspect last, I got a severe shock. Neither of the auras was much distorted—in fact the outer one was almost a perfect ovoid—but they were both so weak as to be scarcely distinguishable. The trouble, however, was with the etheric body ; and if the other photographs were to be considered as more or less natural, this one was a monstrosity.

In the other pictures only the outline of the etheric body had been visible, its edges, since it was apparently very slightly larger than the physical body. But in this picture a whole section, from the hips downward, was extruded ; the etheric feet and legs, perfect replicas of their physical counterparts, were close together, as if held so, to the left of the ordinary figure. The head was only partially extruded, the neck least of all. It was as if some force were straining to separate the etheric body altogether, the latter being still held by a connection at the base of the skull.

" Oh," moaned Valerie over my shoulder, " oh, it's horrible. That's what I meant when I said she seemed stripped."

I see now that a mere description of the picture is far from conveying the impression produced by looking at it. It really was horrible. Although I had certainly never before seen an etheric body, or even a photograph of one, there was a feeling here of unnaturalness and violent mutilation that could not be denied. As near as I can get it, it was like a picture of some one being torn apart right before your eyes. And of course we could recognise from the picture itself who was suffering this fatality.

We were gathered, all of us, about the table. Katoh said, " Ugh, iss bad, bad. Iss magh-ic here by evil man."

Tarrant grunted and, reaching behind him, sat down on a low, upholstered footrest. Now I have seen Tarrant confronted with more than one crisis, with more than one juncture where danger had to be met and met quickly, without much advance information as to its direction or power. He had been calm and certain of his ability. Unbluffed, unruffled. Never had I seen him like this ; there were little beads of sweat on his forehead now and tremors ran along the wrist of his closed hand.

" Look here," I said to him suddenly, " what's the matter with you ? "

He actually groaned. " I should have asked her to marry me long ago. When I had time. My God, Jerry, I love her."

Valerie was the only one who did not appear completely astonished. Quite apart from the fact of this expression from one usually so reserved as Tarrant, I must confess that I had never suspected such a state of affairs. Mary had flirted with him, of course, I knew that, and he had always given the impression of an amused, rather avuncular bandying of compliments. But underneath all this there had been something serious, then ; he had really fallen in love with her. Well ! So that was how it was. I treat Mary a touch flippantly myself as a rule. Of course there wasn't much of that left now.

I hadn't said anything. I was still looking at him with my mouth partly open as he got up and began walking about the room, nervously, turning, pacing. I heard him mutter, " Where is Hor ? Where *can* he be ? "

Valerie murmured, " Oh, Trevis. This is awful . . . horrible." Katoh, after a quick, hissing intake of breath, stood stock still for a moment, then crossed to the divan and squatted there, expression-lessly.

Tarrant paced . . .

With the first peal of the bell Katoh was up on his feet in a flash, pattering toward the door.

. . . . .

Monsieur Hor hardly glanced at the photograph before he sat down in Tarrant's best chair and surveyed us composedly.

" So," he commented, " so. You somewhat per-ceive now what sort of trouble we deal with ? "

No one answered him. I was thinking irrelevantly, isn't that what they call a rhetorical question ? Well, so what ?

He continued, " You must seek to calm yourself, Mr. Tarrant. You are jangling in a very futile fashion."

Tarrant rasped, " What can we *do* ? "

" Take hold of your nerve," said Monsieur Hor

sharply, the first and only time I ever heard his voice above an emotional purl. " Grip it ! " He looked full at Tarrant, held him in a concentrated gaze.

And Tarrant shook himself, pulled himself together. In a moment he spoke perfectly calmly. " We have examined the photograph. But I do not know about these so-called etheric bodies and so it tells me little."

" You still doubt their existence ? "

" There is certainly something there," Tarrant conceded. It was plain that he had succeeded in conquering his terror for Mary for the time and was trying desperately to gain some understanding of what threatened her. He added : " But what it is I I have no notion. What are these bodies supposed to be ? "

Monsieur Hor nodded. " Better," he acknowl-edged. . . . " The etheric body is formed, atom by atom, about the physical body and is a duplicate. It is formed of substances too fine for your ' chemists ' to have dealt with as yet, but it is also entirely physical ; its substance is of the same fundamental octave as your chemical ' elements.' The etheric body is formed by nature, automatically ; except in special conditions it is totally unconscious. . . . The Egyptian name was not *Khu* ; the etheric body is the *Ka* or ' Double.' "

" And the so-called auras ? You think they are bodies, too, corresponding perhaps to those other designations such as the *Ba* and *Sekhem* ? "

" Not at all. The auras are just what they are said to be. They are force fields surrounding the physical body ; they are not material in the sense that the etheric body is material. I see that you have the same smattering of Egyptology possessed by your better ' archæologists.' No doubt you have observed that the outer aura in these photographs is identical in shape with the *earliest* sarcophagi."

" You think——"

" I do not ' *think*,' Mr. Tarrant ; I know. The resemblance is dated by the time when mummification was performed for real purposes instead of the later superstitious ones. . . . Never mind ; it is beside the point."

Monsieur Hor stopped and seemed to be considering. Then he said, " It will be better if I inform you about the question of these bodies. You will kindly not ' believe ' what I tell you ; you have no data to judge of the truth of my statements, and ' belief ' will only muddle your ability to use what I tell you. For you it should be an hypothesis, necessary for understanding the matter before us. No more.

" Normally man has three conscious bodies. Nature supplies him with only the first of these, what you call the physical body ; the other two he must build, or develop, himself, consciously. All three are physical bodies, that is, composed of physical material, although of different fundamental octaves. Man now, being abnormal, fails to develop his two further bodies ; the material for them is present within him but not organically arranged. That he must do for himself, and he has sunk so low that he does not even know the possibilities that exist for him. Your friend, of course, possesses only the first of these bodies.

" In addition to these three bodies there is automatically formed, even in the present state, an etheric duplicate of the physical body ; it is this that concerns us now. The etheric body is unconscious, but through a special effort and by special means it can be rendered conscious temporarily. This can be done not only by its possessor but by others. Furthermore, the etheric body, by virtue of the materials organised in it, has certain uses that you would no doubt call esoteric. These uses necessitate the presence of a relatively large amount of fresh blood, since only under such conditions can the etheric body be freed from——"

Tarrant injected : " Wait. The cerebral anæmia, the laking of the blood into the visceral organs——"

" You are quick," Monsieur Hor admitted. " Yes, that is the cause of the unconsciousness of your friend. And it is closely connected with the etheric phenomena. The blood must be in contact with the etheric body in large amounts. It can be either inside or outside the physical body, in this case inside. In the early days of Egypt it was outside, the origin of their blood sacrifices, which later became mere superstitious rites, like those of the Aztecs. But earlier they slaughtered cattle and, in the presence of the fresh blood, the initiates were able to perform certain necessary acts, using the etheric bodies thus liberated."

" What were those acts ? "

" They were acts that would seriously shock those who must be ignorant of their real purpose. It is not necessary now that I describe them. They cannot be performed until the etheric body has been completely severed from the physical body. And it is this severance that you are concerned to prevent. The initiates made use of their own etheric bodies for these purposes ; they could do so without great harm to themselves because they possessed at least two of the other three bodies of which I told you just now. Because of this they could survive the severance of the etheric body and afterwards re-unite it with their first physical bodies. But your friend has only one body besides the etheric and a final severance of the two will surely mean her death. Incidentally, in her case, the strongest point of attachment between her two bodies is in what you call the subthalamic region and the strain in that place is what has caused the interference with the physical motor functioning ; in short, this strain, resulting from the effort to separate the etheric body, has caused the motor paralysis which was the first symptom."

He ceased speaking. We were all silent, trying to make what we could of the astounding words he had spoken as calmly as if referring to matters of common knowledge. All of us, I suppose, had followed as carefully as we could ; and Tarrant had certainly listened with concentration. After the silence had lasted a minute or more, he looked sharply across at Monsieur Hor.

" If this—hypothesis—of yours should be correct, an obvious deduction follows. There is no possibility that such a series of events was initiated by Miss Phelan, who knows nothing at all about these matters and has never had any interest in them. Some outside agent, plainly some other person, must be causing what has happened. . . . But that implies some one who not only understands these esoteric details but has also acquired the ability to operate in such a field. . . . Frankly," he gave himself a little shake, " the whole subject is so broad and, well, unknown, to me that I can scarcely take all your points as seriously established."

Monsieur Hor's expression underwent no change as he answered, " Mr. Tarrant, all I have done is to tell you a very little about matters you have long felt needed a somewhat more straightforward explanation than is offered by the ' Golden Bough ' school. The idea that really ancient wisdom was less than the knowledge possessed by this mechanical, monkey-on-a-stick civilisation, that idea is itself less than a superstition ; it is evidence of a merely infantile inability to think. You are able to think, to a degree, and your thinking has even a certain objectivity. There are the photographs. I did not need them to tell me of the situation ; I arranged that you procure them for yourself. If Miss Phelan——"

" All right," Tarrant interrupted. " You have presented a theory that is self-consistent. And the photographs constitute some proof. The proof is consistent with the theory, too. Since we can find no other explanation and since—though I don't know why—I agree with you that Miss Phelan is dying, let us proceed on your premise."

" Proceed," invited Monsieur Hor. And just for an instant it seemed to me that his expression might have hinted, very slightly, at mockery.

Maybe it was so, for Tarrant certainly was unable to proceed far by himself. " I presume no ordinary medical remedies would be of avail ? " he asked.

" Not at this stage. Your friend is in a deep coma by now. Injection is the only thing of that kind possible. And I should hesitate to use an injection, even if you had the necessary substances, since you wish to save her life."

" Then we come back," said Tarrant reluctantly, " to the person who we must assume is performing this outrage upon Miss Phelan. Granting all you say, there cannot be many people capable of such action."

Monsieur Hor shook his head. " More than you would suppose, perhaps. There may be a hundred or more in America ; there are probably a score in this city. These abilities are the result of accurate knowledge, careful training and effort."

" But who would deliberately attempt so senseless a crime ? "

" Not senseless, Mr. Tarrant, not senseless. You do not understand the use to which it is intended to put your friend's body, that is all. It will cause her death, true enough, but that use is important, from an objective point of view, none the less. To me it is forbidden to cause objective harm to other beings and, in general, these abilities are not acquired until one's development is already such as to limit their use.

" But this is not a normal planet. It is possible here to develop certain special abilities without having attained a condition of understanding regarding final purposes. I mentioned diabolism to you once. The present circumstances would suggest that some

diabolist is operating upon Miss Phelan for reasons
that have nothing to do with her personally but that
have some objective importance."

"But we must stop him. Can you find out where
this person is, what he is doing ? "

"Most probably I could." Monsieur Hor paused.
"You do not yet grasp the position, Mr. Tarrant.
The man who is attacking your friend is not ' bad ' ;
he is mistaken. Nevertheless, from an objective
point of view, he is already a far superior being to
his victim ; the fact that he is able to attack her in
this particular way, proves it. Undoubtedly I could
defeat him. I do not, however, feel able to attack
him in turn. As between the two, he is objectively
superior."

It seemed to me high time to say something ;
and I raised my voice to say it. "See here, I don't
know what this ' objectively superior ' stuff is all
about. If some one has knocked Mary down like
this, he's a damned dog whatever you call him. It's
all the worse if he never saw her and is just using
her like a guinea pig or something. What the hell
do we care if he's a diabolist or anything else !
We'll get him and we'd better get him before he gets
Mary ! Why, for God's sake——"

I stopped because I couldn't think of anything
more to say. The whole thing was preposterous,
most of all this nonsense about laying off the criminal
if he could really be found. . . . Valerie didn't say
anything ; she was just sitting, looking at this Hor
fellow. She said afterwards that she was completely
stopped, that she felt what she wanted to say would
make no more impression than if she got up on a
soapbox and made a speech to the ocean or to a big
mountain. She knew the premises that other people
accepted just weren't there.

Tarrant said slowly, "You mean that you won't
help us ? Is that it ? "

"I did not say I would not help you," the low

voice went on. " I merely refuse to attack some one else."

" But we have no idea where to find this person you suggest."

" Think a moment, Mr. Tarrant. What you wish to do is to relieve the etheric strain for your friend and restore the normal conditions. This cannot be done by ordinary means through her physical body. But you, too, have an etheric body, my friend."

It was a moment or so before Tarrant caught up with the implication, but he was ahead of me at that. He said, " Oh. You mean that, because there is nothing personal involved, we might be able to transfer the attentions to my etheric body ? It might even be better for these obscure purposes, since I should be willing."

" You understand," remarked Monsieur Hor slowly, " that a severance would be as fatal to you as to your friend ? "

Tarrant looked at him steadily. Tarrant said, " I am willing."

I must have caught my breath at this calm discussion as to who would be killed, for Monsieur Hor was shaking his head at me and smiling. " I make these little tests," he murmured. " It is important to know that he really loves this girl. Since he is willing to give her up, that is the case."

He turned back to Tarrant. " My suggestion is not what you thought ; it is only that if you could transfer your consciousness to your own etheric body, it might be possible for you to accomplish something. Were I to attempt interference, that is what I should have to do."

" But I can't. I don't know how to——"

" With my assistance," the other murmured.

" But what then ? Even if it could be done, I should not know what further action to take."

" It is all I will offer," announced Hor. " I will help you to separate yourself from your physical body. When that is done your consciousness will go over to your etheric body ; in your case it will have nowhere else to go. . . . Something will doubtless suggest itself then. . . . You will have, certainly, quite another view of the situation," he finished.

Tarrant rose and began pacing. " I want to think this over." For five minutes or more he walked up and down while the rest of us sat in a bewildered silence. Monsieur Hor lit another long cigarette and gazed at the ceiling with the appearance of considering other matters altogether.

Finally Tarrant spoke. " I have been over everything. It is only too plain that no ordinary measures are available, I always come back to that. As to this other suggestion, this incredible black magic——"

" Pardon," Monsieur Hor reminded him ; " it is an hypothesis of which we speak. An hypothesis only."

" Very well. This hypothesis, then. It's the only thing we can even guess about. I don't dare wait. Let us try it."

. . . . . .

Tarrant was stretched out on the divan. His collar was off, the neckband loosened. He lay perfectly still. Unconscious.

That is, I suppose, his physical body was unconscious. I mean, if we were to figure according to the " hypothesis " of Monsieur Hor. The whole thing was beyond me, so far beyond me now that all I could do was to sit and stare. When I thought where Tarrant was supposed to be, what he was supposed to be doing—well, I mean ! So far as I can remember, I wasn't even astonished any longer ; if some one had suddenly asked, " What do you think of all this, Jerry ? "—" Huh" would have expressed my feelings fairly substantially.

Katoh, though, was obviously fascinated. I'm sure he had forgotten all about His Imperial Majesty, the Son of the Sun, his Emperor's fell designs upon

the Brooklyn navy yard, and all the rest of it. His
small eyes glittered, lending to his immobile figure
across the room a most curious impression of activity.
Valerie's lips were just parted, her eyes wide, her
pert little nose profiled against the dark hangings
behind her ; under other circumstances a very pretty
picture.

The curious thing was how quickly it was over ;
the whole thing didn't last five minutes. Hor, who
was sitting beside the divan holding Tarrant's limp
wrist, bent forward suddenly. Tarrant's face was
absolutely white ; not pale, dead white with the
positive whiteness of a calcimined ceiling. Hor was
on his feet now, his right hand pressing the region
of Tarrant's solar plexus, his left behind and
under the neck. In complete silence he maintained
the tableau, it seemed interminably ; little ripples,
probably I imagined them, seemed to run up and
down his back under his coat.

Then Tarrant gasped. A peculiar gasp, as if it had
taken untold, concentrated energy to produce this
almost inaudible sound of in-sucked breath. His
whole body tightened, jerked ; then lay still again,
breathing.

Monsieur Hor said very quietly, " You are back.
. . . You are Trevis Tarrant."

Katoh appeared beside the divan with a pony of
amber brandy. He glanced at Hor, received a nod
and held it to the prone man's lips.

Then our attention became concentrated. For
Tarrant coughed once, and a look of grey horror
gathered, spread, stamped his features into a mask.
Automatically I thought of that drowned boatman
at Winnespequam, his expression of final hopeless-
ness intensified.

Even his voice was strange, hollow with the
emptiness of his words. " Oh, my God, *my God* !
I am nothing. I cannot help any one. I cannot
even help myself. . . . I am nothing."

Lying as he was, without trying to raise himself even on an elbow, he took his head in his hands. He lay there, sobbing.

Meaningless as it was, I was shocked. I must have been shocked, for I felt the hair prickle and tingle along my scalp. . . . Tarrant ! Trevis Tarrant ! The redoubtable, the successful. The man who in all the time I had known him had failed only once, and even then had only partially failed. His abasement might have been loathsome, but it wasn't, somehow ; it was shocking but it was so open, so utterly frank and, well, hopeless. It was shocking.

Monsieur Hor's voice sounded a sure, low undertone. The inflection was curiously at variance with the words ; there was no recrimination, certainly no vindictiveness. The tone was one of simple explanation.

" Because you are facile and successful with monkey tricks, because you have been phantasy-ing about serious things in spare time—you speculate in phantasies about the ancient Egyptians—you thought you were Something. And now you realise you are not. It was difficult, very difficult to bring you back at all."

Tarrant groaned, " Bring *me* back ? I—— For me there is no ' I.' Nothing. I tried to do as you told me. Nothing happened, I was a man relaxed on a couch. Then I was, I was pushed. There was a snap. My body lay there. I did not see it ; I *felt* it, experienced it quite differently somehow, all of it, as a machine, *as an automatic, irresponsible machine.* I was nothing. The idea that I have ever controlled it is a subtle illusion. It is talking now, but I am not talking. . . . I am nothing."

" ' You ' are Nothing," murmured Monsieur Hor, " actually. But potentially ' you ' may become Something. Only Being can recognise the absence of being."

In the quiet Tarrant's deep, mechanical breathing

was the only sound. I don't know how long it was before the voice went on, " That is a parodox but only in paradox is any truth glimpsed. I give you an unimportant example, spelled out : it is my custom always to speak in a low voice so that I shall be distinctly heard. The ignorant raise their voices to be heard, the wise speak very low. Thus the attention of their hearers is aroused and, with an *active* attention, no word is missed. To be heard distinctly, speak very low. It is a simple statement of fact, you see. There is no paradox ; the feeling of ' paradox ' is only an evidence of ignorance. It is——"

I found myself looking at Valerie and missed the next few words. She was looking at me. It was as if we spoke soundlessly, suddenly remembering.—
" Mary is dying."

Then I heard Hor's voice repeating the words. " Your friend is dying. Take brandy ; you face a serious decision. There is now a possibility of saving her."

Tarrant gulped the liquor and then he did raise himself slightly. He said nothing, just looked.

Hor looked back at him steadily. " The tests are finished," he spoke, " perhaps in time. I suspected what you are, but only tests make sure. I have confirmed your love for your friend, I have confirmed your ability to realise—what you have recently realised. I have not misled you in this, that there is a certain, objective importance in your friend's death, in the utilisation of her etheric body. But there may be a still higher objective value in re-nouncing its use. . . . That is the possibility."

We waited.

" You," he said to Tarrant ; " the decision is yours. Justice is purely chemical. You have the price, if you wish to pay it."

The other shook his head. With compressed lips, " I have already offered."

" The price is not death. The price is seven years of your life."

" I——"

" You wish to marry your friend. In that time you may lose her. Otherwise you will surely lose her, but then, certainly, no one else will have her."

Tarrant said, " Does that matter ? "

" It was a redundant test," Monsieur Hor acknowledged. " Also, I spoke carelessly regarding seven years. The price is that you, who are now Nothing, must become Something. It may take you seven years, it may take you seventy, you may not succeed before you die. But the price is either that you succeed or that you continue to devote your entire energies to the attempt. In this time you shall not see nor communicate with any one you have known. In any event, seven years. That is the bargain."

" But how——"

" I have already told you what is necessary. First you will have to understand what I have already told you. But I have only told you what, not how. You will have to find out ' how ' for yourself. I shall give you no further help ; that you must seek and find—elsewhere. There is only one condition : you must succeed, or not return. . . . You must decide. Now."

Tarrant said, " I have decided." It would have been, I admit, redundant for him to have added what we all knew.

. . . . .

For a moment the jingle of the telephone seemed utterly unreal.

Valerie answered it. " . . . Yes . . . Yes."

She got to her feet. She said, " Baker. Mary is dying. I am going——" She choked, fumbled with her coat, started across toward the door.

. . . . .

There seems to have been a blank. The next thing I remember is the hospital.

Tarrant, Valerie and I ; we were in the long ward corridor, just outside Mary's closed door. We went in.

Mary lay on the bed. Beside her, across from us, stood Morton Baker holding her wrist and a nurse stood behind him, next to a tank, oxygen perhaps, on some kind of hospital cart. Baker looked up as we came in, then down again. We stood looking down at Mary.

Her face on the pillow was just as it had been the last time we had seen her, whenever that had been, I couldn't quite remember. Eyes closed, calm, but whiter maybe ; not quite as white as Tarrant had been when he lay on his own divan, though very nearly so. I was surprised that I could remember so clearly and be able to distinguish so very slight a difference from memory.

Of course it was my nervousness ; I was upset, plenty. But I seemed able to appreciate the most remarkable shades of significance. I have never been able to since ; no doubt it was largely imagination. No one said anything, but Baker's posture, for instance, spoke as clearly as if he had been talking. There was a stethoscope around his neck over his white coat and I knew that he had no intention of using it for further information. I knew he was convinced the tank was useless, too. I knew he was convinced completely, that he knew there was nothing to be done and was just waiting, waiting for a few minutes more before he would look up and say quietly that she was dead.

Then I realised that every one else knew this, too ; we were all waiting, our only doubt as to whether it would be this minute or the next minute. Hor's words—" On no account must I be disturbed for the next hour. I shall succeed, but you had better go " ; I couldn't think where I had heard them or why I remembered them, but they had nothing to do with this.

And part of me seemed to understand for the

first time that banal phrase about death hovering over the bed. In some peculiar but perfectly definite way death was in the room with us. Death, too, was waiting momentarily. I don't know now quite what I mean by death. Not Mary's death, not in that sense at all. It was apart from Mary and apart from any other person. It was sort of another thing that would touch Mary and then she would be dead. If I tried to put it into words, death was a sort of generalised something but more distinct, less abstract than a verbal generalisation, almost a sort of personification ; but that doesn't mean anything because death was entirely another thing than people.

We all waited, even Mary somehow. All of us in the room, and death, waited. What were we waiting for ? Death could act but none of us could act. Why did death wait ? Valerie raised her head suddenly and involuntarily glanced about the room. There was nothing to see and she looked back again. But I had felt it as well. I don't know what, except that now there was something in the room that hadn't been there before ; somewhere there was struggle. The total energy in this place had been added to ; and not only that but the new energy was in opposition to something or other, I had no idea what.

Not in opposition to death. All at once I knew that while we had been waiting for death to act, death had been waiting for this. Now death was not waiting, death was watching. Watching something we could not see, but only felt, very vaguely.

And that was all there was to it. We stood there a long time ; we must have done because it was dawn when we left. Not much of a climax in that room for, after all, so little happened.

At some point I heard several long-drawn breaths, as if tension had been released. One of those breaths was my own. And just *after* that, Mary's face changed. It had been relaxed but unnaturally relaxed ; now, without the change of a muscle, naturalness crept in, quickly. Where before she had looked as if in a trance, now she seemed normally asleep. I thought I saw her nostrils twitch.

Baker's posture changed, too ; it changed to one of astonished attention. He bent over, his eyes concentrated. He held the palm of one hand just below her nostrils. He laid her wrist back on the coverlet and placed a finger across her opened palm. Mary's fingers gradually curled about his.

He straightened up and looked across at us. With an incredulous smile he motioned us out of the room.

I felt dizzy and sort of hysterical. It was all I could do to keep from laughing out loud because no one had spoken a single word the entire time.

.   .   .   .   .

Morton Baker must have seen my face as I stumbled out. He came into the visitors' room, its big window now grey with dawn, very shortly and he brought brandy and glasses. He gave me a drink first.

He said : " Trevis, she has not only passed the crisis, she is well." He spoke as if he couldn't believe it, yet knew it was so. " Oh, a week in bed maybe, maybe less. I don't want any one to see her for the next two days. No, don't ask me why or how. I don't know ; I suspect we have not known even what the trouble was. I have never seen or heard of a paralysis with so sudden an incidence or so sudden and complete a disappearance. I don't know why but I do know she has recovered. I will stake my reputation on it.

He hurried off before I had finished my second brandy. By that time I had snapped back completely and I was already feeling amazement as I remembered some of the things that had happened that night. They were so utterly screwy.

I grinned rather fatuously and remarked, " So
it was all right all the time. She got well anyhow,
without all that hocus-pocus we listened to."

Then I suddenly remembered Tarrant and the
nonsense he had been involved in. " Say, you're not
going through with any more of this stuff, are you ? "

He turned around from the window. " A bargain
is a bargain, Jerry."

" But my God," I protested, " we were all crazy
sitting around listening to that stuff. We were just
excited, that's all. It was, it was just crazy."

" Perhaps you didn't experience quite what I did."

" But look here. If you take it seriously. If you're
really going to go away, what's to prevent the same
thing happening all over again, if you take it
seriously ? "

He said, " It won't happen again."

" Why not ? "

" Because I know who did it. And a bargain is a
bargain."

" You know——"

" I don't know, but I strongly suspect Monsieur
Hor was responsible for the beginning as well as the
end. He made one slip. He said the advantage, yes
the advantage of the business could be ' renounced '
for a higher value. He was not proposing to attack
some hypothetical diabolist ; he was offering to
give up what he had started. I don't think he
would have carried it out if I had refused. But I
don't know. I couldn't chance it."

I was astonished again. It was some time before
I could stammer, " You're going to live up to this
' bargain ' ? And you made it when it might not
even have been necessary ? "

" Try to get it through your head, Jerry. I love
her. . . . Yes, I am going to live up to it."

" But—but—it was made under threat. It
doesn't hold. Under duress."

" Don't argue, Jerry ; it's no use. I must do this

anyhow. I understand that I am no good to Mary, even to myself, now. This is something I *must* do." He was silent for several minutes. I didn't interrupt because I knew he was trying to think out something important. Finally he muttered : " If I lose, I lose. I may as well include the postage. . . . See here, Jerry. You may tell Mary as much as you wish about last night. Except one thing. Until I come back I don't want you to tell her how I feel about her. She might feel obligated—to something. Don't tell her. Valerie will understand, even if you don't."

Well, I didn't understand, not right then, anyhow. Just then I was more struck by the pain immediately in his eyes.

" You promise ? "

" Eh ? Yes."

Tarrant crossed over the room and stood in the corridor. " I shall see you at the end of seven years. . . . Good-bye." He held out his hand.

I took it. I couldn't think of anything to say. There wasn't anything to say. . . .

I found myself looking at Valerie. She was sitting by the door again, her legs crossed, her tailored skirt falling diagonally half-way to a slim, silk ankle. There was a puckered frown on her face. My God, she was pretty ! And suddenly she was familiar, and dear, and desirable.

I said, " Come on, Val. Let's go home."

THE END

A CATALOGUE OF SELECTED DOVER BOOKS
IN ALL FIELDS OF INTEREST

A CATALOGUE OF SELECTED DOVER BOOKS
IN ALL FIELDS OF INTEREST

THE DEVIL'S DICTIONARY, Ambrose Bierce. Barbed, bitter, brilliant witticisms in the form of a dictionary. Best, most ferocious satire America has produced. 145pp. 20487-1 Pa. $1.50

ABSOLUTELY MAD INVENTIONS, A.E. Brown, H.A. Jeffcott. Hilarious, useless, or merely absurd inventions all granted patents by the U.S. Patent Office. Edible tie pin, mechanical hat tipper, etc. 57 illustrations. 125pp. 22596-8 Pa. $1.50

AMERICAN WILD FLOWERS COLORING BOOK, Paul Kennedy. Planned coverage of 48 most important wildflowers, from Rickett's collection; instructive as well as entertaining. Color versions on covers. 48pp. 8¼ x 11. 20095-7 Pa. $1.35

BIRDS OF AMERICA COLORING BOOK, John James Audubon. Rendered for coloring by Paul Kennedy. 46 of Audubon's noted illustrations: red-winged blackbird, cardinal, purple finch, towhee, etc. Original plates reproduced in full color on the covers. 48pp. 8¼ x 11. 23049-X Pa. $1.35

NORTH AMERICAN INDIAN DESIGN COLORING BOOK, Paul Kennedy. The finest examples from Indian masks, beadwork, pottery, etc. — selected and redrawn for coloring (with identifications) by well-known illustrator Paul Kennedy. 48pp. 8¼ x 11. 21125-8 Pa. $1.35

UNIFORMS OF THE AMERICAN REVOLUTION COLORING BOOK, Peter Copeland. 31 lively drawings reproduce whole panorama of military attire; each uniform has complete instructions for accurate coloring. (Not in the Pictorial Archives Series). 64pp. 8¼ x 11. 21850-3 Pa. $1.50

THE WONDERFUL WIZARD OF OZ COLORING BOOK, L. Frank Baum. Color the Yellow Brick Road and much more in 61 drawings adapted from W.W. Denslow's originals, accompanied by abridged version of text. Dorothy, Toto, Oz and the Emerald City. 61 illustrations. 64pp. 8¼ x 11. 20452-9 Pa. $1.50

CUT AND COLOR PAPER MASKS, Michael Grater. Clowns, animals, funny faces . . . simply color them in, cut them out, and put them together, and you have 9 paper masks to play with and enjoy. Complete instructions. Assembled masks shown in full color on the covers. 32pp. 8¼ x 11. 23171-2 Pa. $1.50

STAINED GLASS CHRISTMAS ORNAMENT COLORING BOOK, Carol Belanger Grafton. Brighten your Christmas season with over 100 Christmas ornaments done in a stained glass effect on translucent paper. Color them in and then hang at windows, from lights, anywhere. 32pp. 8¼ x 11. 20707-2 Pa. $1.75

EGYPTIAN MAGIC, E.A. Wallis Budge. Foremost Egyptologist, curator at British Museum, on charms, curses, amulets, doll magic, transformations, control of demons, deific appearances, feats of great magicians. Many texts cited. 19 illustrations. 234pp.　　　　　　　　　　　　　　　　USO 22681-6 Pa. $2.50

THE LEYDEN PAPYRUS: AN EGYPTIAN MAGICAL BOOK, edited by F. Ll. Griffith, Herbert Thompson. Egyptian sorcerer's manual contains scores of spells: sex magic of various sorts, occult information, evoking visions, removing evil magic, etc. Transliteration faces translation. 207pp.　　　　　　　　　　　22994-7 Pa. $2.50

THE MALLEUS MALEFICARUM OF KRAMER AND SPRENGER, translated, edited by Montague Summers. Full text of most important witchhunter's "Bible," used by both Catholics and Protestants. Theory of witches, manifestations, remedies, etc. Indispensable to serious student. 278pp. 6⅝ x 10.　　　　　USO 22802-9 Pa. $3.95

LOST CONTINENTS, L. Sprague de Camp. Great science-fiction author, finest, fullest study: Atlantis, Lemuria, Mu, Hyperborea, etc. Lost Tribes, Irish in pre-Columbian America, root races; in history, literature, art, occultism. Necessary to everyone concerned with theme. 17 illustrations. 348pp.　　　22668-9 Pa. $3.50

THE COMPLETE BOOKS OF CHARLES FORT, Charles Fort. Book of the Damned, Lo!, Wild Talents, New Lands. Greatest compilation of data: celestial appearances, flying saucers, falls of frogs, strange disappearances, inexplicable data not recognized by science. Inexhaustible, painstakingly documented. Do not confuse with modern charlatanry. Introduction by Damon Knight. Total of 1126pp.
　　　　　　　　　　　　　　　　　　　　　　　23094-5 Clothbd. $15.00

FADS AND FALLACIES IN THE NAME OF SCIENCE, Martin Gardner. Fair, witty appraisal of cranks and quacks of science: Atlantis, Lemuria, flat earth, Velikovsky, orgone energy, Bridey Murphy, medical fads, etc. 373pp.　　　20394-8 Pa. $3.00

HOAXES, Curtis D. MacDougall. Unbelievably rich account of great hoaxes: Locke's moon hoax, Shakespearean forgeries, Loch Ness monster, Disumbrationist school of art, dozens more; also psychology of hoaxing. 54 illustrations. 338pp.　　　　　　　　　　　　　　　　　　　　　　　20465-0 Pa. $3.50

THE GENTLE ART OF MAKING ENEMIES, James A.M. Whistler. Greatest wit of his day deflates Wilde, Ruskin, Swinburne; strikes back at inane critics, exhibitions. Highly readable classic of impressionist revolution by great painter. Introduction by Alfred Werner. 334pp.　　　　　　　　　　　　　21875-9 Pa. $4.00

THE BOOK OF TEA, Kakuzo Okakura. Minor classic of the Orient: entertaining, charming explanation, interpretation of traditional Japanese culture in terms of tea ceremony. Edited by E.F. Bleiler. Total of 94pp.　　　20070-1 Pa. $1.25

Prices subject to change without notice.
Available at your book dealer or write for free catalogue to Dept. GI, Dover Publications, Inc., 180 Varick St., N.Y., N.Y. 10014. Dover publishes more than 150 books each year on science, elementary and advanced mathematics, biology, music, art, literary history, social sciences and other areas.